Still Standing

Still Standing

Nicole S. Rouse

www.urbanchristianonline.com

Urban Books, LLC
78 East Industry Court
Deer Park, NY 11729

ISBN 13: 978-1-60162-807-7
ISBN 10: 1-60162-807-2

First Printing November 2011
Printed in the United States of America

10 9 8 7 6 5 4 3 2 1

Distributed by Kensington Corp.
Submit Wholesale Orders to:
Kensington Publishing Corp.
C/O Penguin Group (USA) Inc.
Attention: Order Processing
405 Murray Hill Parkway
East Rutherford, NJ 07073-2316
Phone: 1-800-526-0275
Fax: 1-800-227-9604

The joy of the Lord is my strength . . .
~ Nehemiah 8:10

This book is dedicated to all the book clubs, women's organizations, ministries, and readers who have supported my novels. The discussions we've shared throughout the years continue to encourage and inspire me. Thank you for your support.

Acknowledgments

Although I put up a good fight, I thank God for surrounding me with people who genuinely believe in me and my dream. This novel, in particular, would not have been possible without the help and encouragement of a community of people.

My parents, Linda and Bernard Rouse, for investing their gifts and talents and implanting the love of writing from birth. The Booker and Rouse families, for their continued love and support.

Sha-Shana Crichton, for standing in the gap and never giving up. Joylynn Jossel, for her patience and dedication. Thanks so much for working tirelessly on my behalf.

Reverends Barbara Y. Glenn and Ayana Newton of First A.M.E. Church of Gaithersburg, for reaching out to me. Your presence in my life keeps me focused.

Zeta Phi Beta Sorority, Inc., especially Eta Chapter (Summer '95 and Fall '96). What God started over fifteen years ago has blossomed into a beautiful friendship that remains untouchable.

While writing this novel, I discovered the true meaning of friendship. I would like to thank those friends who have stood by me through all the trials and triumphs.

~1~

Renee

Without saying good-night to her family, Renee limped barefoot up the stairs and down the dimly lit hallway leading to her bedroom. It had been a long day. She'd been up since 7:00 A.M., finishing a last-minute budget analysis for the newly appointed CEO of the hotel chain she worked for. By 9:45 A.M., Renee had wrapped up the analysis, eaten a light breakfast, showered, and dressed for church. On most Sundays, she'd come home from church and prepare a large dinner for her family, a family that typically included her husband, two sons, one daughter-in-law, and three grandchildren. Sometimes, her oldest son and his wife would be in attendance. That all changed the day she discovered her husband, Jerome, had fathered a child with another woman.

The bottoms of the three-inch heels in Renee's hand rubbed against the white-painted door as she entered the bedroom, leaving a noticeable smudge, and she cringed. Renee tried to remove the marks, but her attempts only caused them to smear, so she gave up. She'd have to try again later, when her feet didn't hurt and she wasn't so tired.

On the way to her walk-in closet, Renee turned on the oblong African lamp by the vanity and then placed her shoes on the rack behind the closet door. As she walked back to the vanity, she unzipped the side of her sleeveless linen dress. Standing in front of the mirror, Renee wanted to cry. The small bags under her eyes and the faded makeup made her look and feel ten years older. The neatly pressed, spotless dress she put on this morning was now full of wrinkles and juice stains, compliments of her grandson. Jerome had decided to treat the family to dinner at a fancy downtown Chicago restaurant. As if that wasn't enough, he also suggested they walk through Grant Park and along Lake Shore Drive. The idea was great, but sightseeing in the midst of an August heat wave was not the way she wanted to spend a Sunday evening. Nor did she want to spend time with Joi, Jerome's sixteen-year-old daughter.

Renee removed her sterling-silver earrings and took a deep breath. "Why does life have to be so difficult?" she whispered as she stared at her reflection. She sat the earrings on the table and accidentally tapped a framed five-by-seven family photograph. In the picture, Renee sat on a hidden wooden stool surrounded by her husband and her three sons. She picked up the picture and stared at the bright smiles on all their faces. Renee was proud of her children.

Reggie, her firstborn, wasn't the easiest child to raise. He hadn't liked school or following rules, so he surprised everyone when he graduated from Northwestern with a degree in sports medicine. And much like his parents, Reggie married his childhood sweetheart. The middle son, Jerome, Junior, or Junior, who was inquisitive from birth, was now an award-winning sports journalist. Though Junior married before he was ready, he was a loving husband and father to Renee's three grandchildren. Joshua was Renee's youngest child, and the only son actually born in Chicago. He resembled Jerome in many ways but had Renee's business sense. He was unlike any child she'd ever known. At the age of fourteen, Joshua developed a plan for his life, and he was determined to reach his goals. In many ways, he was a prime example of what one could do if one set one's mind to it. Joshua was entering his senior year of high school in a few weeks, and he'd already secured a summer internship in the accounting department at the electric company. His dream was to own a Fortune 500 company or work at one as the chief financial officer. There was no doubt in Renee's mind that his dreams would come true.

A faint smile spread across Renee's face. Joshua was her baby. He was conceived after she'd forgiven Jerome for his affair, and after the family relocated to the Windy City, many miles from their Philadelphia hometown and far away from Taylor, Jerome's former lover.

But not even the distance could keep Taylor out of Renee and Jerome's life. Jerome conceived a child with Taylor just a few months before he conceived a child with Renee. The thought of what Jerome had done made Renee sick to her stomach, and she sat the picture down. *What a horrible thing to do,* she thought and plucked Jerome's image, causing the metal frame to fall behind the vanity. Renee started to reach for it but changed her mind. No matter how hard she tried, Renee would always look at Jerome's proud grin and be reminded of his affair and of his illegitimate daughter.

Renee turned around and slid out of her dress. She removed her undergarments and then dropped her soiled belongings inside a hamper by the bathroom door. Physically and emotionally drained, Renee turned on the shower and watched the water fall. The running water soothed her.

The day had been interesting. In church, Renee forced herself to smile as she watched Jerome proudly parade Joi around the sanctuary, introducing her as "Daddy's girl." She'd wanted to stay home, but she had missed the last few Sundays and didn't want the members of Calvary Baptist to make up exaggerated stories about her absence.

After church, the deacons raved about Joi and her resemblance to the family, especially Jerome, while others stared at Renee, searching for any sign of sadness or anger. Renee had been taught to stand by her husband, no matter the situation, but pretending she was happy to have Joi staying in her home *all* summer was more than a stretch. In fact, it was near impossible.

Renee often wondered how Hillary Clinton was able to stand next to Bill during a press conference to address his extramarital affair. Behind closed doors, did she throw pots at him, punch his chest, or scream foul words? Or did she remain calm, exemplify class, and speak her mind in a mild manner? Sometimes, Renee wished she'd taken the classy route, but she didn't have a great track record when it came to controlling her temper. The day she unexpectedly showed up at a recreation center and saw Jerome and Joi together for the first time, she smacked him hard with her umbrella.

Although that day happened ten months ago, to Renee, it felt like yesterday. She'd gone to Jerome's office to pick up a document he'd asked her to proof while he was in Philadelphia, "visiting his brother." As director of community relations for a major basketball franchise, Jerome had developed Future Ballers, a mentoring program for high school athletes. He wanted Renee to review the program documents before he turned them in for final approval. As his wife, Renee was eager to help, especially since she had experience drafting and approving documents for programs at the hotel.

When Renee reached the office, Melanie, Jerome's assistant, had mistakenly given her a folder that contained newspaper clippings and pictures of a female teen basketball player. Something inside told her that the young athlete was more than a player of interest for the mentoring program. For one thing, the girl was wearing a jersey from Engineering and Science, a high school located in Philadelphia. Renee found herself staring at the profile picture longer than normal. It was hard to ignore the girl's soft brown eyes. They were exact replicas of Jerome's. She quickly scanned through the clippings inside the folder and came across an article that mentioned Taylor's name. She nearly fell to the floor for fear that what she was thinking might be true. It was then that she decided to fly out to Philadelphia to confirm her worst nightmare: Taylor had given Jerome the daughter and star basketball player Renee had not.

Renee cleared her mind as she stepped into the shower and let the warm water massage her body. She couldn't believe six months had passed since she found out about Joi. I should've left Jerome that day, Renee thought, but at the same time, she knew a lifetime of memories with him had already been invested, and more importantly, she loved him. He was the only man she'd ever been with, and she didn't want to hastily throw away the history they shared as a couple.

The warm water steamed the bathroom windows and mirror and made it hard to breathe, but that didn't matter to Renee. The water gently beating on her body felt good.

"Hey, babe," Jerome yelled as he entered the bathroom, startling Renee and interrupting her peaceful oasis. "Is it hot enough in here for you?"

Renee heard Jerome lift the toilet seat and rolled her eyes. It was times like this that she missed their old house in Oak Park. There she and Jerome had separate bathrooms. After thirty-five years, he had yet to understand that the bathroom was the only place in the house where she truly felt at peace. Sometimes, she'd sit in the master bathroom and tune everything out until her mind was clear and she felt rejuvenated. Renee was beginning to regret giving up her private bathroom for the luxury of more space.

"Today turned out well, didn't it?" Jerome asked and then flushed the toilet. "Joi seems to be blending in well."

Renee sighed softly. Jerome was floating so high on a cloud, he didn't realize that she wasn't responding.

"She's a good kid. I'm glad she wanted to stay with us this summer," Jerome continued as he washed his hands. "Joi and Josh have a lot in common, don't you think? They could almost pass for twins."

Renee almost stopped breathing. That statement reminded her that Joi was only three months older than Joshua. Jerome must have realized what he'd said as well, because he was quiet for almost a minute. Through the shower curtain, Renee could see his shadow walking toward the door, and she was relieved. She was tired of hearing him talk about Joi, *and* she wanted more alone time.

"You want to watch a movie tonight?" Jerome asked.

Renee pulled back the shower curtain just enough to see him standing by the door. "No, I'm really tired," she answered. "Sleep is all I want to do tonight."

"Yeah, you're right. We did have a pretty busy day."

You think so? Renee wanted to respond, but she just grinned and nodded in agreement.

Leaving the door wide open, Jerome walked into the bedroom. By now, the steam that filled the bathroom had completely disappeared. Renee pulled the shower curtain back in place and showered faster than she'd anticipated. She knew that Jerome would be back if she didn't join him in the bedroom soon. It didn't matter that she had worked long hours all week and had tended to the needs of her family all weekend. Once they were in their bedroom, Jerome expected her attention.

After putting on her favorite pajamas, Renee folded back the sheets and then lay on the bed. Of the many things she asked Jerome to be mindful of, he could never remember to roll down the sheets. She loathed lying on top of a made-up bed but didn't complain. Jerome had been diligent in her other requests. Remembering 90 percent of her quirks was acceptable. Forgetting to roll down the bed was an adjustment she could easily do.

"How's this, babe?" Jerome asked as he stood in front of the new forty-eight-inch flat-screen television he'd bought last night. This was the third time he'd adjusted the settings since this morning. Standing there, with his shirttail hanging outside of his khakis, Jerome didn't look a day over forty. Not even the heart attack he had last year had aged him. He was eating healthier and exercising regularly. With all the time he spent in the gym and playing basketball, Jerome's arms were more defined now than they'd ever been. There was no question that Jerome was handsome, charming, and kindhearted. At fifty-three, he was finally the husband Renee had prayed he'd be, but she was afraid his appeal was losing its effect on her.

Finally satisfied with the settings, Jerome threw the remote on the bed and then removed his T-shirt. "Maybe next Sunday we can drive out to Kenosha. What do you think?"

"You want to drive to Wisconsin?" Renee replied nonchalantly. Though it was roughly a two-hour drive, the family hadn't taken a road trip since Joshua was a toddler.

"I thought we could hit the outlets and let the kids pick out some clothes for school," Jerome said as he undressed.

"I don't know about Joi, but Josh wears a uniform to school." Though she tried not to sound uninterested in his idea, she was.

"They need clothes for the weekend, babe," Jerome answered. "And when have you ever turned down a reason to shop?"

Jerome hadn't realized that Renee was annoyed. She'd normally have to negotiate a deal to get him to spend a family day at the mall. Now that Joi was in his life, shopping wasn't a problem. Renee fluffed her pillow and made herself more comfortable. "Sunday is a week away. Let's revisit this on Thursday and see how the family feels then."

Jerome took his dirty clothes into the bathroom and immediately placed them in the hamper. Renee had trained him well. Long gone were the days when he'd drop his clothes in the middle of the floor, waiting for her to pick them up, as if she were his personal maid. "Good plan," he agreed and started the water for his shower. "Joi and Josh are getting along well. I heard Josh ask her to live with us for a while, especially since Future Ballers is about to start."

Renee wanted to holler. There was no way she was going to let Jerome's love child live in the house where she raised her children. Yes, Future Ballers would be a good program for Joi, but not if it meant she'd live with them for a whole school year. A summer with Joi was too much for Renee, but she tolerated the two-month visit. Spending an *entire* year with her would definitely stretch her patience.

Renee covered her face with the extra pillow on the bed to keep from screaming. Although Jerome didn't say it, she knew he was laying the foundation for his daughter to stay.

The house phone rang, and Renee tossed the pillow aside in order to answer it.

"I bet that's Reggie," Jerome called from the bathroom. "We've been playing phone tag all weekend."

"No, it's Everett," Renee replied after checking the caller ID and then lifted the phone from its base. "Hey, E. What's going on?"

"I hope this isn't a bad time," Everett apologized. "I tried to call your cell, but—"

"No, no problem at all," Renee answered. Hearing Everett's deep, mellow voice tonight lifted her spirits. Over the last few months he'd become a source of strength and peace, and she could use a little of both tonight. "Everything all right?"

Jerome appeared in the doorway with only a towel covering his midsection. He would never admit it, but she knew he was still suspicious of the relationship she had with the CFO of Luxury Inn hotels. On several occasions, Jerome had accused Renee of having an affair with her boss.

Extremely good-looking and intelligent, Everett Coleman had worked very closely with Renee for the last seventeen years. Though he was based at the main hotel in California, Everett traveled to Chicago often. And of all the employees he managed, Renee was his unspoken favorite. Having gone from a college intern to general manager in record time, Renee had proven her talent, loyalty, and knowledge of the hotel business. Together, Renee and Everett had transformed Luxury Inn into a five-star hotel chain across the country, and they were currently leading a team that would build a new international branch in London.

"Darla's flying out to Chicago on Tuesday. She wants to reveal new plans for the Illinois hotels," informed Everett.

"Darla just doesn't know what to do next," Renee said, hoping Jerome would relax knowing that this was a business call. And although Jerome slowly backed into the bathroom, Renee sensed his hesitance to leave the room. "I hope it's nothing major."

Darla Kotlarczyk was the daughter of Randolph Kotlarczyk, the man who created Luxury Inn hotels and was Renee's mentor. Last year Mr. Kotlarczyk, better known as Mr. K to his employees, was diagnosed with lung cancer. With his days left to live numbered, he split control of the business he'd started from scratch between his children. Everyone knew that Mr. K really wanted to leave his empire in Renee's hands, and on his last day in the office, he boldly stated, "If only you were my daughter, this franchise would belong to you." Renee understood and respected the choice he made. Family was important, and if the situation had been reversed, she would've made the same decision.

There were over seventy hotels across the country, and Darla was given control of the Illinois hotels, all of which Renee managed at Mr. K's request. It was an unusual and great responsibility to handle three hotels, but Renee was the ideal person for such an undertaking. Having been in control of the hotels for so many years, and with little to no supervision, Renee didn't readily accept Darla as her new boss. Of Darla's three siblings, she was the least experienced in business. While the others had served as their father's apprentice, Darla had chased her dream of becoming a Hollywood star. Rumor had it that Mr. K wanted Darla in Illinois in hopes that Renee would teach her how to effectively run a hotel. Then, after a year, if Darla demonstrated progress in hotel management, she'd be granted more of an equal share of the family business.

The shift of power hadn't affected Renee while Mr. K was alive. Darla had kept her distance and had given her freedom to run the three hotels as she saw fit. But when Mr. K lost his battle with cancer, his grave was barely cold before Darla revealed her domineering personality.

For reasons Renee didn't completely understand, Darla resented her, and especially the relationship she'd had with her father. There were several moments when Renee wanted to set Darla straight, but out of respect for the man responsible for her successful career, she swallowed her pride whenever Darla was in her presence.

"You called to give me that bad news," Renee teased. "*Please* say you have some good news to tell me."

"I wanted to give you a heads-up. I know you need time to prepare for her arrival," Everett joked.

Renee joined in his amusement. "I appreciate that. Do you have any idea what these new plans are?"

"No, but something's up," Everett replied. "Don't be surprised if she announces her relocation to Chicago."

"Don't play like that," Renee quickly retorted. She could imagine how Darla's constant presence would affect office morale. "She knows she needs to stay in California with you."

"I'm just saying," Everett continued, "don't be surprised."

"I don't know if any of us are ready for that."

"Well, I'm having lunch with her on Tuesday. If I learn anything, you know I'll tell you," Everett said.

Renee knew he would. They had been confidants for years. Unfortunately, their growing friendship was one of the reasons Everett's wife divorced him five years ago. "Thanks, my friend," she said.

"You okay?" Everett asked. "You sound exhausted."

Not very convincing, Renee replied weakly, "Yes, I'm fine."

"I'm not so sure you are."

The water in the bathroom stopped running, making that the fastest shower Jerome had taken since they were married. Dripping wet, Jerome entered the bedroom and dried off in front of the television. Renee chuckled to herself. She knew her husband had come into the room just to eavesdrop. "We'll talk when you get here," Renee whispered carefully.

"Can't speak freely?" Everett said and chuckled softly.

"No, Jerome and I have been busy all day," she replied. Mentioning Jerome's name let Everett know that he was close by. This was a system they had used for almost a year to avoid unnecessary disagreements with their spouses about their business calls.

"Okay," Everett responded. "Have a good night."

"You, too," Renee said and then hung up the phone.

"Good news?" Jerome questioned as he put on a pair of boxers. "You're smiling."

Renee lay on her stomach and closed her eyes. She hadn't realized her good spirits were evident. "Not really. Darla will be in town this week," she said. "I can only imagine what she's coming to do. Everett called to prepare me for the visit."

"Humph," moaned Jerome, obviously jealous.

Jerome knelt by his side of the bed and prayed, as he did every night. Only tonight he prayed aloud. As Renee listened to him thank God for his life, she tuned him out, said a quick prayer of her own, and then planned her workday.

When Jerome was done with his prayers, he crawled into bed and kissed the side of Renee's head. "I love you," he said. "And I love my sons . . . and my beautiful daughter."

Renee sat up enough to turn off the lamp on the nightstand. "Good night, Jerome," she replied. At the moment, she didn't share his loving view of their "new" family.

Hearing the alarm, Renee opened her eyes and reached for the clock to stop the irritating buzzing. Still tired, she lay still and stared at a tiny bird resting on a branch outside the window. With so many concerns weighing on her heart, she'd had a restless night. How much longer could she put up with Darla's outright dislike of her? Would she ever be able to accept Joi as her stepdaughter? Could she *really* trust Jerome again? Too many unanswered questions were beginning to take a toll on her, and she didn't know how much longer she'd be able to handle the unknown. As she watched the bird fly away, Renee prayed for guidance. If she wasn't careful, her life would slowly spiral out of control, and that wouldn't be good for anyone.

Renee rolled over on her side and faced her sleeping husband. Over the years, he'd become immune to the buzz of the alarm clock. No matter what time Jerome fell asleep at night, every day he woke up by 7:00 A.M. like clockwork.

The peaceful look on Jerome's face bothered Renee this morning. How could he be so happy when she was in a state of internal turmoil? Did her feelings not matter to him anymore? Did he *really* think that all was forgiven? Why was it so easy for him to forget what he'd done? Had he been scarred at all by the effects of his affair? Renee thought she had moved past the hurt, but the wound she'd closed years ago reopened the day she came face-to-face with Joi. And this time, the pain of his affair was fresh and stronger than before.

Elise, Renee's best friend, constantly reminded her to "let go, and let God." Jerome and Taylor had apologized on many occasions and seemed genuinely remorseful, but for Renee, it was hard to accept the apology of a woman who had repeatedly slept with her husband, and to forgive the man who had vowed to love her unconditionally. Rehashing those memories, Renee realized that it was going to be hard getting over the hurt. And, if she couldn't get over all that had happened, how could she honestly move forward in her marriage to Jerome?

~2~

Jerome

When Jerome woke up that same Monday morning, he was surprised to see his wife still lying in bed next to him. For a moment, he thought his internal alarm was off, but when he looked at the digital clock on his nightstand, he realized it was indeed Renee who had overslept. This was not like Renee. She was usually up and partially dressed by the time his feet hit the bedroom floor every morning.

Jerome reached for his wife, but the unsettled look on her face bothered him, so he slowly pulled back his arm. Maybe Renee planned to sleep in late, he thought. The summer was busier than usual. Renee was in the middle of a project that could boost her career. Though she had a dependable staff, she made sure she was available at all times. This week alone, Renee had worked over sixty hours, and instead of resting over the weekend, Jerome had kept her busy with the family. He had to admit that it felt good to see her resting, since he felt partially responsible for her fatigue.

Making an effort not to disturb her, Jerome gently eased out of the bed and tiptoed to his closet. He grabbed the custom-made Chicago Bulls robe that Renee had given him for his birthday two years ago and slipped it on. As he tied the belt around his waist, Jerome closed his eyes and thanked God for another day.

After his heart attack last year, he realized that life was a precious gift, a gift that he'd shamefully abused many times. He'd taken the love of his family for granted, especially the love of his wife. Not many women would have forgiven their husband after an affair. Even fewer would have stayed when they discovered a child had been secretly conceived. Yes, Jerome was blessed, and he knew it wholeheartedly.

Keeping his daughter, Joi, a secret was never part of Jerome's plan, but he could never find the right time or the right words to reveal his shame. *Disgrace* wasn't a strong enough word to describe how he felt, but with everything now out in the open, he tried his best to make up for his indiscretions.

When he met Taylor, Joi's mother, many years ago at a popular after-hours lounge in Philadelphia, Jerome never imagined their relationship would be more than a casual friendship. It didn't take long before Taylor's lively, carefree spirit captured his heart. She was exactly what he needed at that point in his life. At the time, he and Renee fought over the simplest things—what to cook for dinner, which movie to watch, keeping the gas tank full, leaving a dirty fork in the sink. . . . There was nothing they could seem to agree on. With Taylor, everything seemed easy and stress free.

Taylor was supposed to be a temporary friend, and Jerome never promised her any more than that. Even on the worst days at home, leaving his wife was never a consideration, nor did he believe that she'd ever leave him. Jerome was certain the marriage would get better over time, but he could have never been more wrong. As one year turned into two, the feelings between Jerome and Taylor grew deeper. Without a formal conversation, Taylor assumed he wanted a divorce, and Jerome never corrected her thinking. Looking back, he wished he had. Eventually, Taylor verbally demanded more from the relationship every day. She wanted all the things Jerome knew he couldn't deliver—more time, more commitment, and signed divorce papers.

Ending the affair after Renee found out wasn't easy, but Jerome couldn't risk losing his family. He tried to let go, but the guilt of what he'd done to Taylor wouldn't let him rest. In what should've been a quick visit to apologize and say good-bye, his emotions weakened and he slept with Taylor one last time. That was the night she became pregnant with Joi.

The day Taylor shared the news of her pregnancy, Jerome was stunned. Not only had he impregnated her, but Renee was also pregnant with their youngest son. More out of fear of losing Renee for good than anything else, Jerome begged Taylor to keep quiet. "If the baby is mine, I'll send you money every month. Just please, please don't say anything to Renee," he told her that day. Taylor did keep her promise, but there were some things God didn't keep hidden in the dark forever.

Jerome rubbed his upper body. Every time he thought about what he'd done, he could feel the muscles there tighten. No matter how many times he lay on the altar and repented, he couldn't seem to forgive himself. Having known each other since high school, Jerome and Renee had grown up and matured together. They were high school sweethearts and undeniably soul mates.

Jerome closed his eyes and massaged his chest until the growing tension subsided. When he reopened them, he noticed a family picture lying on the floor between the vanity and the tall dresser. *How long has it been there?* he wondered and walked toward the dresser. Jerome leaned down to pick it up, and before putting the picture back in its place, he took a moment to admire his family. Although he was proud of his sons, it was time for an updated portrait, one that included his daughter.

Jerome put the picture on the dresser and shook his head. He couldn't imagine Renee agreeing to sit through a photo session with Joi. She hadn't said or done anything outright against Joi, but Jerome knew Renee still needed time to adjust to the new family dynamics. Joi had been in Chicago for six weeks now, and yesterday was the first time they'd all been to church together.

"I don't want to deal with the humiliation," Renee told Jerome each week.

To which he'd reply, "It doesn't matter what everyone else thinks. As long as we're okay, everyone else will be okay, too."

Renee didn't agree, but instead of belaboring the point, she created opportunities to be out of town on business every Sunday. Family outings were also a challenge. All summer Renee chose working extra hours at the hotel over spending quality time with the family, and when she did accompany them on an outing, it was as if she wasn't there at all. Jerome ignored Renee's growing distance, convincing himself that they'd eventually get past the awkwardness. She just needed more time to get used to Joi. But how much time?

Jerome sighed silently and slid into his house shoes. After all he'd put his wife and family through, he'd have to give Renee all the time she needed. It was the only fair thing to do. Heading downstairs, he saw lights flickering in the family room and realized that the television was on. When he reached the family room, he was surprised to see his two youngest children sound asleep. Joi was on the long couch, under a blanket, cradling the autographed basketball he'd given her for Christmas, and Joshua was stretched out on the leather recliner. Wedged between him and the side of the recliner were two family photo albums. They must've been up all night. Newspaper clippings and empty soda cans littered the coffee table, and open bags of pretzels and cheese curls, mixed in with DVDs, were scattered across the floor. Jerome stepped over the objects on the floor and turned off the television. Renee would gasp if she saw the family room in its present state, but Jerome was relieved to witness the evidence of his children bonding before she could discover the mess.

To a stranger, the two siblings looked as if they'd known each other all their lives. No one would believe that they met for the first time last December. They were inseparable. During the week, they volunteered at the church basketball clinic. When they weren't in church, Joshua and Joi could be found lounging around the house or hanging out with a group of friends. As close as Jerome was to his brother, and as close as his sons were, Joshua and Joi had them all beat. What more could a father ask for? Especially a father who had abandoned his only daughter until her teen years.

Jerome leaned across Joshua and turned off the lamp behind him, then walked to the kitchen. As he did every morning, he set about brewing a fresh pot of coffee, then took the nondairy creamer and a mug out of the cabinet and sat them on the counter. Although he'd changed his eating habits to include healthier foods, Jerome couldn't completely give up coffee with extra cream. At least the coffee was decaffeinated.

While Jerome waited for the coffee to brew, he began cutting up a cantaloupe and half of a small seedless watermelon.

"Morning, Jerome," a sleepy voice said from behind.

Being called by his first name bugged him, but hearing Joi call his name brought an automatic smile to Jerome's face. "Hey, baby girl," he replied as he turned around. "You and Josh were up late, huh?"

"Yes, he was telling me all the family secrets."

"And you're still here?" Jerome laughed. "That means you must really love us."

"You can't help who God chooses to be your family," Joi said playfully.

"So true," Jerome replied, touched by his daughter's insightful remark.

Joi stood next to Jerome and put one arm around him. "Need some help?"

"Can you make pancakes?" he asked as he put cubes of fruit in a ceramic bowl on the counter.

"I sure can," Joi said confidently. "I cook for my brothers and sister at home sometimes."

Jerome took a box of pancake mix out of the cabinet. "Great. Everything you need should be in the fridge," Jerome replied, taking a clean bowl and spatula from the dishwasher. "Let me know if you need my help."

The timer on the coffee machine buzzed, and Jerome poured himself a cup. Before taking a seat at the table, he mixed in three heaping teaspoons of creamer and then turned on the small television set sitting near the edge of the L-shaped counter. As he listened to the latest in sports, Jerome watched his daughter prepare breakfast. Having missed the first sixteen years of her life, he took advantage of even the smallest moments to observe her. Joi was more like him than any of his children in looks, interests, and demeanor. That filled him with pride.

"You don't have to stare at me, Jerome. I'm not going to set the house on fire or anything," Joi said as she poured batter into a hot skillet.

"I know," Jerome replied, unashamed of his actions. "I only have two more weeks to look at you. Is that a crime?"

"Ten days," corrected Joi. "The time did go too fast, though. I feel like I didn't really get to know anyone but you and Josh."

"There's plenty of time for that," Jerome assured her. "Besides, you'll be back again. Aren't you interested in the University of Illinois?"

"I don't know where I'm going to college," replied Joi. "Mom wants me to go to Temple. You want me to attend U of I. . . . I might go to the University of Hawaii to make both of you mad."

"Please don't go that far," Jerome begged. He was just beginning to know his daughter, and he didn't want them to lose touch. Hawaii was too far away to visit regularly.

"I'll take the best offer," Joi said, flipping the first set of pancakes, "but I hope I can come back here before next summer."

"You never need an invitation to come see your father, sweetheart." Jerome took a sip of his coffee and noticed Renee standing in the hallway outside the kitchen with a scowl on her face. Before he could speak, Joshua ran around Renee and into the kitchen.

"Morning!" Joshua shouted to everyone as he plopped his 130-pound body in a chair at the table. "Joi's cooking breakfast?" he asked with a grin.

"Yes, your sister is the chef this morning," Jerome answered and then faced his wife. He wondered how long she'd been standing there. "Morning, babe."

As Joi placed a pitcher of orange juice on the table, she chimed, "Good morning, Renee."

Renee mumbled something too low to hear when she entered the kitchen, and Jerome sensed that she was in a bad mood. What had happened between the time she went to sleep and the time she woke up this morning? Had he done something to anger her, or was she upset about work?

Renee stepped around Joi to get to the patio doors and then opened the shades to let more sunlight into the room. When she turned around, she almost bumped into Joi, who was carrying the bowl of fruit to the table. Joi chuckled at the near blunder, but Renee remained expressionless. She stopped cold in her tracks and waited for Joi to get out of her path before continuing.

"You okay, babe?" Jerome asked, concerned.

Renee took a small glass from the cabinet and then opened the refrigerator. "I'm fine."

"I put orange juice on the table, Renee. Want me to pour you a glass?" Joi asked kindly.

"No thanks. The acid in the orange juice may be too much for my stomach today," Renee replied as she placed a container of cranberry juice on the counter.

Jerome stood up and poured the remains of his coffee into the sink. He rubbed Joi's shoulders and then stood next to his wife. "Not feeling well?" he asked, careful not to agitate her given her sensitive mood. It sounded like Renee was on her monthly cycle. She was in the early stages of menopause, so every few months she experienced some spotting and mild cramping. That had to be why she wasn't herself this morning.

Renee poured cranberry juice into her glass and left the open jug on the counter. "I'm fine," she repeated and then walked to the computer in the corner of the room.

Something was definitely wrong. Renee would never leave an open container of anything on the counter. Jerome took the liberty of putting the cap on the cranberry juice and returning it to the refrigerator. "Are you working at home today?" he inquired curiously.

Renee picked up a small stack of unopened mail and, as she sifted through it, mumbled, "Yes."

"I cut up some fruit for us. That cool for you, or would you like some cereal?" asked Jerome.

Renee sat in the chair next to Joshua and started to open her mail. "Fruit is good. I'm not that hungry."

Without asking, Joi refilled Jerome's coffee mug. "Thanks, sweetheart," Jerome said and leaned against the counter.

Joi removed a small plate of sausage from the microwave and placed it on the table. "Breakfast is ready."

Jerome took a sip of his coffee. "Smells good," he said and sat his mug on the countertop. "Why don't you say grace this morning, Josh."

Without hesitation, Joshua did as his father asked. He blessed the food, using the traditional grace, and then ended with a word of encouragement for the day. When he was done, he was the first to put a stack of pancakes on his plate. "What time are we leaving for my driving test today, Pop?" he asked as he buttered his hotcakes.

"I did promise to do that today, didn't I?" Jerome said and then looked at Renee. "Do you mind dropping Joi off at church?"

Renee nearly dropped the fork in her hand. "Take her to church?"

"I guess I was so focused on my meeting today, I forgot about the driving test," Jerome explained.

"Mom, you know I've been waiting to get my permit," Joshua interjected. "We talked about this yesterday, remember? I said I'd be your personal chauffeur."

Renee half smiled at her son as she put a few pieces of fruit on her plate.

"I need to get him there early in case there's a line," said Jerome. "I'm meeting the principal at—"

"Fine, Jerome. I can take her," Renee interrupted and grabbed her plate and unopened mail. "Josh," she continued in a softer tone as she got up from the table, "make sure you clean up the family room after you eat."

"Mom gets like this when she's stressed," Joshua said after Renee left the kitchen.

Joi glanced his way. "I'm sure that's it," she said with mild sarcasm and continued to eat.

Jerome excused himself from the table and went after Renee. By the time he reached her, she was halfway up the steps. "Babe," Jerome called, but she didn't stop. "Babe," he said again, a little louder. "Are you *sure* everything is okay?" He was beginning to think her mood was more than frustration about her menstrual cycle.

"Everything is fine," Renee stressed as she climbed the stairs.

"C'mon, babe. I know when something's going on with you. Did something happen at work? Did Darla do something?" he asked.

Renee stopped at the top of the stairs. If looks could kill, he would've dropped dead to the floor. "This has nothing to do with work," she snapped. Jerome looked confused, and that angered her even more.

"You have to help me out, then, babe, because last night you were fine and now—"

"That's where you're wrong," Renee shouted. "I was *not* fine last night, but you were so into how happy you're feeling now that Joi is here that you didn't notice *my* feelings." She put her hand on the banister. "You can't really think I'm okay with all of this, can you?"

Jerome was speechless. He hadn't expected Renee's explosion.

"Why can't you inconvenience yourself?" she continued, pointing at him for effect. "Why ask *me* to transport *your* daughter? It was *you,* after all, who lay down with Taylor, unprotected. This isn't easy, Jerome, and I need you to stop acting like everything is okay, because everything, *especially* you and me, is *not* okay."

Jerome had no defense. It was he who had had the affair, and it was he who had kept Joi a secret for more than sixteen years. It hurt that Renee stressed that Joi was *his* daughter, but he had to accept the blame. "I understand," he began, "and I'll do what—"

"You shouldn't have slept with Taylor," Renee huffed. "And I don't think there's anything that you can do at this point to make this situation better."

Jerome didn't really know what to say. "If you don't want to take her, I can make other arrange—"

"It's too late for that now. I said I'll take her," Renee angrily replied and then stomped to the bedroom.

Jerome stood at the bottom of the staircase until he heard the door slam. It was clear that Renee was still uncomfortable with Joi's presence. In fact, Jerome could safely say that she was angrier now than she was eight months ago. Feeling tense, Jerome gently rubbed his chest with his hand as he prayed for God to show him how to ease his wife's pain. What he'd been doing the last few months was obviously not good enough.

Once Jerome got himself together, he walked back to the kitchen and joined his children at the table. He wondered how much of the conversation they'd heard. Though the television was on, he wasn't sure the volume was high enough to drown out Renee's words.

"Is Mom cool?" Joshua asked, nibbling on a piece of sausage.

"She's fine," responded Jerome. "Work is a little hectic right now, that's all."

Jerome couldn't look his children in the eyes. His response was far from the truth, and he had a feeling they knew it. As they all finished breakfast in silence, Jerome tried to convince himself that everything would be all right. He just had to give Renee more time.

~3~
Joi

Joi struggled to get her thick, unpermed hair into a bushy ponytail. On most days, she had little trouble taming her hair. Now that she was under pressure, she couldn't get the band in place without unwanted lumps and uncooperative stray hairs. After the fifth try, Joi gave up. Renee was taking her to church this morning, and she didn't want to make her wait too long. Without taking a last look in the mirror, Joi grabbed the studded belt hanging on the doorknob and began threading it through her jean loops as she ran downstairs.

Before going into the kitchen, where she thought Renee would be waiting, Joi pulled out the crisp white sneakers she kept at the bottom of the hall closet. With her sneakers in hand, she went into the kitchen, to find Jerome unloading the dishwasher. "Hey, Jerome. Have you seen Renee?"

Jerome turned around. "No. Did you check her room?"

"The lights were off," Joi responded, and a faint line appeared between her brows. "Do you think she fell asleep?"

"I'll go check," Jerome offered and closed the dishwasher.

Joi followed him out of the kitchen, and while she waited for his return, she double-checked the family room. She wanted to make sure Joshua hadn't forgotten to clean up, as his mother requested. She'd learned in a short period of time that Renee was the boss of the house, and her rules were to be followed without debate.

Last week Joshua had taken Joi on a tour of downtown Chicago. The day had been great. By the time they reached Navy Pier, the sun had gone down and the temperature had dropped to a comfortable eighty-four degrees. Joi was so excited that she'd convinced Joshua to stay out later than his normal curfew. It was hard to persuade him to stay out, and at some point Joi saw beads of sweat form on his nose, but that didn't stop her. She pressed the issue until he gave in. After only an hour of extended fun, Renee called Joshua's cell phone and ordered him to go to the hotel where she worked. "No child of mine travels on public transportation this late at night," Renee scolded when she picked them up from the hotel that night.

Joi didn't understand why Renee was so stern. Was she really that uptight all the time, or was she upset that Joshua was enjoying his time with his half sister? In Philadelphia, Joi was allowed to use the bus as long as she was with someone or one of her parents was meeting her at the last stop. Why wasn't this an acceptable option for Renee?

Joi wanted Renee to like her, but it was more important that she strengthen her relationship with Jerome, which she had. In the weeks that she'd been in Chicago, he felt more like a father than a friend. She'd even considered calling him Pop, which she knew he wanted.

Joi's half brothers were coming around slowly. Reggie and his wife lived in New York, but they made sure they talked to her at least once a week. Junior was a little more resistant. He didn't go out of his way to speak with her but would occasionally entertain brief conversations, mostly about sports. Joshua was the only one of Jerome's sons with whom Joi had connected instantly, and that was odd to Joi, because Joshua was very close to his mother.

Jerome walked back downstairs with a puzzled look. "She's not upstairs, and I've been in the kitchen all this time, so I know she can't be in the basement."

"Did Josh see her?" Joi asked meekly.

"He said she was dressed," Jerome said as he left the hallway.

Joi sat at the bottom of the staircase and waited. There was nothing else she could do. She'd overheard the disagreement between Renee and Jerome earlier this morning. Renee wasn't happy that Joi was visiting for the summer, but would she really make her late for work at the church?

"Where are you?" Joi heard her father say from the kitchen. Joi guessed he was on the phone, because she didn't hear Renee reply. "Okay, she'll be right out."

Jerome returned to the hallway, holding the cordless phone, and Joi looked up at him as she tied her shoelace, waiting for an answer. "She's sitting in the driveway," he said with a hint of disappointment.

Joi jumped up nervously. "How long has she been there?"

"Not long," Jerome replied and opened the door leading to the garage.

Joi moaned under her breath. She didn't understand why he had asked Renee in the first place. Jerome could've dropped her off before heading to the DMV, or she could've taken the bus.

"Don't worry. Renee just wanted some fresh air," Jerome said, trying to assure her that Renee wasn't mad at her.

Jerome stepped into the garage first, and Joi followed. The main garage doors were rolled up, and Renee was sitting in a lawn chair at the top of the driveway, reading a magazine. Jerome walked to the driveway and whispered something in Renee's ear. Whatever it was, she didn't want to hear it. Renee closed the magazine in her hand and stood up. Jerome tried to pull her close, but Renee pushed back. It was painful for Joi to watch their interaction. *This is all my fault,* she thought. *I'm the reason why they're not getting along.*

Renee tried to fold her lawn chair a few times, but Jerome stopped her at each attempt. Finally, Renee gave up trying and walked away, leaving Jerome to fold the chair and return it to the garage himself. Without saying a word or looking in her direction, Renee unlocked her car, and Joi reached for the passenger-side door handle.

The engine started, but before getting inside, Joi looked at her father, hoping there had been a change in plan. But "Have a good day, sweetheart," was all he said.

"You, too," Joi responded, then eased into the passenger seat. She could tell Jerome was upset.

Joi adjusted her seat belt as Renee backed her Infiniti out of the garage. As the main garage door lowered and Jerome disappeared from her view, Joi was thankful it was only a twenty-minute drive to the church.

Right away, Renee turned on the radio, and for the next ten minutes she and Joi listened to NPR in silence. Joi decided to take a chance and start a conversation. Maybe if they talked about what had happened, things would get better. At least that was her stepfather's theory. "Did I ever tell you about the day I found out about Jerome? I was at my Mom's clothes store," Joi said, even though Renee didn't seem interested. "I was trying to get out of there, and then one of her friends came in. The lady told me I looked like my dad, and I thought she meant Lance. That's my stepfather's name. But then she said Jerome's name, and my mother looked like she'd seen a ghost, so I looked at my Mom like, what is she talking about?" Joi laughed for amusement, though she knew the situation wasn't funny.

Pausing for a moment, Joi hoped Renee would say something, but when she didn't, Joi finished her story. "Mother and I weren't on good terms for a while after that." Joi saw Renee grip the wheel tighter, but she kept going. "I told her I wanted to meet Jerome, even if I had to come to Chicago by myself. I wanted to see him and tell him off," Joi said and chuckled. Running out of words to say, Joi thanked Renee for welcoming her this summer. "Jerome and I are getting closer. Me and Josh, too."

Focused on the road, Renee turned onto Madison Avenue. Only five blocks until they reached the church. Joi tried one last time to make a personal connection. "How did you find out about me?" she asked, not really expecting a response. "I know I was surprised, but how—"

"That's a conversation for adults," Renee said abruptly, never taking her eyes off the road.

Taken off guard by Renee's reaction, Joi replied, "I didn't mean any harm. I just want everyone to get along."

"I don't see that happening," Renee responded gruffly. "You can't force people's feelings. There are things that have happened that you can't understand. You're too young, and you really just met all of us. You don't have any idea of the history between Jerome and me, or Jerome and your mother. Jerome was a married man, and your mother sle—" Renee stopped mid-sentence, realizing she might have gone too far.

Joi was stunned. No, she didn't know everything about her mother's relationship with Jerome, but she shouldn't be punished because of their actions. Her mother had moved on, and so had Jerome. When was Renee going to accept that and move on, too?

Renee pulled into the church parking lot, and when the car came to a complete stop, Joi opened the door. With one foot on the concrete, Joi turned to face her stepmother. "Do you think you'll ever think of me as part of the family?"

"Look," Renee began and then let out a deep sigh. "This isn't your fault. But I honestly don't know how I feel right now or how I'm going to feel in the future."

Teary-eyed, Joi stared out the window and wondered how adults expected children to forgive when they couldn't themselves. Somehow, Joi had managed to forgive Jerome and her mother for keeping the truth from her. Though Renee was experiencing a different kind of pain, in Joi's mind pain was pain.

Understanding that she couldn't control Renee's attitude toward her, Joi got out of the car. "Thanks for the ride," she said somberly and, without looking back, walked into the church.

~4~

Renee

Renee slammed the garage door and threw her purse and strapless sandals on the stair landing. She couldn't explain why she was so angry. What happened in her marriage was not Joi's fault, yet every time she saw her face or heard her voice, nothing but resentment and sorrow surfaced.

It took a lot of heart for Joi to start a conversation during the drive to church, but Renee wasn't open to bonding with a stepchild she hadn't known a full year. In her heart, Renee knew she was wrong for the way she treated Joi, but something inside her refused to allow a relationship between them to develop. Maybe she was being selfish and immature, but Renee honestly doubted that she would ever accept Joi as a part of the family. And if that was truly how she felt, what did that say about her marriage?

Renee opened her purse and grabbed her cell phone. Rather than stress about something she couldn't change, she wanted to enjoy a quiet, peaceful day at home, starting with a bowl of oatmeal. The fruit from breakfast wasn't enough to hold her until lunchtime.

Once inside the kitchen, Renee connected her cell phone to the charger, then opened the cabinet and reached for the Quaker oatmeal box, only to find that it was empty. *Who would do such a thing?* she asked herself and threw the box back inside the cabinet. The person who ate the last packet could have thrown the box in the trash. Though anyone could be the guilty party, Renee couldn't help but blame Joi. In all the years that she'd lived with Jerome and the boys, this had never happened.

Since oatmeal was no longer an option, Renee settled on Honey Nut Cheerios. There was at least enough left in the box for one bowl of cereal. Renee sat the box on the counter and opened the end cabinet. "What happened to all the bowls?" she said aloud. There were several small plates and a few teacups, but no bowls. She took a deep breath. Things had certainly changed since Joi came to stay for the summer.

Renee moved down a few paces to the dishwasher and opened the door. Someone had taken the time to wash the dishes but not put them away. That wasn't going to be Renee's job today, either. After removing a large bowl and spoon from the dishwasher, she poured the cereal into the bowl. Just as she was about to open the refrigerator, her cell phone vibrated against the countertop.

"I hope that's not Jerome," Renee moaned as she picked up the phone, and she was relieved to see Everett's number. "Good morning," she said cheerfully and leaned against the kitchen sink.

"Morning, beautiful," Everett said. "I got your e-mail. It's not like you to take a day off on short notice. You okay?"

Lately, Everett's gentle baritone voice seemed deeper and more sensuous. Had it always been that way? Or did the stress in Renee's life make his voice seem more soothing?

"Nothing new, Everett," replied Renee. "I had a busy weekend with Jerome and the kids. I guess I need some me time today. Sometimes I feel like I'm losing my mind around here."

"What can I do to help?" Everett asked. "I can't have you losing anything until the London hotel opens next year."

"Don't worry. I'm on top of our plans. You know I'm not going to let you down."

"Okay," Everett said, with a little concern in his tone, "but you haven't been yourself for a while now. I don't like to see my partner this way. Every day I wonder when the real Renee is going to show up."

Hearing Everett say that, Renee remembered the talk she had had with her husband. Jerome had, in so many words, said the same thing this morning in the driveway. She wondered if her children, friends, and other colleagues had noticed a change in her, too. "I'm trying to feel normal again," Renee said and heard her voice crack, "but I can't seem to breathe long enough to deal with Jerome's daughter." Renee paused long enough to control her emotions. "Do you know he asked me to take Joi to church this morning? If my son hadn't been sitting next to me, I would've hit him. But that's not me anymore," she said and told him about her day.

Everett grunted playfully, and that made Renee smile. He knew about Renee's past high-strung be-havior and had given her the nickname "Short Fuse." That was when she was in her thirties and forties. At fifty-three, Renee liked to believe that she was more reserved now, but sometimes, like this morning in the car with Joi, her patience was thin.

"You do know that was the old Renee coming out, right?" Everett said with care when Renee finished. "Look, I'm not going to play games with you. No one should make you go backward. Your husband should bring out the best in you. The old Renee understood that," Everett lectured. "Don't let this situation get out of hand and make you lose sight of what's good for *you.*"

Renee stared at the smudges on one of the patio doors as she listened to Everett talk. It was easier to focus on what she needed to clean than on what he was saying. Renee took a few squares from the roll of paper towels on the counter and grabbed a bottle of Windex from the cabinet below the sink. "You're my counselor now?" she half joked and walked to the patio doors.

"I really care about you, Renee," Everett admitted. "I mean that. We're more than colleagues, and most days I feel like we're more than friends," he continued. "I think you know that."

Renee swallowed hard and squirted a generous amount of Windex on the patio door. She didn't know how to reply, and with all the problems she was dealing with, Renee wished he would stop sharing his feelings. She rapidly wiped at the same spot until small particles of the paper towel left faint streaks across the glass. Renee knew she'd be fooling herself if she pretended not to know how he felt. The chemistry between them had been evident since the day they met. It just wasn't a good time to discuss those feelings.

"I respect your marriage, but it hurts me to see you this way."

"Ev, I know," she began. "The truth is, I can't shake what Jerome has done to me, and to this family. I'm trying to take care of this. I've been praying, but I feel like God isn't listening, because I'm still so mad." Renee squirted more Windex on the glass door and wiped it clean. "As for your feelings . . . Ev, despite what Jerome and I are going through . . . we're still married, and I don't—"

"Renee, it wouldn't be right for me to speak against your marriage. I only want what's best for you," Everett declared. "It's hard for me to sit by and watch him do this to you for so many years when I know I can do better."

Hearing his words brought back memories of their first business trip together many years ago. Though they were attracted to one another, Renee did her best to stay professional. She'd heard rumors about intimate encounters between colleagues on these types of trips. Renee wasn't that kind of woman, despite the fact that Everett appeared to be the man of her dreams. Even when he leaned in to kiss her good-night one evening after a Chicago boat ride, Renee held her ground. "We can't do this," she told him reluctantly. After that night, Renee feared that she'd offended him and that their relationship moving forward would be awkward. But Everett didn't change. Instead of becoming distant, he respected her wishes and over time became one of her closest friends.

"Everett, I—" Renee closed her eyes. She didn't want to say the wrong thing and risk ending their friendship. He'd been a part of her life for seventeen years. She had shared things with him that she hadn't even told her husband or Elise.

The day Renee told him about Joi—and then, days later, about Jerome's heart attack—Everett had reacted like a true friend. Though it was the holiday season and she should've been with her family, Renee couldn't stand to be near her husband. Everett instantly dropped his plans and flew to Chicago. Jerome was recuperating in Philly, so he didn't want Renee to spend Christmas and New Year's alone. Everett had been a godsend; he knew exactly what to do and what to say. There was never any pressure in their friendship, but at some point, everyone's patience wore thin.

"Everett, I don't know what to say," Renee finally said. "I didn't know—"

Everett stopped her. "Renee, we're both adults. I apologize if I made you feel uncomfortable, but I needed to put my feelings out there. We can go on as normal and talk whenever you're ready."

Go on? How can we go on? Renee thought.

"I'll be in Chicago in a few days to help finish the media center proposal," Everett said, changing the subject. "Call me if you want to throw around some ideas."

"Okay," mumbled Renee, glad the conversation about them had ended. She didn't have the energy to deal with another issue.

"I'm here for you, Renee," he said. "I always will be."

There was a moment of silence, followed by a weak good-bye, and Renee disconnected the call. *What do I do now?* she asked herself and stared at the cell phone. Part of her was afraid to explore her feelings for Everett. If she stopped to think about how much his friendship meant to her, she'd allow her mind to wander. Everett had the qualities most women revered in a mate. His poise, demeanor, and business savvy were attractive on many levels.

Maybe what was happening was all her fault. Maybe she shouldn't have allowed a friendship to develop in the first place.

Renee reconnected her cell phone to the charger. Had she really been naive all these years? Was she foolish to believe that a man and woman could have a pure friendship?

Still hungry, Renee took a gallon of milk from the refrigerator and removed the cap. As she put the cap on the counter, she noticed a slip of paper with dates and names on it. Curious, Renee examined the paper more closely. It looked like Jerome was making plans to have the family get pictures taken at Sears. On the paper, he'd listed the cost of various package options. Next to the prices, he'd scribbled ideas for poses. There were several with him and Joi, some with him and the boys, a few with him and the grandchildren, one with him and his daughter-in-laws, and two with the entire family. Renee's name was circled next to a darkened question mark.

Puzzled, Renee turned the paper over, hoping to find more information, but the other side was blank. *Why the question mark?* she wondered. Was Jerome planning to have pictures taken without her? Before Renee realized what she was doing, she ripped the paper into small pieces and tossed them into the trash. There had to be a logical explanation, but nothing she came up with seemed to be a reasonable excuse. Renee poured milk over the cereal and then returned the gallon to the refrigerator. There was only one way to stop her mind from racing. She needed to speak to Jerome and ask him directly.

Using her cell phone, Renee dialed his number. After four rings, Jerome didn't answer, and she had to leave a message. "Hey, it's me. Call the house when you have a moment." Renee hit the bright red button to end the call and then sat the phone on the table.

Normally, Renee would put all her energy into work when she wanted to avoid dealing with marital problems, but today she decided to exercise. Donna Richardson's latest workout video had been sitting on the entertainment center, unopened, for weeks. On the way to the upstairs Renee stumbled over Joi's basketball. "What's this doing in the hallway?" she moaned. Agitated, she picked up the ball and tossed it into the hall closet. "And why are there so many shoes down here?" she questioned, staring at a disorderly arrangement of sneakers and shoes at the bottom of the closet. "Didn't Jerome tell his child that only one pair of shoes is allowed at a time?" Feeling her frustration build, Renee slammed the door, grabbed her purse and sandals, then stomped upstairs and down the hall to her bedroom.

Already disturbed by the events of the morning, Renee sat on the edge of the bed and let her sandals and purse fall freely from her hands. One thing was certain. Renee was tired. Every aspect of her life seemed to be out of control, and for a person who prided herself with maintaining order, she was finding it hard to cope.

Renee kicked the sandals across the floor and inhaled deeply. Something in her life had to change, and soon. Feeling overwhelmed, she thought about calling her best friend. Though Elise knew about Jerome's affair, she had no idea that Renee had a sixteen-year-old stepdaughter. Just the sound of those words sent a chill through her spirit. *I'm a stepmother,* Renee told herself. *I have a stepdaughter.*

"God, why did this happen to me? Did Taylor *have* to get pregnant?" she said aloud and continued in a one-sided conversation with an imaginary friend. "Haven't I been a good wife and mother? I've compromised, sacrificed, and learned to forgive, all to be betrayed, taken for granted, and lied to."

Minutes passed, and Renee was still staring into an unmarked space, waiting for something to happen. Then, out of nowhere, her heart began to ache like it never had before, and slowly she began to cry. Her soft whimpers turned into moans, and her moans escalated into cries that she belted from deep within her soul. Renee felt like she was crying for every woman who ever experienced betrayal in her home or in the workplace. "Why does this have to hurt so bad?" she shouted and continued to cry until she couldn't produce another tear. "What do I do now?" she moaned. "I can't go on this way. Lord, please, *please* help me."

Renee had always been able to handle problems. Often referred to as Superwoman, Renee was ready to turn in her cape for one that fit the loyal sidekick.

Staring at the phone, Renee dialed Elise's work number. The phone rang twice before she answered.

"How are you, honey?" Elise asked after hearing her friend's voice.

"I'm living," Renee mumbled. "How's Florida?"

"Hot!" exclaimed Elise. "What's up with you? When are you coming to visit?"

As hard as Renee tried, she couldn't contain her emotions. There was still a load of tears inside of her to release. In less than five minutes, Renee gave Elise a summary of the last eight months of her life.

"What do you mean, he has a daughter the same age as Josh?" queried Elise.

"You heard me right," said Renee. Seconds passed, and Elise had yet to reply. "Elise, are you still there?"

"Wow. I can't believe what I'm hearing," Elise answered. "I want to tell you the right thing to do, but the girlfriend in me wants to say the opposite. This is heartbreaking."

"I know," Renee said, sniffling. "The harder I try to accept it, the angrier I become."

"That's because you haven't really had a chance to let this sink in. It's not just his affair anymore. I'm so sorry, Renee. I really don't know what to say, and who knows what I'd do if it were my husband instead of Jerome," Elise replied. "Why did you keep this from me for so long?"

"Embarrassed, I guess. And I knew you had a lot on your plate with your own family. I didn't want to be a burden."

"That's nonsense," Elise countered. "No matter what I'm going through, I'm always here for you. We're like sisters."

"I don't think we're gonna survive this one," confessed Renee.

"As a child of God, you know prayer is your weapon. Miracles aren't a thing of the past."

"I've been praying, and my feelings haven't changed one bit."

"They will," Elise assured her. "Your wounds are still fresh, that's all."

"It's already been eight months," Renee replied.

"His daughter is sixteen. You can't put a limit on the healing process," explained Elise. "It could take years."

Renee stared out the window. That was the last thing she wanted to hear. "Sometimes I don't want to try and make this work," she admitted. "Joi walks around like she's the queen of *my* house. She talked Josh into staying out late last week. He knows better than that. She leaves her shoes in the downstairs closet and lets her basketball roll free throughout the house. I can't take anymore, Elise."

"I know you're hurt, but this isn't Joi's fault. You're upset with Jerome. He could've said no to Taylor, and none of this would be happening, but let me not go there," Elise retorted, trying to remain focused. "Why don't you try talking to Joi again? You might find that you like her."

Renee had a better solution. "Maybe I need to move out until she leaves."

"That might make matters worse," Elise said quickly. "Let God help you through this. Isn't keeping your beautiful family worth fighting for?"

Renee couldn't answer. She loved her original family, not the new, extended one.

"I need to go," Elise said. "But why don't I come out to Chicago in October. We can work through this in person. Would that be okay?"

"Sure," Renee replied, though she was unsure that she could wait that long. She had to make a move. The two friends confirmed a date for the visit and then wrapped up the call.

Renee put the cordless back on the nightstand. Although Elise lived in Florida, the distance hadn't changed their friendship. They had supported and encouraged one another in the best and worst of times. That was why Renee had called her today. The conversation was supposed to make her feel better about her situation. It was supposed to give her some encouragement, even if it was only enough to get through the day. But the conversation did neither. It only confirmed how tired Renee was of the mess her husband had created.

Renee was tired of trying to make things better. She was tired of asking God to change her heart. She was tired of feeling guilty about the way she treated Joi. She was tired of sacrificing her time, of being strong, and of pretending. She was just plain tired.

Closing her weary eyes, Renee counted to ten. When she reopened them, her eyes gravitated to a suitcase under the window. It had been there, untouched, since her last business trip. "God!" she called out. *It sure would be good to get away now.* Renee stood up and brought the suitcase to her bed. As she unzipped the side pocket, she thought more seriously about leaving the house for a few days. Elise didn't think leaving would solve any problems, but Renee feared that if she didn't escape, she'd lose her mind. Her emotional rampages were getting worse. Without thinking anything through, Renee picked up the cordless phone again and dialed her assistant. What harm would two weeks away do?

"Luxury Inn, Carmen speaking."

"Hi, Carmen. This is Renee. I need to book a room for today. Can you check to see if any suites are available for the next two weeks?"

"Sure, Mrs. Thomas," replied Carmen. "Give me a minute to check availability."

While on hold, Renee emptied the suitcase and removed two duffel bags from her closet. That should be enough to hold two weeks' worth of clothes and accessories.

"Mrs. Thomas," Carmen said, now back on the line, "the Governor's Suite is available. Did you say two weeks?"

"Yes," responded Renee. "Two weeks."

"Okay. Hold on one more moment."

Renee stuffed an armful of clothes inside the suitcase without neatly folding them. She stuffed several pairs of shoes inside one of the duffel bags and noticed a restaurant brochure sticking out of a side flap. Renee removed the brochure and smiled. Bahama Breeze was one of her favorite restaurants. The menu selection was average compared to that of many of its competitors, but the service and environment were always top notch. The only bad experience Renee had there was the day Taylor rudely interrupted her business lunch with Everett. That afternoon Taylor had the audacity to blame Renee for the affair she'd had with her husband. How dare she embarrass her in room full of patrons? Renee was the wife, not the other woman.

"Mrs. Thomas," Carmen said when she returned. "I have you all set for two weeks in the Governor's Suite, starting today."

"Perfect," Renee said as other instances of Taylor's boldness flashed through her mind—the time she approached her during an altar call, the time she appeared in the bathroom at a prayer breakfast. . . . "You know what?" Renee said before Carmen hung up. "I'm not sure how long I'll need the suite, actually. Can you keep the room open for me?"

"Open?" Carmen sounded surprised. "Uh . . . I guess that should be fine. If the governor needs the suite, I'm sure we can make other arrangements for you."

"Not a problem," answered Renee. More encounters with Taylor were something Renee wasn't looking forward to. She wanted Taylor out of her life forever, but because of Joi, what she wanted could never be. Two weeks was not enough time for her and Jerome to mend their marriage, so she thought it might be best to stay at the hotel until they had a chance to figure out how to move forward.

"All right, you're all set. The room is reserved under your corporate card."

"Thanks, Carmen. I'll see you shortly," Renee said and hung up. She wanted to leave before Jerome came home and tried to change her mind. Renee knew she should've prayed before calling the hotel, but she didn't want God to talk her out of leaving, either.

After checking to see if she had everything she needed, Renee carried her bags downstairs. Though packing was easy, it was going to be hard telling the children why she decided to leave. "I forgot my jewelry," Renee said aloud as she sat her bags on the floor. She rushed upstairs and headed to her bedroom to get a few pieces of jewelry.

"Renee?" Jerome asked, and Renee jumped. She hadn't expected him to be home for at least another couple hours. "What's going on? I heard your message and came home. Are you going on another business trip?"

Renee continued to load her jewelry into a small carry-on bag. "I don't want to drag this out, so I'll get to the point." She turned around to face Jerome and with confidence said, "I'm leaving."

Jerome fell to the bed. "Leaving? Is this about what happened this morning?"

At this point, Renee thought it best to be honest. No more pretending or catering to Jerome's feelings. "After church yesterday, I thought about Joi's visit," she said. "This may be selfish, but at this point in my life, I don't want to rearrange my world to include a child I didn't give birth to. And there's no other explanation I can give you for my feelings. I just don't want to deal with this. I love you, but I need to move on to a new chapter in my life."

"Are you saying you want a divorce?" Jerome asked in a high-pitched tone.

"I'm saying I need a fresh start, and right now I don't know what that means for us."

Jerome seemed stunned. "Is this really about you and Everett? Is he the reason you're not giving this a real try?"

"Are you kidding me?" Renee snapped and zipped the carry-on bag. "Trying is all I've been doing since I found out about Joi. I've tried to be understanding. I've tried to accept the fact that you had an affair. I've tried to accept that you need time with her. I've tried to cope with her bonding with my kids and my grandbabies. I'm sick and tired of trying, Jerome." Renee put the strap of the bag on her shoulder and walked out of the room.

Jerome jumped up and blocked her path. "Please, you can't leave."

"I have to," Renee said and pushed her way out the door and down the stairs. Jerome followed close behind her, nearly stepping on the back of her heels. When Renee reached the last step, she turned around. "Why did you put that question mark by my name?"

"What?" Jerome asked, confused.

"The family portrait you're planning? There was a question mark by name. Why?"

"Is *that* why you're so upset?"

"Yes, Jerome," Renee retorted. "I'm upset about the family portrait you don't want me to be a part of—"

Jerome touched Renee's arm. "Baby, then this is all a misunderstanding. I had that there because I wasn't sure about your schedule. I would never consider doing anything without you."

"You know," Renee said and picked up one of the bags, "it really doesn't matter. I'm not happy anymore. I'm not happy about the way I feel or that I'm losing control of my life. I have to do this for me, Jerome. Please understand that."

"How long will you be gone?" queried Jerome, clearly defeated.

Renee opened the garage door. "I don't know."

"What am I supposed to tell the boys . . . and Joi?"

"I don't care what you tell Joi," Renee wanted to shout, but instead, she took a deep breath and said, "You figure out what to say. I'll give the boys a call tomorrow."

Fighting for another chance, Jerome grabbed Renee's waist. "I can't let you go, not like this." He held Renee's face in the palms of his hands and kissed her passionately, hoping she'd feel the love.

Renee kissed him back, but when they were done, she looked into his eyes and said, "Good-bye. I'll be back for more clothes in a couple weeks."

"God wouldn't want us to do this. Please, Renee," pleaded Jerome. "Don't go."

"I'm not so sure God wants me to spend my golden years unhappy, either," she replied and then gathered her belongings.

Though she struggled to get out the door with all of her luggage, Renee didn't ask for help. Once in the garage, she threw her bags in the backseat of her car and then got in on the driver's side. As she backed out of the driveway, Jerome stood at the side door with pain in his eyes. Though her heart ached, too, Renee believed she was doing the right thing and prayed her family would understand her reasons for leaving.

~5~

Jerome

"Good morning," Melanie said loudly as Jerome passed by her desk.

Avoiding eye contact, Jerome opened his office door. "Sorry, Mel," he said with little enthusiasm. "Good morning."

Without looking at the keyboard, Melanie continued to type on the computer. "Judging from the bags under your eyes, you had a rough night," she said. "Everything okay?"

"I'm a little tired," Jerome replied as he loosened the tie around his neck.

"A little tired" was an understatement. After Renee left the house last night, he'd slept for a total of fifteen minutes, three quick five-minute naps. How could he sleep? When he woke up yesterday, he was a happily married man, and today he was unhappy and separated from his wife.

Jerome closed his office door and walked to his desk. He dropped his briefcase beside his specialized leather chair and sat down. It was no secret that Renee was struggling to adjust to Joi's presence in the house, but he'd had no idea she was contemplating separation.

Last night, after a spaghetti dinner, Joshua asked if Renee was working late. It was hard to look him in the eye and lie, but Jerome felt he had no choice. It was, in his eyes, the best thing to do until he and Renee had a chance to talk this through. He only prayed God would forgive him. "Your mother's working around the clock on a project," Jerome had told his son. "She doesn't want to stress us out, so . . . she'll be staying at the hotel for a while." Joshua didn't respond, but Jerome had a feeling he knew there was something more to his mother's absence.

There was a light tap at the door, and Jerome quickly hit the power button on the computer. "Come in," he said blandly.

Melanie opened the door and entered with a cup of hot coffee in her hand. "You bypassed the coffee station this morning," she said and sat the cup on Jerome's desk. "Something is *definitely* going on. Want to talk about it?"

"No," Jerome replied and focused on the creamy drink in front of him. Melanie had mastered how to prepare his favorite breakfast drink.

"Don't lie to me, Thomas," Melanie answered as she eyed Jerome's computer. Out of everyone in the entire building, she was the only one that called him by his last name. "You barely spoke when you came in. You didn't stop for coffee," she continued, "*and* you've been in your office for a good ten minutes and you're just now turning on your computer. I'd say those are clear signs that *something's* going on with you."

Jerome logged into his work e-mail account without staring at his assistant. Not only was Melanie easy on the eyes, but from time to time she'd drop subtle hints to let him know she was attracted to him. Considering his history, Jerome knew better than to give any woman reason to believe that he'd cheat on his wife. "I was looking over some paperwork," he told her.

"I may be a lot of things, but I'm no fool," Melanie stated. "I don't see any paperwork on your desk. If you don't want to talk about it, just tell me you're having a bad morning."

"I'm having a bad morning," Jerome responded and pretended to read his e-mail messages.

Melanie sat her small frame on the edge of a chair in front of Jerome's desk. "Should I send Renee flowers?"

Jerome looked up from the computer, and Melanie's lean, sculpted legs caught his attention. It was rare that she wore skirts below the knee. "Who says Renee is the reason for my bad morning?" he asked.

"Please," Melanie said and crossed her legs. "I know that sad look well. That's a face you have only after arguing with someone you *love*."

"You're something else, Melanie," Jerome said with a grin.

There wasn't much that could get by Melanie undetected. She was a little rough around the edges professionally, but she was observant and intuitive at all times. In the time they'd been working together, she'd been careless only once, and that one time was major. Melanie was the reason Renee found out about Jerome's secret child. In a hurry to complete another assignment, she'd given Renee the wrong folder. That folder happened to contain a wealth of information about Joi. "The material inside could've been confidential information," Jerome had said when he reprimanded Melanie that day. "We're lucky Renee isn't a threat, but you have to be careful with anyone not employed by the company." Though the lesson he taught Melanie was valid, Jerome knew he had to accept part of the blame. In his rush to make a flight to Philadelphia, he'd forgotten to put the folder in the file cabinet under lock and key.

Melanie had accepted Jerome's criticism with dignity, though it was clear he was venting because of his mistake. They never mentioned that incident again, but somehow Melanie could now smell when trouble involving his daughter was brewing.

"If you must know," Jerome continued, "Renee and I had a rocky night. So, I guess sending flowers wouldn't hurt." Melanie scratched her back, drawing Jerome's attention to her snug V-neck sweater, and he forced his eyes back to the computer screen.

"How bad was the argument?" she asked.

"What difference does that make?"

"Well, you *always* send flowers. Depending on the level of the argument, you may need to try something new," explained Melanie.

"An argument is an argument," he replied and meant it.

"That may be true, but it makes a difference when you're trying to make up. A new outfit, a spa day, a night out downtown, a weekend trip, a cruise—"

"A cruise?" Jerome interrupted. He liked the sound of that.

Melanie shook her head and stood up. "That bad, huh?"

"Thanks for the suggestion. I'll take it from here," Jerome replied, ignoring her remark.

"Don't be silly. It'll be my pleasure to follow up," Melanie said and picked up a thick pad of sticky notes and a pen from Jerome's desk. "I just need to know where you want to go, when, and for how long."

Planning ahead without Renee's input was often hit or miss. Jerome could never keep up with her schedule, and she rarely allotted time for spontaneity. But making the effort this time was worth a try. His marriage was on the line. "A five-day cruise anywhere interesting around the holidays would be good," he said and prayed his wife would agree.

"Great!" Melanie exclaimed and scribbled on the notepad. She was always excited about new projects. "I'll have something for you by the end of the day."

By 2:00 P.M. Jerome had finished everything he needed to accomplish. Although he didn't want to go home, he needed to do something to keep busy. Staying idle only made him concentrate on his problems at home. To make matters worse, Renee hadn't called him all day. Nor had she sent an e-mail or text message. This was the longest he'd gone without hearing her voice since they were teenagers. Even after Renee made him move out of their Philadelphia home because of the affair, he still spoke to her at least once a day. Jerome was tempted to call but also understood that his wife needed space. He wanted to respect that but feared giving her space would create too much distance between them. And if there was too much distance, Renee might never return home.

Jerome lowered his head in his hands. *God, please tell me what to do to save my marriage.* Someone at the door cleared their throat, and Jerome lifted his head.

"I don't mean to disturb you," Melanie said and escorted a young man with dreadlocks hanging past his shoulders into Jerome's office. "This is Denver McBride. He wanted to ask you a few questions about Future Ballers. Is that all right?"

It was more than all right. He welcomed the distraction. "Sure," Jerome said and stood up. He walked around his desk and shook Denver's hand. "Come on in and have a seat."

"Let me know if you need anything," Melanie said as she eased out of the office, quietly closing the door behind her.

"So, Denver, how'd you hear about the program?" Jerome asked and sat on the edge of his desk. He was curious to learn more about the man sitting in front of him. With his athletic build—strong arms, wide shoulders, and large hands—Jerome wondered if Denver had any real skills on the basketball court. Sometimes looks could be deceiving.

"I volunteer at Marshall High School and heard Coach Brown talking to some of the students about it," Denver said with a strong island accent. Jerome could tell that he talked slowly on purpose, so that he pronounced his words clearly. "It sounds like a great mentoring program. I wish something like this was around when I was playing ball in high school."

"You play ball?" queried Jerome. "Do you play for a college now?"

Denver frowned but talked to Jerome firmly about his past and future plans. He discussed his accomplishments as an athlete, his disappointment when he turned down the opportunity to play college basketball, his volunteer responsibilities at Marshall, and his determination to pursue his dreams a second time.

In Jerome's line of work, he encountered many young, talented basketball players. He rarely forgot a name or a face, but for some reason, he was drawing a blank when it came to Denver McBride. "So, Denver . . . how long have you lived in Chicago?"

Denver stretched his long legs forward. "Almost four years. I'm originally from Kingston."

"You've been at Marshall all four years?"

"Yes, sir," Denver answered politely. "I had a scholarship to Georgetown but had to decline to help my

mother. I've been out of touch for a while, but basketball is in my blood. Everything is good at home now,
so I'm ready to try again before I get too old." Denver's
eyes radiated with hope as he talked about his plans. "I
think volunteering at Future Ballers would be good for
me. It'll help keep me focused, and I'm sure I'll learn a
few things from the younger generation."

Impressed by the young man's maturity and initia-
tive, Jerome offered Denver a paid part-time position
if his references checked out. "Do you mind me asking
why you didn't try to play college ball locally?"

There was some hesitation, but Denver spoke with
confidence. "My father got into some trouble my senior
year and moved out of the house. My mother hadn't
worked in years, so I stepped in to help raise my sisters
and brother."

"That was noble of you," Jerome said.

"I didn't have a choice," replied Denver. "My mom is
working full-time now, so it's a good time for me to try
my luck again. I'm going to apply to a few colleges, so
I'm hoping one of them will give me a chance."

"That all sounds great, Denver, but while you're looking for a second chance, I hope you and your father
make amends, too. Every man makes mistakes," Jerome
told him from experience.

"With all due respect, Mr. Thomas," Denver replied,
"it's hard to respect a man who cheats on his wife, especially a man that calls himself a pastor."

Ouch, Jerome thought, then talked to Denver as if he
were one of his sons. "Don't be so hard on him. If he is
a man of great faith, I'm sure he understands the mag-
nitude of his mistake and is sorry. God forgives us all
the time, and at some point, you're going to learn how
to forgive your father as well."

"My father stood before his congregation and humiliated my mother and our family. I'm not sure I'm ready to forgive."

All of a sudden, Jerome's memory was coming together. "You say your father was the pastor of a church here in Chicago?" he asked.

The young man nodded.

Denver McBride, he said to himself. *McBride. McBride. McBride?* "Wait a minute," Jerome said. "You wouldn't happen to be Reverend Lewis McBride's son, would you?"

There was a faint look of shame in Denver's eyes. "I'm afraid I am."

Lewis McBride was once the pastor of Word of Life Church. Two years ago he had the largest congregation on the west side of town. Jerome remembered Pastor McBride well. Local and national news stations aired the established pastor's shame for an entire week. The segment showed the pastor in the middle of preaching a sermon about redemption. Out of nowhere, a young woman, no more than twenty-five years old, wearing an oversized knit poncho and dark shades approached the pulpit. McBride continued to preach as if he didn't see the woman standing there. Slowly, the woman lifted her knit garment and revealed a tiny baby wrapped in a blanket.

Security guards immediately rushed the altar, but that didn't stop the woman's mission. "Are you gonna deny your daughter in front of everyone? In front of God?" she cried repeatedly.

Pastor McBride was frozen by her words, and the media ministry's cameras zoomed in on his face, capturing his awestruck reaction. Security escorted the wailing woman and child out of the sanctuary, but the damage had already been done. As a few members in the congregation walked out, the tape ended with the pastor's last words, "God forgive me."

"Now I remember you," Jerome recalled, and Denver clenched his teeth. "You won the city's slam dunk contest two years in a row. I always wondered what happened to you. You had great talent."

Denver smiled softly. "I still do."

"Well," Jerome replied, "I once needed a second chance, so I think I'm going to help you. If you work hard, I may be able to put you in touch with a few coaches." Denver beamed with gratitude, and that warmed Jerome's heart.

"I really appreciate this."

"Like I said, I remember what it feels like to be in your shoes." Jerome searched for a pamphlet about the program on his desk. "You'll still be able to volunteer at Marshall some days. You'll learn that I'm very flexible."

Unable to find a pamphlet, Jerome wrapped up his meeting with Denver and then escorted him outside. On the way back to his office, Jerome stopped by Melanie's desk and excitedly told her about his plans for the new recruit.

"Sounds great," she said. "I'll get his application and forms ready in the morning. I need to leave in a few minutes to meet the printer. But before I go . . ." Melanie handed Jerome a sheet of paper. "Here's a list of cruises to consider. Let me know which one you like, and I'll go ahead and make all the arrangements."

"Thanks, Mel," Jerome replied as he scanned the list.

Melanie removed her purse from the file cabinet behind her desk and put it on her arm. "Renee's a lucky woman," she said. "She'll forgive you. I know she doesn't want to lose a good man."

There was an extra bounce in Melanie's walk to the stairwell, and Jerome found himself in a temporary trance. "I pray you're right, Mel," he whispered as she disappeared from his view.

Still seated at his desk a few hours later, Jerome stared at the telephone. He couldn't believe Renee had let an entire day go by without trying to contact him. Longing to hear her voice, he picked up the receiver and dialed her direct line.

"This is Renee Thomas," she said after one ring.

Jerome could tell by her tone that she was busy, and today he didn't care. He needed her to make time for him. "Hi, Renee," he said. Jerome was certain he heard a soft sigh, but ignored it. "How are you?"

"I'm in the middle of something. Can I call you back?"

Jerome didn't trust that she would, so he kept talking. "I won't hold you," Jerome told her. "I just wanted to know if you were coming to dinner on Friday. Reggie and Zora will be in town for the weekend."

This time Renee sighed louder. "I forgot about that. I'm not sure if I sh—"

Before Renee could come up with an excuse not to be there, Jerome cut her off. "The boys have a lot of questions about us. It would be nice if we talked to them together. Don't you think so?"

Renee was silent for ten seconds before giving in. "I guess I can make it."

"I understand," Jerome said, happy that she would be there. "I think it's important for us to be on the same page when we talk to the children. I also think they need reassurance that this is only temporary." Jerome waited for Renee to respond, but she didn't. "Renee . . . this isn't a permanent situation . . . is it?"

"It's too soon to tell," Renee answered carefully.

"This isn't right," Jerome said out of frustration. "And Joi thinks this is her fault."

"Then you need to tell her this is *your* fault. It's not my job to make her feel better."

"Think about the children, Renee. What is this doing to them? Joi will take this hard."

"You need to think about *me*," Renee commanded. "When am *I* going to matter in this situation? I mean, really . . . what do you expect me to do? Embrace her like I do the children I gave birth to? You want me to hug and kiss her? Take her shopping? She's *your* child, Jerome. *Your child.* A child you had while we were married. So, please spare me. I think I *deserve* some space."

Jerome didn't say anything.

"Look, I'll be there on Friday for dinner, but I can't stay all weekend," Renee announced.

"Okay," he said dryly. He didn't want to pressure Renee any further for fear that she'd change her mind altogether. "I'll see you on Friday."

~6~

Renee

Renee opened her compact makeup case and freshened up her eyeliner and lipstick.

"Yes, you are beautiful, Mrs. Thomas," said a friendly voice. "No need to stare at yourself."

Renee closed her compact case and smiled. Everett was standing at the door, staring back at her in one of his designer tailored suits. They'd been friends so long, Renee hadn't paid much attention to the way his clothes draped his body. Every bulge and ripple was apparent with little effort. "I thought you were flying in tomorrow?"

Everett entered the office like a runway model and stopped in front of Renee's desk. "I decided to come in early because I was concerned about a friend."

Not wanting to stare too long, Renee quickly looked him up and down as she put her compact case back into the top drawer. "That friend is very grateful."

"Like I said the other day, Renee . . . I'll always be here for you." Everett sat down and rested his manicured hands on each arm of the chair. "So . . . I received a call last night," Everett continued. "I hear you're staying in the Governor's Suite."

Somehow gossip always found its way to Everett's ear. One of the cleaning ladies had probably leaked the information, and by now all the employees knew she was staying in the suite.

"C'mon, you know word travels fast around here," he said and flashed his crisp white teeth.

Renee wouldn't normally justify her actions, but Everett was a friend. She could tell him the truth. "I need space to find the old Renee, that's all," she explained.

Everett lowered his hands to the top of his legs. "I'm glad to hear that. I miss my old friend."

"Listen, Ev . . . about yesterday . . . I don't want you to think that I blew you off. It's just that . . . now isn't the right time."

"It's never a good time," he replied, "but I understand. What can I say? I saw an open window and went for it."

Renee tried not to blush. "Well, I'm using this time to figure things out. I promise we'll talk once I'm clearer about my situation."

"I can respect that," Everett said, and he stood up. "Now, let's grab something to eat. My treat."

Although Everett had stood in front of Renee many times, today her mind entertained exotic thoughts. What would it feel like to lie on his chest while his strong, inviting arms hugged her? "Okay," she answered, hoping she wasn't making a mistake by accepting his invitation. Their relationship could not cross the lines of friendship, at least not at this time. "How about—"

"This is great!" Darla shouted as she marched her frail body into Renee's office. "I've got both of you in one room. I know it's after six, but do you have a minute? I just got off the phone with one of our investors, and there are a few questions I couldn't answer about the London hotel."

Both Renee and Everett looked confused. Why was Darla talking to the investors about London?

"Sure, we have a few minutes," Everett said as he pulled two chairs close to Renee's desk.

Darla hesitantly studied the look on their faces and, as she hesitantly sat down, asked, "Was I interrupting anything?"

"Not at all," Everett answered with a straight face.

"Okay . . ." Darla replied and scooted her chair closer to Everett. "Well, the investors are crazy about branching out to London, but there are a few things we may need to reconsider."

"Was there a problem to begin with?" Renee asked. "I'm not sure I understand why you'd talk to an investor without Everett's or my presence."

Darla looked directly at Everett and answered as if he'd asked the question. "There's no problem at all. I was asking about the changes to this hotel, and we casually started talking about London. All the investors are excited about moving into the international market."

"That's fine," asserted Renee. "But you shouldn't be discussing any details with anyone without one of us present—"

"Let's hear what Darla has to say," interrupted Everett. "I'm sure she wouldn't make decisions about London without us."

You're smooth, my friend, Renee thought. But this wasn't the time to be gentle. She and Everett had built solid relationships with all the investors. They were well respected, and Renee didn't want Darla to tarnish their reputation or interfere with their progress with her imprudent ideas.

For the next fifteen minutes, Darla rambled on about concerns she should've been able to address, but because she was a novice hotel manager, she needed Renee's and Everett's help. As Renee listened, she wondered when Darla was going to invite her into the conversation. Did she forget that Renee was in the room, too? Did she forget that the London hotel was a project Renee and Everett were working on *together?* Annoyed, Renee drew geometric shapes on a notepad until Darla called her name.

"I was looking for the renovation budget this afternoon," Darla stated as she stared at Renee's doodles. "Did you send it?"

With slight sarcasm, Renee covered the notepad and answered her boss. "Not yet. I've been working on the financing for London due on Thursday, remember?"

Darla's silly grin turned into a frown. "Are you having trouble managing all your responsibilities?"

"Not at all," Renee replied, a little offended. "I did send you an e-mail saying that I'd have it to you before your status meeting."

"I didn't see the e-mail," Darla retorted. "Do you think I can get it before tomorrow afternoon so I can review it?"

Renee didn't understand why she needed to review the budget so far in advance. Budgets, especially in the format in which she presented them, were not hard to follow. Unless Darla was conducting her own personal audit, Renee didn't see the point in completing the budget analysis more than a day early. "I don't think so. Status is on Friday. It's only Tuesday. I can have it done Thursday morning."

Darla was stunned, and her eyes watered as she struggled to come up with an appropriate response.

"I have some time," Everett interjected. "I can get the report to you in the morning."

Renee shot Everett an unpleasant glare. She knew he was trying to end the power struggle between the two women, but she didn't like that he'd interfered.

Darla pleasantly redirected her attention to Everett. "I'd appreciate that. Thank you," she said and stood up. Without saying good-bye, Darla smoothed the wrinkles from her dress and left the room.

When Darla was gone, Everett put her chair back in the corner of the room. "Before you say anything," he began and grinned, "I only offered to help because you two were about to throw punches."

"I know," Renee huffed and leaned back in her chair. "That woman can push my buttons with little effort. But in case you're wondering, I really did send that e-mail."

"I'm sure you did," he replied. "Now, let's forget about Darla and go eat. I'm starving."

"Okay. I'll meet you in the lobby in ten minutes. I need to wrap up a few things before I leave."

Everett nodded and then left Renee alone to work.

To ease her conscience, Renee logged into her e-mail account and searched through the sent folder. She was positive she'd sent that e-mail. But as she looked through the messages sent on Monday, she didn't find any that were sent to Darla. Just in case there was a mishap with the computer, she checked to see if the message was sent on Sunday. Again, nothing to Darla. Renee was confused.

Something in Renee's spirit told her to check the drafts folder. She closed her eyes and said a quick prayer as she hit the ENTER key. Sure enough, when she opened her eyes, the message she'd created for Darla was at the top of the list. How did I forget to hit the SEND button? she asked herself silently.

Frustrated, Renee turned off the computer. If Darla were an easier boss to work with, Renee would apologize, but there was no point in admitting her mistake now. The damage was done, and Everett had come up with a solution. Going forward, she'd have to remember to be more careful when sending e-mails.

Instead of catching a cab, Renee and Everett decided to walk the few blocks to P.F. Chang's. Being stuck inside the building all day, Renee welcomed the chance to enjoy the fresh air and scenery. Along the way, they stopped at Nordstrom. There was a huge two-day sale on shoes happening, and neither of them could pass up the chance to find a bargain.

"What do you think about these?" Everett asked as he held up a leather shoe made by an Italian designer.

Renee was impressed. If only her husband had Everett's natural sense of style. "Put those on now and you'll be ready for a *GQ* ad."

A salesman who had been arranging a new shoe display nearby joined the harmless banter. "If your wife can give you a compliment like that," he said, "you must buy those shoes."

Everett smirked and laid the shoe back on the display stand. "We're not married . . . at least not yet."

Renee lightly smacked his arm. "I thought you were going to back off."

Flushed with embarrassment, the salesman couldn't tell if they were serious or playing around.

"Don't worry, my friend," Everett said, relieving him of any discomfort. "I'll be back tomorrow."

"We better go, Ev," Renee said after looking at her watch. "We don't want to be out too late. Dragon lady will be breathing down our necks tomorrow if we don't finish our homework."

Everett let out a hearty laugh. "Dragon lady?"

"That's what I said," replied Renee. "But you have nothing to worry about, because she *adores* you."

"Jealous?"

"Not even a little," Renee answered as they walked down the center aisle of the department store.

"You know . . . I can't put my finger on it, but there's something weird going on at the hotel."

That was the first time Renee had heard Everett voice concern about the hotel. "Should we be worried?"

"Life's too short for us to worry," he said. "We'll just let things unfold as they may."

As they neared the main doors, Renee recognized a woman from church who was searching through a pile of handbags on a sale table and stopped abruptly.

"What's wrong?" Everett asked, confused. "You forget something?"

Of all the people to see, why did it have to be Sister Gloria Barnes? Gloria was a self-proclaimed deaconess at the church, and although she was younger than Renee by many years, she presented herself as a woman who was much older. One with high expectations, Gloria gave the impression that she'd been saved all her life. As such, she expected everyone else to live clean, holy lives with ease. "Living for the Lord is the only way to live," Gloria quoted every Sunday after service. Renee didn't mind her dedication to her beliefs. The problem was her inability to keep quiet about other people's personal matters. "There shouldn't be any secrets in the Kingdom of God," Gloria would say each time she was accused of having a gossiping spirit.

Though she was doing nothing wrong, Renee worried how Gloria would present what she saw to the church family. Holding on to Everett's suit jacket, Renee gently tugged his arm. "Can we go out a different door?"

Though perplexed, Everett didn't ask any questions. Whatever was bothering Renee could be discussed once they left Nordstrom.

"Sister Thomas?" Gloria called before Renee could walk the other way.

"Hey," Renee said and unbuttoned her linen jacket. The temperature in the room had definitely risen a few degrees.

"How are you?" she asked cheerfully, her long summer dress dusting the marble floor as she walked toward Renee. "My husband is speaking at a conference at the art school, so I decided to tag along. I haven't been outside of Oak Park in almost a year. We're staying at that fancy hotel on the corner," Gloria shared and then suspiciously eyed Everett. "What about you, Renee? What are you doing downtown?"

"I work at Luxury Inn, a few blocks from here," Renee replied, though she was certain Gloria already knew that. "You should've told me. I would've given you a discount."

Gloria slowly shook her head and cut her eyes in Everett's direction, giving the hint that she wanted to be introduced.

"Where are my manners?" Renee said. "This is Everett Coleman, CFO of Luxury Inn. We're on our way to a business dinner."

"Nice to meet you," Everett said as he shook Gloria's hand firmly.

"Praise the Lord. The pleasure is mine," Gloria responded and eased her hand away from his. "So, Renee, I haven't seen you in church in a very long time."

It was clear Gloria was starting trouble. Renee had missed a number of Sundays, but she was in church last week and did speak to her. "Everything's good," Renee said. "I've been traveling a lot for work."

"So . . . are you in town *this* Sunday?" inquired Gloria.

Renee knew better than to lie. She had no intention of going to church. "Not exactly."

"Oh, okay," Gloria remarked. "Well, we miss seeing you. Jerome and the children all look well. I see them every week and some Wednesday nights, and, oh, that Joi, she sure is—"

"I hate to cut you off," interjected Renee, "but we really need to go." She wasn't about to entertain a conversation about Joi with the church gossip. Gloria said she understood, but Renee sensed that wasn't true. "Enjoy your time downtown," she said and charged out of the department store, forgetting that Everett was with her.

Everett had to jog slowly to catch up with Renee. "That went well," he said.

"This isn't funny," Renee answered. "By the time Gloria gets back to her hotel room, half the church will know I was shopping with a man that isn't my husband."

"We didn't doing anything wrong," assured Everett.

"I know," she sighed, but Renee knew that she was guilty. Just not for the reasons Gloria thought. She was guilty of not going to church, of a weakened relationship with God, and of walking out on her husband.

Exhausted, Renee parked her car in front of her River Forest home and turned off the ignition. It was Friday, and she hadn't spoken to Jerome in three days. After a long and grueling week, she prayed the evening wouldn't be as dramatic. The status meeting Darla had pressed her about lasted all of twenty minutes, and she only glanced over the budget she and Everett had worked on all Tuesday evening. To top things off, Darla had Renee adjust a simple document three times in less than an hour. Analyzing budgets and drafting proposals had become second nature to Renee. It was her expertise, but she needed more than an hour to create an effective report.

Darla's last-minute assignment also messed up Renee's lunch plans with Everett before his flight back to California. In a way, she was glad the lunch was canceled. Although they had a wonderful time together during his visit, Renee no longer trusted herself when it came to him. Being away from Jerome gave her too much time to consider what life could be like with another man.

Renee got out of her car and walked to the front door. Out of habit, she put the house key inside the lock and paused when she realized what she was doing. *Should I ring the bell?* she asked herself. Though she'd been gone for only a week, it felt like a month. Joshua reminded her of that every day. Jerome had told them she needed space because of a deadline at work. Renee didn't go against him. Of the three, Joshua was the only one who believed the story, and that she was coming back soon.

I still pay half the mortgage, and this is still my family, Renee told herself and unlocked the door.

Right away, familiar sounds greeted her when she opened the door. The grandchildren were running around upstairs, full of joy. The boys were debating about sports in the family room, and Junior's wife, Grace, was sharing funny stories about the kids with Zora. Renee didn't hear Jerome, but she smelled the evidence of his special barbecue coming from the backyard grill.

"Gama!" Renee's oldest grandson shouted and jumped into her arms. Lucky for him, Renee was standing within reach. He often thought he was an invincible superhero. Hearing her name, Renee's only granddaughter carefully walked downstairs. It hadn't been a full week since she'd seen them last, but Renee missed them. She grabbed them both and hugged them tight.

"There's my workaholic mom," Joshua said as he emerged from the family room with his brothers and ten-month-old nephew.

Slowly releasing her grandchildren, Renee hugged her children, and then they all walked into the kitchen, where Grace and Zora were enjoying a small bag of veggie chips. There was no sign of Joi, but traces of her presence lingered throughout the house. On her way in the house, Renee had noticed a fuchsia key chain dangling from the closet door, a pair of clogs by the stairs, and fancy pink shades on the hall table.

One of the patio doors opened, and Joi entered from the backyard, holding a metal tray full of corn halves. *Back to reality,* Renee thought. Joi greeted her like they were best friends and sat the tray on the counter. Renee didn't know why Joi was so happy, but she acknowledged her with a warm hello and then continued talking to her children. It was hard to concentrate when Joi was in the kitchen, organizing things, the way Renee once had. It was even harder to watch her go back outside and serve as Jerome's assistant by the grill. That was a role Renee used to play. Watching father and daughter interact annoyed her. *Get yourself together!* Renee commanded herself as she watched them walk back inside together.

Carrying his cooking tools and seasoning bucket, all gifts Renee had purchased over the years, Jerome strolled over to his wife. Smelling of smoked barbecue and charcoal, Jerome leaned down and kissed her on the cheek. "I'm glad you made it," he whispered in her ear.

"Would anyone like some tea?" Joi asked, and Renee felt her blood pressure rise. Everyone, including the grandchildren, accepted her offer.

"Renee," Joi said, "how about you?"

Although she was thirsty, Renee declined. She was beginning to feel like a stranger in her own home. Joi had quickly taken on the responsibilities that once belonged to her. "So, what's for dinner?" Renee asked, to take attention away from her temporary replacement.

Unusually happy, Jerome ran down the items in each of the trays lined up along the countertop. "Fried catfish and grilled salmon. Grace made the potato salad. The mac and cheese was made by Zora, and the grilled corn is Joi's first attempt on the grill," Jerome explained. "The garden salad is from the grocery store, so I hope you have a big appetite."

Everyone positioned themselves around the table, ready to consume the meal that had been prepared for them. After pouring several glasses of iced tea, Joi handed Jerome a wad of napkins. "Can you put these on the table?"

"Sure, baby girl," he answered. "Are we all set?"

Until last year, Jerome had acknowledged his daughter only through monthly financial commitments. Looking at them today, one would think Joi had been a part of his life from birth. On some level, Renee knew Jerome should be commended for what he was doing. Though Renee grew up in a two-parent household, she'd heard about the struggles children from single-parent homes faced and the long-term effects that often surfaced in their adult lives. Jerome was doing a good thing, but there was an emotional wall keeping Renee from embracing his efforts.

Joi removed a pan of hot buttered rolls from the oven and then gave Jerome a thumbs-up.

"Okay, let's get ready to eat!" Jerome said in a weak Bill Cosby impression.

As was their tradition, the family held hands while he blessed the food. It wasn't his custom to talk more than a minute, but today was an exception. Standing next to Renee, he held her hand firmly as he thanked God for the meal, the love of his family, and the power of reconciliation. It felt more like a mini sermon than a preparation to eat.

"Pop sounds more and more like Deacon Arrington," Junior teased when his father was done.

Agreeing with Junior, everyone laughed as they formed a line at the counter. Renee remained in her seat while the others filled their plates with food. She thought about Deacon Arrington and his long-winded prayers. A man of sincerity, who had a passion for people, Deacon Arrington had been married to the same woman for more than forty years. In that time, no affairs had surfaced. His wife didn't have to sit next to a child he'd conceived with another woman and struggle to focus on the pastor's sermon every Sunday, or worry about what the members were thinking. *No,* Renee thought, *Jerome isn't like the deacon at all.*

"So," Junior began as he carried his plate to the table, "you all know that I'm not good with holding stuff in." Junior sat down and cut a piece of catfish in half. "We all know what's going on and have the same questions. I think it's best that we ask them now since we're all together."

"What's on your mind, son?" Jerome asked as he nibbled on a piece of corn.

"It's not just me," Junior said. "I think we all want to know if you and Mom are separating."

Renee got up from the table and walked to the counter with the food. At the same time, Jerome slowly put the corn in his hand down on his plate. Everyone was silent as they moved around the kitchen. Though a separation had not been formally discussed, Renee couldn't honestly say that she hadn't seriously considered it.

"Your mother is very busy at the hotel," Jerome answered for both of them. "Because there is so much going on around here, we agreed that she should spend a couple weeks away to focus on her latest project. You know how your mother is about her job. She wants to do her best, and we want to support her."

Renee filled her plate with salad and then placed a piece of salmon on top. Telling a half-truth wasn't the best plan, but she decided to let Jerome take the lead.

"Think of this as her vacation away from home," Jerome added. "This is a good thing."

"If it's a good thing, why aren't either of you smiling?" Junior questioned sharply.

Still silent, Renee poured herself a glass of water and then returned to the table with the rest of the family. She prayed no one would ask her a direct question she'd have to avoid answering.

"I'm not sure I understand why Mom has to stay at the hotel. I mean . . . there's plenty of space in the basement," Reggie added, "and she has a private office."

"You sure that's all that's going on?" Junior asked. He then put a piece of catfish in his mouth and directed his next comment to Renee. "You've been busy before, and you never had to leave the house. What's *really* going on?"

Time seemed to stand still, and Jerome was at a loss for words. Renee took a sip of her water and stared at her plate of food. She refused to say anything and risk lying to her children. Seeing that Renee wasn't going to respond, Jerome offered another excuse. "Your mother's under a great deal of pressure with Mr. K's daughter," he said, hoping his reply would suffice.

"We're all adults here. Mom's an excellent manager. The awards on her wall prove that," responded Junior. "This is about Joi, isn't it? Well, not really her . . . It's about what Pop did with her mother. Is that why you're leaving, Mom?"

"Let's not throw Joi's name around," Jerome blurted. "And your mother isn't leaving me. She's taking a couple weeks to finish a project. You know how your mother is about work."

"I also know that her heart was broken," Junior snapped.

"That's enough, Junior," Reggie said.

"Junior," Renee began, breaking her vow of silence.

"I'm sorry, Mom," Junior replied. "I just think it's best to be up front. Our family has had enough of secrets." Junior paused to swallow the food in his mouth. "Besides, you two have been married too long for a separation . . . or divorce."

"Mom said this is temporary," Joshua interjected with optimism and chuckled. "And if they are having problems, absence will make the heart grow fonder, right?"

"This is no time for jokes, little brother," Junior retorted and then looked at his father. "Pop, you and Mom have always been able to work through the toughest problems. Have you done something else to hurt her?"

"Now, hold on," Jerome said. "I'm still your father, so you need to respect me. I'm not one of your basketball buddies."

"Let's all calm down," Renee said and stood up before things got out of hand. It was time to tell the truth. Enough was enough. "This is supposed to be family night. We haven't argued all these years. Let's not choose tonight to start. The bottom line is, I have a lot on my plate, including our new family situation, and I need some space to focus. To ease all your minds, there's been no talk of separation or divorce. Just a little time apart."

Unsatisfied with his mother's reply, Junior broke off another piece of catfish with his fork. "This has nothing to do with work, and you know it, Mom."

Renee grabbed her glass of water and left the kitchen before she said something about Jerome or Joi that she'd regret later.

"Let's just eat our food before it gets cold," Renee heard Reggie say as she sauntered down the hall. "We need to be better examples for the little ones. They do listen to our every word."

Settling in the living room, Renee sat on the rust-colored suede sofa and right away noticed a spot on the middle cushion. It looked like it had been there awhile. Her guess was that one of the grandchildren had been in here unattended. What happened in the kitchen should've been avoided. Perhaps she and Jerome should've been honest. With all the back and forth, there was a feeling that the children were going to have to take sides, and it was clear that all the odds were against Jerome. That was not what Renee wanted. Though she was upset with her husband, she didn't everyone to be.

Renee pulled a long ottoman toward her and rested her legs on top of it. She couldn't remember the last time the living room had been used to entertain guests. Since Jerome's heart attack, Renee hadn't been in the mood to cater to anyone.

"You okay, Mom?" Zora asked as she entered the room.

"You know me," sighed Renee. "Once I get control of everything, I'll be fine."

Zora sat next to her mother-in-law. "I'm not so sure about that this time."

Renee patted Zora's leg. Zora was only in junior high when she met Reggie, and thus she'd been around for all the disputes and outbursts in the Thomas home, especially when the arguments were regarding Taylor. Nonjudgmental from the very beginning, Zora knew the family well and never criticized Renee for her reactions, or Jerome for his infidelity. She was beautiful both inside and out, but everyone had at least one flaw. In Renee's eyes, Zora's flaw was her hesitation to have children. Months ago, when Renee asked about it, Zora said they were waiting for the right time. Both Reggie and Zora were in their thirties and were well established in their professions. They seemed to be in the ideal position to become parents, so why they weren't ready was something Renee couldn't comprehend.

"We all understand that you need some space. We're just concerned about you," Zora said sincerely. "You are the matriarch of the family. Although we love and need you, we want you to do what you need to, to be happy."

"Thanks, sweetheart," Renee replied and took a sip of her water.

"I know from experience," Zora shared. "Reg and I had a small 'issue' in college and separated until he got himself together. He's been good ever since. So no matter what the boys say, you do what you feel is right."

Hearing Zora's words was confirmation for Renee's spirit. "I needed to hear that," she told her. "But I better go. As long as I'm here, things are going to be weird."

"The boys aren't going to like that."

Renee nodded as she finished her glass of water. "I know, but come by the hotel tomorrow. We'll spend time together then. I just don't think being here tonight is a good idea."

Renee stood in front of her office windows overlooking Navy Pier, munching on pretzel thins. It was a nice day, and several people were out enjoying the mild summer weather. It had been over two weeks since Renee left the house and three days since Joi had gone back to Philadelphia. Now that Joi was out of the house, Jerome and Joshua were expecting Renee to come home tomorrow morning. Though Renee had packed her bags last night, she wasn't ready to leave her suite. Having never lived alone, she'd grown accustomed to the space and freedom. She missed the comfort of her house in River Forest, but in the suite there weren't any reminders of Jerome's affair or of his precious daughter. There were no empty cereal boxes, no shoes thrown in the hall closet, and no loose basketballs rolling around. Renee had peace of mind in the suite, and that luxury alone was priceless.

There was a knock at the door, and Renee turned around. It had to be her assistant. Earlier in the day, she'd asked Carmen to hold all calls so that she could work on another round of budgets for Darla. "Yes," she said loudly.

"I'm sorry to bother you, Mrs. Thomas," Carmen said as she opened the door. "There's a call from Taylor Belle on line one. I told her you were at lunch, but she said it was an important family matter. Would you like me to put her through, or should I take a message?"

"What does *she* want?" Renee mumbled and closed the near-empty bag of pretzels in her hand. Taylor should've been a private detective. Last year she disguised herself as Renee's sister-in-law in order to find out her hotel room number. Taylor had insisted she wanted only to share her reasons for keeping Joi a secret and to apologize, but Renee believed she just wanted to gloat about the fact that she'd given Jerome a daughter. "Put her through," she sighed and sat down at her desk.

Seconds later the phone rang, and Renee answered immediately. "Hi, Taylor," she said wryly and put the pretzel bag in the trash.

"Sorry for interrupting your lunch."

Renee doubted she meant that, but said, "It's okay. What's going on?"

"I wanted to say thank you for letting Joi stay all summer," Taylor answered. "I know how difficult that must've been."

"No need to thank me," responded Renee. "She is Jerome's daughter."

"Well," Taylor added, "Joi really appreciated getting to know her father's family. I hear she's even an auntie."

Renee rolled her eyes. She didn't know where the conversation was headed, but she hoped it would end soon. They weren't friends or acquaintances. There was no unfinished business between them, and she was too busy for small talk. "Are you sure everything is all right, because I really need to—"

"I understand," Taylor said and took a deep breath. "I wanted to apologized for—"

Renee cut her off. Whatever she was sorry about this time didn't matter. "No apology needed, Taylor," Renee stated. "What's done is done."

"I know, and now that Joi's a part of *our* lives, I wanted to make amends. I made a lot of mistakes in the past, but there's no reason we can't be cordial toward one another."

Was she serious? As far as Renee was concerned, they never had to speak to one another again. She and Jerome could raise their daughter without her input. "This really isn't needed," she insisted.

"Renee, I can only imagine how you feel, but—"

"Let's not do this again, Taylor. You *can't* imagine how I feel, so please spare me," said Renee. "And is that what you called to tell me? Is *that* what was so urgent?"

"No, Renee, it isn't. I'm trying to establish a mature relationship with you, but I see you're going to make this hard," Taylor replied more forcefully.

"It doesn't have to be hard at all," Renee retorted. "There's no need for us to have a relationship."

"Look, I understand why you're angry with me, and Joi told me not to say anything," Taylor began, her tone now void of any kindness, "but I have to say I don't appreciate the attitude you gave my daughter during her visit. She's just a child, Renee. She has nothing to do with what happened between me and your husband."

Taylor was really starting to get on Renee's nerves, so she tuned her out, hoping she'd finish what was on her mind and then leave her alone for good. Renee checked her e-mail as Taylor talked, and stopped when something caught her attention. "What did you say?" Renee asked. "Repeat that last sentence."

"I said . . . if Joi is going to live with you her senior year, I'd feel better knowing you wouldn't mistreat her," Taylor repeated. "She's my firstborn. She's tough on the outside, but she takes things personally, and I won't—"

Renee sat up straight in her chair. "What do you mean, she's staying with us her senior year?"

Taylor was silent.

"Taylor?"

"I—I'm sorry," Taylor replied. "Jerome didn't discuss this with you? I thought . . . well, he . . . I talked to him last night and . . . Renee, I really am sorry. I thought you and Jerome were in agreement on this."

To keep from raising her voice in the office, Renee got up and walked to the window to watch boats sailing on Lake Michigan. Was this how things were going to be from now on? Was Taylor always going to have the inside track on what was happening in her personal life? Renee hadn't signed up for that, and it definitely wasn't a part of her wedding vows.

"I know that you were staying at the hotel, but Joi's been home for a few days. I thought that was enough time for you and Jerome to talk about this," Taylor continued. "I mean, Joi just mentioned this to me, and I called Jerome to let him know I was thinking about it. Nothing's been made official."

Though Renee had been out of the house, Jerome knew he could call her at any time about serious matters. Why hadn't he mentioned this?

"Renee?" Taylor asked. Renee hadn't realized she'd been quiet. Her mind was busy trying to figure out why Jerome would keep this from her. "If this is going to be a problem, Joi can stay in Philly," Taylor said. "I definitely don't want to upset your life any further. It's really the only reason why I called, and—"

"I've heard enough, Taylor," Renee said irately. "You and Jerome can make whatever plans you feel are best for *your* daughter. You don't need my stamp of approval. Now . . . are you done?"

"C'mon, Renee, I . . . I really—"

"Taylor, please," Renee said, annoyed. "I asked if you were done."

"Yes," Taylor answered, and though Renee was clear that she wanted the conversation to end, Taylor continued to plead Joi's case. "Jerome's new program is going to be good for Joi, and although I don't want her to go, I have to do what's best for my child. She's a good player."

"I'm fine. Future Ballers will be great for your all-star daughter. You and Jerome made a wise decision. Now, I need to go." Before Taylor could reply, Renee hung up. "I can't deal with this," she mumbled under her breath and logged off of her computer.

In need of some fresh air, Renee removed her suit jacket. If she stayed in the office, she would call Jerome and they would argue. In order to avoid that, she decided to take a quick walk down Michigan Avenue.

"I'll be back in fifteen minutes," Renee told Carmen when she stepped out of her office.

As Renee walked over to the elevator, Darla poked her head outside of her office door. "I thought I heard your voice," she said and joined Renee by the elevator. "Did you finish the Northbrook assessment? I thought I mentioned I needed it by noon."

Renee was offended that Darla would talk to her like a child in front of Carmen. Despite Darla's rudeness, she controlled her temper. "I sent it to you last night," she stated confidently and hit the elevator down button. Unlike the last time, Renee made sure the document was sent before exiting her e-mail.

"And I sent it back. I asked you to use the form I created."

"I replied to that e-mail as well. I reviewed your format and used my thirty-plus years of experience to determine that it's best to use the form we approved for this kind of task," Renee said with authority. "We never had any complaints, so I don't see a need to change."

Taken by surprise, Darla stared straight ahead as her jaw dropped slowly. This was the first time Renee hadn't gone along with one of her whimsical changes. "There are going to be a lot of changes around here, and I need you to be on board."

Renee was already working on something that needed to be finished by the close of business. She didn't have time to fool around with Darla's demands; however, the fact remained that Darla was her boss. "If you insist on using your complex format, you'll need to give me until tomorrow."

"But I need it today," Darla barked, trying to assert her position.

"Do it yourself," Renee wanted to say but held back. "I don't have time . . ." Renee began, then stopped when the elevator doors opened. As she entered the elevator, Renee realized that using Darla's complicated format was the least of her worries today. "I'll need until three. What time is your meeting?"

"I guess I can push it ahead to four. Is that acceptable to you?" Darla said, bargaining.

God give me the strength, Renee thought. "You'll have it, but I want you to know how unreasonable I think this is."

As the elevator doors closed, Darla made another comment. "I hear you're occupying the Governor's Suite."

Renee quickly pressed the hold button, and the elevator doors bounced back open. "I am, temporarily," she replied, wondering where Darla was going with her statement.

A silly smirk appeared on Darla's face. "Glad you're enjoying it. It pays to be the general manager of *three* hotels, huh?"

"The company isn't paying for the room. I am," Renee clarified. "Do we need to discuss this inside your office?"

"Take advantage of your perks for as long as you want," Darla said with false sincerity.

The elevator timer buzzed, and Renee released the hold button. "I'll be out in a week," she retorted, though she had no concrete plans.

"Suit yourself," she heard Darla say as the elevator doors closed.

After a fifteen-minute walk, Renee decided to work in the suite for the rest of the day. She wanted to complete Darla's assignment without unnecessary interruptions. It took over an hour, but Renee finished the assessment by 2:30. Once she confirmed that Darla had received the correct document, she walked into her living room and stretched out across the sofa. It had been a long day, and she still needed to talk to Jerome. Renee grabbed her cell phone from the coffee table in front of the sofa and dialed his office number. Without a "Hello," "Good afternoon," or "How was your day?" Renee immediately jumped to the point. "Is there a reason why I'm the last to know Joi is planning to live with us?"

"Hey, babe. I—I know we talked about the possibility, but Joi didn't say she wanted to move," Jerome replied, clearly taken off guard.

"Well, that's not what Taylor told me today," informed Renee.

"Taylor?"

"Yes, Taylor, Jerome. That woman never ceases to amaze me. She had the nerve to call my job to let me know that *your* daughter is moving in."

"Wait a minute, Renee. I didn't know she was going to call you, and of course, I would've talked to you first," Jerome said, desperately trying to defend himself.

"Taylor said she talked to you last night," Renee explained. "So, which one of you is lying?"

"No one is lying. I did talk to her last night, but she was drilling me about colleges and scouts. Taylor said she'd *think* about letting Joi stay here," said Jerome. "She said she'd give me time to talk to you first. I was going to do that once you were back at home. I didn't want to spring something like this on you right away, and I didn't think Taylor would call you this soon, or at all, for that matter."

"This is exactly my point. Taylor doesn't know when to take her place. She thinks she's the head woman in charge. She always did, and now that she has your daughter, who looks like you, acts like you, plays ball like you . . . she's always going to think she's in charge." Renee was quiet, as was Jerome. "I shouldn't have to answer to another woman when it comes to my husband."

"You don't have to," Jerome answered firmly.

Renee spoke slower to make herself clear. "I don't think you understand. As long as Taylor is a part of our lives, there's going to be a battle between us."

"I'll talk to her," Jerome promised. "I'm sure we can come up with a reasonable solution."

"Jerome, the last time you talked to Taylor, Joi was conceived."

"That's not fair."

Renee's words came out mean, but those were the facts. "If this is the way things are going to be . . . I don't think I want—"

"Don't say another word, Renee. This isn't a problem. Let me have a word with Taylor and Joi before you make any more rash decisions, okay?"

"I don't know," Renee began, "but I think I should stay at the hotel until you figure this out."

"This has gone on long enough, babe. Come home and we'll work it out," Jerome pleaded. "I don't even know if Taylor will let Joi stay with us."

"She will, and you know it," Renee remarked. "School has already started, so my guess is that she'll be moving here soon. If we're going to work anything out, it'll have to be while I'm at the hotel."

There was a long stretch of silence before Jerome spoke again. "What if we try counseling? Will you come home then? Pastor can set up—"

"I don't want to talk to the pastor about our problems," Renee responded. Reverend Hampton was a good man and a great pastor, but he had also become Jerome's friend. If counseling was going to work, they needed a neutral therapist.

"We can see whomever you want to. Just come home."

Renee held her ground. "I'll agree to counseling, but I'm not coming home yet. Right now, I think you need to handle things with Taylor and Joi."

"What am I going to tell Josh?"

Renee hated to disappoint him, but she couldn't settle just to make him or Joshua happy. "I'll talk to Josh tomorrow," she said.

Rather than argue, Jerome agreed. It was best to end the call peacefully. Renee said good-bye and then hung up. Now she just needed to find a place to live.

Downtown Chicago was known for renting apartments to busy professionals in need of three- to six-month leases. Three months was a fair commitment for what Renee needed. Six months would work, too, if her marriage was still in limbo. From the looks of things, Renee might not go home until the school year ended. She wasn't about to cohabitate with Joi, and though Jerome thought counseling would help Renee resolve her issues toward his daughter, Renee doubted any therapist could convince her to do otherwise.

Renee put her cell phone back on the coffee table and walked to the kitchen. On top of the microwave, a welcome basket filled with goodies, compliments of the hotel, caught her attention for the first time. Inside, there were flavored tea bags, premium coffee bags, Godiva chocolates, and a bottle of wine. For some reason, the wine was calling her name. She removed the wine from the basket and read the label. Pinot Noir.

Renee looked through the drawers for a wine opener and then played around until she figured out how to remove the cap. "It's just wine," she whispered when the cork popped. After pouring half a glass of the deep red liquid, Renee walked back to the living room and sat in the chair closest to the window. Renee sniffed the wine, like she'd seen people do in movies. She didn't detect an odor and had no clue as to whether or not that was good or bad. This was the first time she'd had red wine. Renee had enjoyed a modest amount of champagne at weddings and social gatherings, but never had she tasted anything as potent as the glass of liquid in her hand. Renee took a deep breath and sipped enough to wet her palate. *Very bitter,* she thought and swallowed more. *I don't see what all the fuss is about,* she mumbled. *It's just okay.* Renee gulped the wine, drinking a great deal at a time, and minutes later felt a little lightheaded. As she leaned back deeper into the chair, her muscles relaxed. "One glass of wine isn't going to hurt anything," she told herself and closed her eyes. "One glass of wine isn't going to hurt at all."

~7~

Jerome

The slam of a car door coming from the driveway caught Jerome's attention, and he put down the newspaper he was reading and headed to the front of the house. As he approached the door, he realized that it could be Renee coming home. Maybe she wanted to personally apologize for missing the launch of his Future Ballers program. The boys had gone on a mini vacation right after the launch three days ago, something they did together once a year. He wasn't expecting to see them for at least another two days. Jerome moved as fast as he could to open the door, not bothering to peek through the window. *It has to be Renee,* he convinced himself and swung the door open.

Holding the autographed basketball he'd given her for Christmas, Joi stood on the porch, smiling wide. Behind her were Reggie, Junior, and Joshua, standing proudly in front of a small U-Haul truck.

"What's going on?" Jerome asked.

"Mother talked to Renee last week," Joi said. "She isn't sure if she's coming back, but she said that I was welcome to stay here for my senior year. She thinks I'd be a great candidate for Future Ballers." Joi placed the basketball under her right arm. "So, what do you think, Pop? Can I move in?"

Jerome started to cry. He'd waited a long time for those words to come out of Joi's mouth. As he watched his boys fuss over unpacking the U-Haul, Joi stood beside her brothers, begging them to be careful with her things. It was going to be a good year, indeed. God had brought his daughter into his life. Maybe He'd place it on Renee's heart to come back, too.

With two of his children by his side, Jerome proudly strutted into church on Sunday. He hadn't planned on attending service this morning, but even though Joi had barely unpacked her belongings, she insisted they go.

Standing by the sanctuary doors, Gloria Barnes handed church bulletins to members as they walked in. As she gave each person the one-page document, she quietly scolded a junior usher for wearing baggy pants without a belt. "Good morning, Brother Thomas," she said and handed Jerome a bulletin. "Good to see all of you. Renee's not joining us again this morning?"

"She's working today," Jerome answered and tried to enter the sanctuary behind his children, but Gloria stepped in front of him. The young usher backed away quickly without Gloria realizing it.

"That's one working woman," Gloria said, falling back on her duties. "Did she mention that I saw her in Nordstrom with a Mr., um . . . I think his first name is Everett, but his last name escapes me."

If Gloria was trying to get a rise out of him, it wasn't going to work today. Renee had warned him that Gloria was a gossip, but he'd often ignored her. So, before he replied too hastily, Jerome checked himself. Though he had his suspicions, he knew that Renee and Everett often worked through lunches. They'd been doing it for years. Renee had never given him a concrete reason to believe they were more than friends, and he had tried his best not to let his insecurity and guilt make him believe she was telling him a lie. Though he had to admit, whenever they had a serious disagreement, he often wondered if Everett consoled her in the same way Taylor used to console him. "Renee is working on a big expansion for her hotel. Everything needs to be completed before January."

"Yes, she mentioned an important project," Gloria said and handed a bulletin to a couple standing behind Jerome. "That's one *hardworking* woman."

Jerome didn't like that Gloria tried to plant doubt about his wife in his children's minds. "We're very proud of her," he replied and then excused himself. "Enjoy the service."

Joshua put his hand on his father's shoulder. "Mrs. Barnes got the spiritual gift of gab."

Without turning around, Jerome knew that Gloria was already interviewing her next victim. "I agree," he told his son as they walked to their seats.

Easing into the row, Jerome said good morning to everyone seated nearby. A woman behind Jerome leaned close to his ear and whispered, "I hear Renee's been traveling a lot."

News travels fast, Jerome thought. Then, sounding like a broken record, he said, "She's working on a big project."

"You know," the woman continued, still close to his ear, "I live only a few blocks away. If needed, I can bring dinner over sometimes."

Jerome turned around to get a better look at the woman. *Funny,* he said to himself. The woman sat in the same section every Sunday, yet she never said more than good morning to him. He didn't know her name, how long she'd been a member, if she was married or had kids, but somehow she felt comfortable enough to offer dinner while Renee was gone. "I appreciate that," he responded, and the woman smiled wide, "but my daughter is a good cook."

The grin on the woman's face faded as she leaned back in her seat. "Well, in case you change your mind, or if you need anything, give me a call. My number is listed."

"Thanks," he said and was glad the choir had started to sing.

It was hard for Jerome to focus during praise and worship. While the congregation sang along with the choir, he sat as still as a statue. Though the lyrics of each song were inspiring, he wasn't moved. He sat through the announcements in the same state and stood only to read a scripture from his Bible. When the pastor called people down to the altar, Jerome twisted his body so that others trying to make it down the aisle could get by.

"C'mon, Pop," Joshua said.

Not wanting to disappoint his son, Jerome headed to the altar. As he knelt, he tried to shake his melancholy mood. Though he was a praying man, Jerome was lacking words to say.

"Bring your concerns to the altar," Reverend Hampton told the congregation. "It is at the altar where God will give you the strength and peace you need to face your challenges and fears. It is at the altar where God will seal his promise to you. I invite all who need to hear a word from the Lord to the altar."

Slowly, Jerome let the pastor's words sink in. Soon, his body surrendered, and his thoughts ran a course of their own. The noise in the room suddenly decreased. The wailing saints and prayer warriors behind him were only muffled sounds in his mind. The medley of praise coming from the choir was nothing but a faint hum in his ears. In this solitude Jerome began to weep, and as God revealed Himself, he became transparent. All his strengths and weaknesses were exposed. "Forgive me, Lord," Jerome cried out. "Make me the man I need to be for my family. Show me how to lead."

A ray of light appeared and warmly filled his spirit with love. Unconsciously, he stretched his arms wide across the altar and humbly received all the knowledge and strength God deposited into his soul. When the light disappeared, Jerome lowered his arms and slowly regained awareness of his surroundings. The music had stopped playing, but there was a melodious tune coming from the cries and prayers in the congregation.

Feeling hands on his back and shoulders, Jerome looked to his left and right. To his surprise, he was the only remaining person at the altar. "How long was I praying?" he asked himself and looked up. Above him, Reverend Hampton stood in the pulpit with his hands reaching toward heaven. Jerome wasn't sure what had happened, but he was certain that God was there.

Jerome stood to his feet, and the sanctuary rejoiced, adding more fuel to his rejuvenated spirit. There was power in the shouts of praise that filled the church, and Jerome knew that his family would be together as one again soon.

After the service, Jerome sat inside the pastor's office. He wasn't in a hurry to go home and hoped that he could spend time with his friend. Joshua and Joi were going to dinner with friends in celebration of Joi's return. If Renee were around, the family would've been together, enjoying a huge Sunday meal. But she wasn't, and the tradition he and Renee had started stopped the day she moved out of the house.

"I hope you weren't waiting too long," Reverend Hampton said apologetically as he walked into the warm room. "It's picture day for our young adult ministries," he explained as he took off his robe. "So I haven't seen Renee in a while. What's going on?"

"It's not good," Jerome sighed.

Reverend Hampton sat behind his desk and removed his tie. "I take it she's not away on a business trip."

"I'm afraid it's deeper than that," Jerome confessed. "She's been staying at her hotel since August."

"She's been out of the house an entire month?" the pastor asked, alarmed. "What brought this on . . . if you don't mind me asking?"

The last time Jerome talked to Reverend Hampton, he was getting ready for Joi's summer visit. So much had changed since then. Taking his time, Jerome explained what happened the morning Renee left—how she hesitated to take Joi to church, then became infuriated when she believed she'd been excluded from a family portrait. "To make matters worse," Jerome said, "Taylor called her before I had a chance to discuss the possibility of Joi moving to Illinois."

"You sure have a lot on your hands, my friend. You're dealing with two strong-minded women," the pastor said and shook his head. "But if you don't set boundaries for Taylor, Renee will always feel threatened."

"She kind of said the same thing," Jerome replied, "but I don't understand. Taylor isn't, and really *never* was, a threat."

"We've been through this many times," Reverend Hampton reminded him. "You have to approach this situation from Renee's point of view. Trust has been broken. While you're building a relationship with your daughter, don't forget that you're *rebuilding* a relationship with your wife, too."

Jerome thought about his altar call experience. "God's going to bring my family back together. All I have to do is stand. I know it's going to be tough, but Renee is worth fighting for. But I believe, as husband and wife, we should work out our problems while living under the same roof. Living in two different places could drive a permanent wedge between us. Don't you agree?"

"Well, Jerome," the pastor began, "I would agree with you. However, you have to understand that Renee feels like she's been betrayed *twice*. Give her what she needs for now, and while you are apart, trust that God will bring her closer to you."

"If only I could turn back the hands of time," Jerome stated.

Reverend Hampton laughed aloud. "Don't we all. But I've learned to embrace my mistakes. Mistakes become testimonies, and testimonies become teaching moments. You never know how many lives will be saved because of your teaching moment."

As he listened to his pastor and friend share his wisdom, Jerome thought about the teaching moment he'd one day share with men who succumbed to infidelity.

Later that night, Jerome lay in bed alone. Half asleep, he reached for the pillow beside him and held it tight. The pillow was a poor substitute for Renee, but it helped him sleep at night. Jerome tried to get comfortable, but his substitute failed to soothe him. Renee's warm body was the only cure.

Jerome set the timer on his television and yawned. It was only 10:38. Knowing Renee, she was still awake and working on her computer. Jerome grabbed the cordless lying next to his leg and dialed his wife's cell phone number. With any luck, she was missing his warm touch, too, and would invite him to her suite.

"Hi, Jerome," Renee answered, a little groggy.

Disappointed, Jerome changed his original plan. "I didn't mean to wake you. I just wanted to say good-night."

"Okay," Renee replied. "Have a good-night. I'll talk to you tomorrow."

"Renee," Jerome said before she hung up. "I never said I'm sorry for the Joi situation, but I am. And I want you to know that I heard everything you've been saying. I'm going to talk to Taylor soon about her boundaries."

"What's done is done, Jerome," sighed Renee. "Like I told Taylor, all we can do is move forward from here. Joi lives here now, so just make the best of it."

"I know you don't want to hear this, but I often think about the damage I caused Joi and her mother. I can't make up for lost time, but I can try to make things right now," explained Jerome. "I don't want to lose you. You've been by my side through all the ups and downs in my life, and I know this is hard, but I want you to be by my side now. I love you, Renee. You're good for me and good to me. I'm sorry that I hurt you, but please let me try to make things right for you, too."

After his mini speech, Renee was silent. Jerome expected her to give him some feedback, even if it wasn't what he wanted to hear. But all he heard was her television in the background. "Renee, are you there?" he asked, praying she hadn't fallen asleep.

"I'm here," she answered softly, "and I think this is a great start for our first therapy session. It's too late to dig into all that's on your mind tonight."

Rather than feel rejected, Jerome chose to highlight the positive—Renee was looking forward to counseling. And to Jerome, that meant he was one step closer to saving his marriage.

~8~
Joi

Joi walked down the hall of her new high school, beside the vice principal. Next to him, she didn't feel like an Amazon, the way she did with most of her peers. The tall, lanky man resembled Abe Lincoln and talked more like a politician than the school administrator of John Marshall High School.

It was the third week of school. Joi had wanted to start sooner, but her mother wouldn't let her move to Illinois without Renee's approval. "I'm not sending you to an unhealthy environment," Taylor had told Joi after speaking to Renee one day. Joi had moped around the house for days, until Taylor gave in and called Renee a second time. It was unclear how the conversation began and ended, but Joi didn't bother to ask for details.

Being away from family and friends for an extended period of time was going to be a challenge. No matter how unfair Joi thought Taylor could be, she was her mother. For better or for worse, they'd been connected for nearly seventeen years. It would be hard to break that chain without some degree of sadness. She was also going to miss her twin brothers and her sister, Leah. The adjustment would be difficult, but Joi prayed this would be a decision she would never regret.

"Here we are," the vice principal said and stopped in front of a classroom door. "Remember, my door is open if you need anything."

Joi looked up at the heavily bearded man and thanked him. She wondered if his statement was the truth or just a line for all new students. When the vice principal opened the door, a woman about the height of Joi's eight-year-old sister gave him an unwelcomed look.

"Ms. Morris, this is Joi Belle. She'll be joining this math class," he said, immune to her apparent displeasure. There were already close to thirty students in the room. The last thing the teacher wanted was another student to be responsible for.

The young teacher took a deep breath and forced a closed-mouth smile. "Glad to have you, Joi," she said as she scanned the full room. "Please, take a seat. There are a couple of empty desks in the back."

Joi slid her backpack off her shoulder and carefully eased down the narrow row to the back of the room. She sat in the first available seat and quickly settled in. When the vice principal left, Ms. Morris retied her curly blond hair into a puffy ponytail and continued to teach like nothing had ever interrupted her. For a woman who looked to be just a few years older than her students, she had them well under control.

Although Joi sat among several students, she felt alone. All the friends she'd made over her summer visit attended other schools. At least Joshua was nearby, at Whitney Young, a magnet school students had to be accepted into. John Marshall, on the other hand, was well known for its sports program. The school was a perfect fit for students pursing athletic careers, and since Joi lived and breathed basketball, Marshall was where she needed to be. There she'd face strong competitors and receive training from top-notch coaches. With this combination, at the end of the school year, Joi would emerge as a smarter, tougher power forward.

She yearned to be the best and believed that she was on the right path to reach her goal.

"Can anyone figure out the answer for problem five on the board?" Ms. Morris asked.

Joi looked at the algebraic equation and, without writing anything on paper, solved the problem in her head, but she kept the answer to herself. No one liked a know-it-all new student. Coming from a small magnet school in Philadelphia, she learned how to solve simple quadratic equations in an advanced tenth grade math course. As she patiently waited for a classmate to come up with the answer, Joi browsed the room, trying to identify possible athletes. The girl in front of her was way too short to play basketball, and judging by her complicated but stylish hairdo and long, intricately designed fingernails, cheerleading was probably a better fit.

The girl to Joi's right was a strong candidate. She was husky and tall, but with the micro braids that hung midway down her back, and the plaid skirt that showcased her solid leg muscles, she exhibited a sense of femininity.

Before anyone solved the problem on the board, a bell rang throughout the building, indicating that it was time to move on to the next class. "Since you couldn't figure out the answer in class," Ms. Morris said in a loud voice, "maybe you'll be able to solve all the problems on the board for homework." The students groaned but copied the three problems in their notebooks.

After writing down her first assignment correctly, Joi hurriedly left the classroom. Though she had had a brief tour of the building before math class, there were too many floors and classrooms for her to remember anything with accuracy. A bit overwhelmed by the mass of students in the hallway, Joi stayed close to the wall, where she could see the room numbers on the doors. *Two-seventeen, two-sixteen, two-fifteen,* she counted to herself. *Good. I'm going in the right direction.*

Joi's concentration was broken when a student rushed from inside a classroom and bumped into her. The books in her hands fell to the floor, and when she reached to get them, her backpack slid off her shoulder.

"My bad. Let me get those for you," a gentle and calm voice said. "Are you okay?" he asked.

Besides the muffled snickers she heard from those who had witnessed her blunder, Joi was fine. The sudden contact hadn't broken any bones or bruised any part of her body. The friendly student's shoulder-length dreadlocks grazed her arm as she stood up and took the book from his hand. "I'm fine," she said nervously. The warning bell rang, alerting everyone still in the hallway that there was one minute left to get to the next class. As the students scurried around her, Joi lost her sense of direction.

"Do you need some help?" the young man asked, seeing that she was confused.

Joi studied the young man in front of her. He didn't look like a student at all, at least not one that attended high school. "My class is in room two-oh-seven," she managed to say.

Before he could reply, the girl that had sat next to Joi in math class grabbed his arm. "That's the new girl. The guard can help her from here."

"Be nice, Jamila," the young man said and then faced Joi. "Two-oh-seven is at the end of the hall and around the corner. You better get moving. Mrs. Bryant locks people out if they're late."

Jamila made a smacking sound and then pulled her friend with her down the hall.

"You're a mess," Joi heard him say as he followed Jamila's lead.

Taking the young man's advice, Joi hurriedly followed his directions, only to find the door closed, just as he had said it would be. Joi didn't know what to expect when she opened the door, but prayed she wouldn't be the subject of another embarrassment.

"I hope you have a note," a security guard remarked as he walked by.

Joi placed her hand on the doorknob and sighed as the guard chuckled underneath his breath. Ignoring him, she turned the knob slowly and quietly walked inside. All eyes were on Joi as she closed the door behind her.

Without a warm stare or pleasant smile, the teacher looked up from the book she was reading aloud and asked, "Are you looking for English Honors?"

Joi double-checked the miniature roster in her hand and nodded. "I'm sorry for being late," she said. "I had trouble finding the room."

A few students giggled at Joi's last statement and waited for Mrs. Bryant's reply.

"You must be a new student," Mrs. Bryant said and smirked. "What's your name?"

Joi cleared her throat and spoke clearly. "Joi Belle."

The teacher checked the official roster on her desk and then welcomed Joi into her class. "For future reference, unless you have a written excuse for being tardy, don't enter this classroom once the door is closed." Mrs. Bryant walked to the front of the room and sat on a wooden stool. "I don't like interruptions."

"Yes, ma'am," Joi responded and sat in an empty seat in the front row. Joi couldn't wait for the day to end. Her first day of school hadn't played out the way she had imagined it would.

~9~

Renee

Dressed in the mauve Ellen Tracy suit she'd purchased on sale at Filene's Basement, Renee sauntered into Baldwin and Stroud with mixed emotions. Counseling wasn't something she wanted to add to her already cramped agenda. This was Jerome's idea. He thought a counselor could help them solve their issues. Renee wasn't so sure anyone could salvage their marriage but hoped the therapist could help her work through other areas of concern in her life.

In all honesty, she didn't want to deal with her emotions surrounding Jerome's involvement with Taylor, and she didn't want to learn to love Joi. What she really wanted was to be happy. The kind of happy she felt before Jerome damaged his knee, and before he lost his first real job after they were married. She would even settle for the happy times after she'd forgiven him for the affair.

It was hard for Renee to believe that kind of happy would ever exist for them again. Selfishly, she had hoped that Jerome would tell Joi that she couldn't live in Chicago for a year. But that didn't happen. Joi had officially moved into the River Forest home, and Renee had serious doubts about moving back in.

When Renee reached the open receptionist area, Jerome was sitting by a large fish tank, looking through his cell phone. Since the start of his mentoring program, Jerome had been working as much as she did. His high-tech cell phone had become a necessary addition to his life. Though he had more responsibility at work, Jerome refused to upgrade his attire much. Wearing a suit and tie all day would be torture, so he'd upgraded his wardrobe only with more expensive pairs of slacks and silk ties.

"Hey," Jerome said and stood up when he saw her. "You look great. Is that a new color for you?"

Jerome kissed her cheek, and she halfheartedly placed her hand around his waist to hug him. "Thanks. I bought this last week," Renee replied and then sat on the edge of the sofa. "How's the mentoring group going?"

Jerome was glad that she asked, and his eyes lit up. "Really well. You should come by and see Josh in action," he answered. "I have the kids starting their own basketball team, and Josh has emerged as the star. He's already figured out who to hire, and how to get the best players for the best salary. He's negotiating deals for uniforms, and . . . Well . . . you know our son's personality. He just has that special way about him. He has great business sense, like his mother."

"And his father's charisma," Renee replied, proud to hear of her son's accomplishments.

"Maybe he'll forget about accounting and go into sports management."

Renee couldn't recall the last time she'd seen Jerome this excited. "Maybe," she agreed, "but the choice belongs to Josh. Remember, he worked hard to get that internship."

"I know, but I can get him one, too."

Renee's cell phone vibrated in her purse. *Perfect timing,* she said to herself. She had sensed the conver-

sation with Jerome was heading in an unpleasant direction. With phone in hand, Renee pressed the green
button, but it was too late. The call had gone to voice
mail. She checked the call log and discovered that Everett had called. Normally, she would wait to dial him
back, but there was a big meeting today, and she was
on call in case of an emergency. Before she left the office this morning, Renee gave clear instructions to her
staff, and although she trusted that they would execute
her wishes, she didn't trust Darla. Darla had a knack
for changing things at the last minute. Renee was starting to dial Everett's number when she noticed that he
had sent her a text message.

> Good luck at your meeting this afternoon.
> I know you'll keep Darla on the right track.

Glad that she didn't have to put out a fire, Renee
quickly thanked him in a text and then put her phone
away. She hadn't told Everett that she was meeting Jerome for counseling, and she wasn't sure she wanted
him to know.

The office door opened, and a woman with thick,
shiny black and gray twists appeared. "Mr. and Mrs.
Thomas?"

"Yes," Jerome responded as he stood up.

"I'm Annette Stroud. Nice to meet you," the fifty-
something woman said. "Come on inside."

Jerome stepped aside to let Renee walk ahead of him.
Once they were both inside the office, they paused. It
was the cleanest office they'd ever seen. Almost picture
perfect. It was furnished with a classic black leather
sofa and chair, an executive-style desk, and spotless
glass tables, which looked like they hadn't been used
in years. The beauty of the black-and-white paintings

along the wall would've been lost without the thick black frames around them. The scent from the white roses in a clear vase on her desk added a pleasant smell to the room. The only splashes of color came from the red accents in the large area rug.

Afraid to take a seat, they looked at one another and smiled. If Mrs. Stroud hadn't been highly recommended by Reverend Hampton, they would've turned around. From the looks of the office, the neatly dressed woman needed a therapist of her own. Jerome often teased Renee about having OCD (obsessive-compulsive disorder) syndrome, but standing in Mrs. Stroud's office, they silently agreed that Renee wasn't even close.

Mrs. Stroud removed her leather portfolio from its place on her desk and sat in the high-back leather chair. "Please, have a seat," she said, pointing to the long sofa.

Renee carefully positioned herself an arm's length apart from her husband and prepared for the first session. She wasn't sure what to expect, but she quietly prayed that she'd have an open mind.

"Well now," Mrs. Stroud continued. "Before I get to know you, let me share a little about myself." As she talked, Mrs. Stroud picked at a few tiny lint balls on her skirt. "I've been married to my second husband for three wonderful years. I have one daughter and two grandsons, Irish twins, Ricardo, and Rayvon. My daughter graduated in the top five of her class from Columbia University, and I graduated from Chicago State. For many years, my daughter and I worked at various agencies throughout the city. Seven years ago, we decided to join forces, and we started this practice because we wanted more control of who our clients are. We care about people and their well-being."

Mrs. Stroud dropped the few lint balls in the trash can by her chair, and the thin silver cross around her neck reflected off the light coming through the window. "That's my résumé," she said with pride. "Now, what brings you to Baldwin and Stroud?"

Jerome waited for Renee to speak, and when she didn't, he jumped at the opportunity to tell his story. He talked about his birthplace, his career, and his children. "I don't think my wife cares for my daughter. That's why she moved out."

In response to his statement, Renee replied, "I never said I didn't like Joi, and she's not the *main* reason I'm not in the house. You're leaving out a lot of important details." Jerome had an astonished look on his face, but Renee paid him no attention. "We're here to be honest," she charged. "So, let's tell all of the truth and not just pieces of it."

"That is correct," Mrs. Stroud agreed. "You're paying me to guide you through a difficult situation. It would help a great deal if all the cards were on the table."

Renee started to lean on the arm of the sofa, then sat up. She didn't want to accidentally scratch the leather with the button on her suit jacket sleeve. Since Jerome wasn't going to be honest, she took the lead. "I'll sum things up for you. After seventeen years of marriage, he had an affair. I eventually forgave him, and we moved to Chicago to start over, only to learn that he had one last fling and got her pregnant," she rattled in one breath. "And it gets better. Jerome knew about the child and didn't tell me about the child. Now she's living in my home."

Mrs. Stroud jotted a few notes in her portfolio. "Well, that's certainly a lot of *stuff* going on."

"That's why we're here," Jerome added. "We want to save our marriage."

"I'm not sure what I want anymore," admitted Renee. "There's a lot going on with me right now."

Mrs. Stroud wasn't quite ready to address Renee's confession. "How are your children dealing with what's going on?"

"Josh is an optimist. He thinks I'm coming home soon. He's immune to the tension between me and his father," Renee responded. "Junior's only concern is my happiness, and Reggie is pretty neutral."

"I agree with my wife," Jerome said, jumping in. "But I would also add that Junior is trying to hide his anger toward me. He doesn't come right out and blame me, but I know he thinks this is all my fault. Joi, on the other hand, she's a lot like me."

At the sound of Joi's name, Renee immediately stopped Jerome from talking. "Excuse me, but we didn't come here to talk about Joi this soon."

"I understand," Jerome sighed, and that annoyed Renee.

"Did I mention that I found out about Joi by accident?" Renee rambled, and Mrs. Stroud wrote something in her portfolio again. "Yes, I found out, and right after that he had a heart attack. I forgave him for that, too, and took care of him, and months later, his daughter is spending the summer with us. I wasn't ready for that." Renee paused to keep from crying. When she was able to hold back the tears, she continued. "And now I'm in the middle of the hugest project of my career, with a woman who tries to make me feel incompetent to cover up her ignorance. There aren't enough hours in my day to get things done, so when I take time out to make an effort to patch up this marriage, I don't expect to come in here and talk about how great Joi is."

Mrs. Stroud kept her portfolio open as she spoke and took notes. "We will need to talk about all your children, including Joi, at some point. I asked about your children because I believe it's important to have a strong support system," Mrs. Stroud said. "But why don't we refocus? Let's start from the beginning and talk about how you two met."

Slightly embarrassed about her outburst, Renee didn't know what had gotten into her. When she woke up this morning, she was in control of her emotions and ready to sit through the session. But somehow, the feelings that had been bottled up inside of her for years had exploded without warning.

"We met in biology class," Jerome began but was cut off by Renee.

"Why did you do it, Jerome?" Renee questioned, now warm with fury.

"Mrs. Thomas," the counselor said when Jerome didn't answer. "We should probably—"

"Tell me why?" Renee asked, talking over Mrs. Stroud. She needed an explanation from her husband. "After all we've been through together. Why did you do it?"

No one said anything for two minutes. Mrs. Stroud sat in her seat and scribbled in her portfolio, waiting to see how the interaction would play out, and Jerome stared at the floor.

"I was afraid to tell you," Jerome finally admitted. "I messed up so many times and didn't know how to tell you that I had a daughter."

"I'm not talking about Joi," Renee stated and clutched her purse tight. "Why did you carry on a relationship with Taylor for *two years*?"

Jerome was looking for a way out, but there was no escape this time.

"I know this is difficult, Jerome," Mrs. Stroud said, noticing his struggle to express the truth, "but I don't think we're going to make any progress until your wife gets the answers she needs."

Uncomfortable, Jerome fidgeted in his seat. "I was young and—"

"Being young isn't an excuse," Renee snapped, interrupting him again. "I was young, too. We're the same age, remember? We graduated from the same high school at the same time. Do you know how many decent and attractive men I turned away from? Do you?" Renee's voice cracked. "You're not the *only* man that thought I was special. But I was married to *you*. I made a commitment to *you* and to *our* family. *That* meant something to me."

"It means a lot to me, too," Jerome replied. "That's why I suggested counseling. There was so much going on at that time. I didn't have a real job. You were paying all the bills. We weren't spending time together like we used to. I was feeling lonely and lost. Before I knew what was happening, Taylor had become a part of my life."

Renee couldn't stop her tears. "I wouldn't have done this to you," she cried. Mrs. Stroud handed her a box of tissues and put a trash can near her foot. Why hadn't Jerome shared his feelings with her before he ran to another woman? Was she that unreasonable? Did he really think that she wouldn't support him? Renee sobbed as she took a tissue from the box. "I wouldn't have hurt you like this."

"I know, baby, and I'm sorry," Jerome said and touched Renee's hand. "I know I failed you. I was too immature and stubborn back then."

"Even if all you said is true," Renee replied as she pulled her hand from under his, "you went back to Taylor after I forgave you. Why, Jerome?"

Painfully, Jerome explained that he visited Taylor one last time to apologize. "She started crying, and then one thing led to another. God knows I wish I could change what happened, but you've got to know that I *never* wanted to leave you to be with her. *Never.*"

Renee wiped her face with the tissue in her hand. "You could've picked up the phone to say good-bye."

Jerome didn't have a reply for her comment. Deep inside, he knew Renee was right. A phone call would've spared him all of the drama that followed.

Mrs. Stroud closed her portfolio and laid it on the glass table next to her chair. She placed her pen neatly beside it and then folded her hands in her lap. "This wasn't what I envisioned our first session together would be like, but sometimes you have to deviate from the script." She looked at her watch and then crossed her legs. "There isn't much time left, but why don't you take a moment and jot down some of the earliest memories of your life as a couple . . . before you were married," she said and directed Renee's and Jerome's attention to a neat stack of notebooks and pencils in a leather container next to the sofa. "I'll have you share your memories the next time we meet."

Renee couldn't switch gears that fast but tried her best to cooperate. Maybe reminiscing about the past, before she became a wife, was a good idea.

Thirty minutes later Mrs. Stroud wrapped up the session, and Renee rushed to her car in a better mood. During the session, she had dug up memories that were long forgotten—basketball games Jerome played in when he was in his prime and study sessions that lasted for hours. Together, Renee and Jerome replayed the corny lines they used to feed each other, and joked about their chaperoned dates. Renee wished that time could stand still, but she had to get back to work and save her employees from Darla's impromptu madness.

"Time for a quick lunch?" Jerome asked, struggling to keep up with Renee's pace.

"I've got a meeting in two hours," she responded. "With all that's going on, I don't want to risk being late."

"I understand," he answered weakly.

In silence, Jerome escorted Renee to her car. After a rocky start, they'd ended the morning on such good terms that Renee felt bad for turning down his lunch offer. "Look," she said when they reached her car, "I'm not trying to avoid you. I really do have a busy afternoon." Renee unlocked her door and got inside the car. "What about dinner tomorrow night?" she asked as she started the engine. "Josh and I are going to Pappadeaux. Why don't you join us?"

"That sounds great!" exclaimed Jerome. "I guess Joi can have dinner at Junior's house."

"I guess you're right," Renee wanted to say but refrained. Did he *really* think she wanted to go out to dinner with his daughter? "Okay, I'll meet you there at seven," she said and headed to the hotel.

Renee got off the elevator and noticed people leaving the big conference room. *That's strange,* Renee thought. Why would Darla schedule another meeting in that room today? Afraid that her original preparations had been altered, Renee took a deep breath and searched for Carmen, who wasn't at her desk, to get answers.

Before Renee had Carmen paged, she checked all the empty rooms on the floor. She poked her head in the two small conference rooms first and then walked to Everett's office. The lights were on, so she slowly pushed the door open. Everett was in California this week, so no one should've been in his office without Renee's approval.

Inside Everett's office, Carmen was sitting in the corner of the room, blowing air into an assortment of blue, white, and silver balloons.

"Hey, Carmen. What's going on?"

Practically in tears, Carmen dropped the balloon in her mouth on her lap, and the air inside it slowly seeped out. "Darla asked me to blow up all these balloons," she strained to say as she pointed to a large bag.

"For what?" Renee questioned, confused. Blowing up balloons on company time was a waste of money. Didn't Darla know there was a more efficient way to handle this?

"I've been trying to call you," Carmen replied. "Darla's been asking for you all morning. She rescheduled the meeting to an earlier time to accommodate some potential investors. I asked if I could sit in and take notes for you, but Darla needed me to run all kinds of errands. Now, she needs these balloons for some party she's having tonight in the atrium."

Renee's mood turned sour. "You can go back to your desk, Carmen. This isn't your job."

Carmen quickly got up. "I tried to call you on your cell, but it kept going to voice mail."

"No problem," said Renee. She must've been so immersed in the counseling session that she didn't feel her phone vibrate. "I should've checked my messages, but . . . what is this about rescheduling the two o'clock meeting?"

"Darla said she sent you an e-mail, but I wasn't copied, so I didn't know until everyone showed up."

Renee charged out of the room and into her office down the hall. *How do you change a meeting time without the general manager knowing?* What was Darla up to? In record time, Renee logged into her e-mail and browsed her incoming messages. There was nothing from Darla. Before addressing Darla, Renee called Everett. Maybe he knew what was going on.

Everett answered right away. "Hey, Renee. Calling me for a pep talk?"

"Were you aware that Darla pushed up the meeting?"

"The managers' meeting?" he asked, unsure of where Renee was headed with her question.

"There was a lot more than managers there," fired Renee.

"Humph," Everett moaned. "She didn't say anything to me. Was Bianca there?"

"I think so. I'm going to call her after we hang up. Can you believe—" Renee stopped abruptly when Darla walked into her office and closed the door behind her. "Darla just walked in. I'll give you a call later," she told Everett and hung up before he could say good-bye.

"Are you all right?" Darla asked, pretending to sound concerned.

"I'm fine, but what's this about changing the meeting time?" Renee inquired.

"Didn't you get the update? I'm sure you were on the group e-mail."

"No, I didn't," stated Renee. She wasn't in the mood to play games. Darla knew her name wasn't on the list.

"I sent it last night," Darla said coldly.

It really didn't matter what time the e-mail was supposedly sent. There was no excuse for conducting a meeting without her knowledge. "When you didn't see me this morning, why didn't you call my cell?"

"I didn't know you were going to be in late," Darla retorted. "You didn't mention you had a prior appointment."

It had been a long time since Renee had to answer to anyone. In fact, Mr. K was the only person besides Everett she had been accountable to. "Carmen knew where I was," she answered.

"Didn't Carmen try to call you?" Darla inquired snidely.

If Renee didn't put an end to their verbal tennis match, she and Darla would go back and forth for hours. "In the future," Renee stated, "we shouldn't reschedule important meetings without one another's consent."

"I'll keep that in mind. However . . . I do expect my executives to be on top of things."

Renee wanted to tell her to go to college and earn a business degree so she could be on top of things, but held her tongue. "Should we debrief?"

"I don't have time right now," Darla said as she walked to the door. "I'm hosting an investment group social tonight. I need to go prepare for it. By the way, did Carmen finish what I asked her to do?"

"Carmen is my assistant," Renee wanted to say but refrained. "Carmen's helping me with a project," she said. "If you ask Mrs. Tina from the flower shop, I'm sure she'll let you rent her helium machine."

Darla smiled crookedly. "I better go," she said and paused for effect. "But you'll be happy to know that I've asked Everett to relocate to Chicago . . . at least until we close the London deal."

"What does that mean?" Renee questioned and crossed her arms.

A tiny smirk crossed Darla's face. "Just that the two of you work well together." Darla opened the door, and in plain view there was an unfamiliar woman talking to Carmen. "Hi," Darla sang and motioned for the woman to come inside Renee's office. "Renee, this is Cybil Gates, our newest employee."

Renee eyed the forty-something-year-old woman, curious about her position within the company.

"Hi, Renee," the woman greeted in a voice an octave higher than that of Renee's teenage son. "I'm looking forward to working with you. I've heard wonderful things."

Renee walked to the new employee and extended her hand. "I wish I could say the same about you. What department are you working in?"

"We're still working on those logistics," Darla answered. "At the meeting you missed, I shared the new vision of the Illinois hotels. Since I don't have time to talk, I'll send an update via e-mail to you and Everett. Would that be acceptable?"

Renee didn't like her tone but chose not to reply too sarcastically in front of the new hire. "I'll be sure to look out for it this evening," she said and then faced Cybil. "Please excuse me, but I have a deadline to meet. I'm sure we'll have a chance to talk soon."

When Darla and Cybil left the room, Renee sat at her desk and turned the chair toward the window. There was an unsettling feeling in her spirit. Darla was doing more than changing the face of the hotel. She was changing personnel, too, and Renee's gut told her that Cybil was her replacement.

If her intuition was true, what did that mean for her future? She'd been a faithful employee of Luxury Inn since college, and in less than five years she would be able to retire. By the world's standards, Renee was too old to go on job interviews or make a career change. "Time changes all things," Renee mumbled softly. First in her marriage, and now in her career. The one place she could go and maintain order and control would soon be stripped from her, too.

***

"Did I wake you?" Jerome asked when Renee answered her phone.

"Hey, Jerome," she said, half asleep, and then glanced at the time on her cell phone. She couldn't believe that it was after eight and she was still in bed. Renee touched the side of her head and slowly sat up. The last thing she remembered before falling asleep last night was the opening scene of a *Law & Order* episode. She swung her legs to the side of the bed, and her foot knocked over an empty bottle of wine.

"I didn't mean to wake you. I actually thought you'd be in the office by now," Jerome responded, curious. "Are we still on for dinner tonight?"

"My day is busy, but I promised Josh, so I'll be there." Renee picked up the wine bottle and sat it on the nightstand.

"Okay, we'll see you there," replied Jerome. "Are you okay?"

"I overslept, that's all. So, I should get moving," she replied with a slight attitude. Her head was throbbing, and Jerome was trying to hold a lengthy conversation. "I'll see you tonight."

Renee ended the call and sat the phone beside her. How she had consumed an entire bottle of wine was baffling, and her body was paying for the overindulgence. Concentrating on maintaining her balance, Renee got up and inched her way to the kitchen. She really needed some fresh air to wake up and to get rid of her headache. There were no windows she could open in the suite, so for now, Renee would have to settle for a cup of black coffee.

There were a number of things Renee had wanted to do before going to bed that she'd have to follow through with this morning. As she fixed her coffee, she replayed her to-do list in her head. She needed to talk to Everett about relocating to Chicago, meet with Bianca to discuss what happened in the meeting she missed, and check her e-mail for Darla's summary notes. Checking for Darla's e-mail was at the top of her list.

The premium coffee in the suite wasn't one of Renee's favorites, but it was all that was available. Renee made herself a cup and then walked into the living room. While her coffee cooled, she logged into her e-mail and sent Carmen a message to let her know that she would be working at the Northbrook hotel today. It pained her to copy Darla on the e-mail, but after the mishap yesterday she thought it was best that she try to cooperate. After sending the e-mail, Renee was surprised to see that Darla had sent the meeting notes at 2:00 A.M. Everett had sent an e-mail at seven this morning as well, and she opened his message first.

Time to update our résumés.

Renee chuckled. Something in Darla's notes must've rubbed him the wrong way, because Everett would never consider leaving Luxury Inn. Before she replied to his e-mail, Renee downloaded Darla's document and read it carefully.

It was professionally written, and Renee questioned if Darla had composed any part of it. In the document, plans to completely renovate the three Illinois branch hotels over the next two years were discussed in detail. When everything was done, the hotels that Renee had worked hard to establish would only be a memory. Darla wanted to create a mega conference center. That wasn't a bad idea, but Renee wasn't sure it would be wise to eliminate their special events division. There were so many adaptations to the building, Renee doubted the budget could justify keeping the same number of staff on payroll.

Renee closed Darla's file and reopened Everett's e-mail. Before she typed in a response, she thought about the implications of having Everett in Chicago every day. It was going to be good to have him in the office to help combat Darla's craziness, but she was afraid how it would affect her marriage. Though she tried to fight it, Renee was becoming more attracted to him.

> I think you're right. This hotel is a sinking ship. So . . .
> she's moving you to Chicago? I'll be in Northbrook today,
> if you need me.

Renee responded to a few more e-mails and then shut down her computer. If she didn't make it out of the suite within the hour, she'd get stuck in the morning rush hour traffic.

Before going into her private Northbrook office, Renee stopped at Bianca's door. She needed to hear what took place in yesterday's meeting from her protégé. Other than Everett, Bianca was the only employee that she trusted.

High strung and determined, Bianca had been Renee's intern back in Philadelphia. Over the years their relationship had developed beyond the workplace. Outside of the hotel, Renee was more like her aunt. When Renee announced she was moving to Chicago, Bianca eagerly offered to join her. Not one to grow attached to employees, Renee couldn't ignore the young assistant's drive and approved her relocation. She reminded Renee so much of herself. And Bianca was far from a disappointment. In less than two years, the bright-eyed intern had been promoted to the manager level.

Renee tapped on the door, and Bianca jumped from behind her desk. "I'm so glad you're here!" she exclaimed and embraced her mentor with a warm hug. "I called you twice last night. Did you get my calls?"

Not wanting to tell the whole truth, Renee said, "I fell asleep and didn't hear the phone." That sounded a lot better than "I drank a whole bottle of wine and fell into a stupor." Renee stepped into the office and closed the door. "Do you have time to talk?"

"Of course I do," Bianca responded. "What's up with your girl, Darla? When I didn't see you at the meeting yesterday, I got worried."

"She conveniently forgot to send me the new meeting time," Renee replied as she sat in the chair next to Bianca's desk.

Bianca couldn't sit still. This was one of the major differences between the two women. Most of the time Renee was calm in troubling situations. Bianca, on the hand, was quick on her feet, and fiery in the way she handled difficult matters. As she told Renee about the unfamiliar people at the meeting and about Darla's vision, she pranced around the room. "It was weird. Darla went over these changes, and all that the other managers could think about was where you were. Then that Cybil started asking us questions," Bianca informed her. "I felt like I was being interviewed informally. Do you know what's going on?"

"I don't know what's going on, but keep your eyes and ears open," replied Renee.

"Well," Bianca responded, "if you leave, you know I'm right behind you."

"I appreciate your loyalty, but don't mess up your career because Darla doesn't like me."

Bianca sat on the edge of her desk and placed her hands at her side. "Enough about Darla. How about you? We haven't talked since you moved into the suite."

Bianca didn't know about Jerome's affair until the one Friday night she ran into the Thomas' family at an ice cream parlor. At first, Bianca thought Joi was Jerome's niece, but he proudly dispelled that belief by introducing her as his daughter. Unlike many of Renee's acquaintances, Bianca didn't pressure her to share the details. It was obvious that Jerome had been unfaithful. There was no need to make her relive that painful fact. Renee loved that about her young friend. Sometimes, a person needed a friend that knew when to speak and when to be silent.

"I've seen better days," Renee sighed. "But things are good. Jerome and I started counseling, so who knows what's next for us."

"I'm praying for you," Bianca said and hopped off her desk. "You know how much I love your family." Bianca strolled to a long bookshelf by the window and took a picture out of what looked like a school yearbook. "You know I've been visiting Philly a lot lately, and now I can tell you why. I've got a new beau," she cooed and handed Renee the picture.

Renee studied the photograph and smiled. It was good to see two people in love. Bianca and her friend were at an outdoor festival. Judging by their expressions, they were having a great time. Renee wondered how long that happy feeling would last. "He's handsome, Bianca," Renee told her. "Where'd you meet him? And is it serious?"

"I think so," Bianca said and blushed. "His name is Sharif, and we dated very briefly in college. I ran into him at a friend's wedding, and we've been talking ever since. It's been three months so far."

"You can handle the long distance?" Renee asked out of curiosity. She remembered how difficult it had been to be away from Jerome for a few days while on business trips. She couldn't imagine being away from him for long stretches of time back then.

"It gets rough at times, and it is expensive," Bianca replied. "Those trips to Philly add up. If you leave this place, I think I'll quit and move back home."

"Don't go making any plans," Renee snapped, without realizing the sharp tone in her voice. "It's good to be loved, but always be smart. Don't move for a man unless you're absolutely positive he feels the same way about you."

The sparkle in Bianca's eyes dimmed. "I know. I have to put me first. We're taking things slow, so . . . we'll see where God leads."

Renee laid the picture on the desk. She hated to put a damper on Bianca's high, but at the present time she'd lost hope in fairy-tale endings. "Yes, trust God," she said and stood up. "And when He shows you that something's not right, don't ignore it."

"I won't let him hurt me. I promise," Bianca responded solemnly.

"It's getting late," Renee said. "I have a few things to do before meeting Joshua tonight. We should go to lunch soon. We've got a lot to catch up on."

"You got it," Bianca replied, trying to maintain some enthusiasm.

Renee walked out of Bianca's office and headed down the hall to her office. She closed the door, and when she sat down, she started to cry. Though she wished Bianca well, Renee had to admit that she was a little jealous. It had been so long since she was really *in love* with her husband. She'd give anything to feel the way Bianca and Sharif looked in the picture.

In spite of her slight jealousy, Renee had given her advice from her heart, and she prayed Bianca had listened with an open mind. When she was young, her mother had tried to enlighten her about love, but Renee had refused to listen. "The heart can't control who you love, Mom," Renee had whined one night after dinner. While she still believed that statement, Renee wished she'd been wiser in choosing a husband. "Love doesn't pay the bills," she'd heard a comedian say one morning on the radio. Renee couldn't have agreed more. A successful relationship needed more than love to hold it together, in her opinion.

Renee removed a folder from her briefcase and tried to focus on work, but her mind was in another place. Every time she thought about Jerome, she cried a little harder, and every time she thought about Darla, her body tensed up.

I need you, God, Renee thought, sobbing. *If You don't show up, I don't think I can make it another day.*

An e-mail alert caught Renee's attention, and she opened the new message from Bianca.

I know this is a hard time for you, but hold on. No matter how low you feel, no matter how crazy your life becomes, God is there. He loves you, and because He does, the best is yet to come.

Renee thanked Bianca for the encouragement and then thanked God for sending an angel to plant hope in her spirit. Though her heart was still full of sadness, she could reflect on those words and make it through the rest of the day.

~10~

Joi

Joi had never seen her half brother so excited. When Jerome picked her up from school, Joshua jumped out of the car and practically pulled her inside. "Junior's giving me his old car!" he exclaimed.

That was exciting news. If Joshua had access to a car, they would be able to get around the city without relying on other people or catching public transportation. *Maybe Josh will teach me how to drive,* Joi thought as they pulled into a hidden alley full of modern-day townhomes.

Junior was outside watering the lawn when Jerome parked the car in the driveway. Joshua charged out of the car and ran up to his older brother, nearly knocking him to the ground. The water hose fell from Junior's hand and sprinkled the side of Joi's leg before it slithered into the grass. As she approached the front door, behind Jerome, she wondered if Junior would ever give her with a warm reception. Before Renee moved out, Junior was beginning to accept Joi, but after the family dinner with Renee, that all changed.

Joshua ran to the alley at the back of the town house to look at his "new" car, and Junior greeted his father as he picked up the hose. Barely looking at Joi, Junior acknowledged her and then walked to the front door and turned off the water valve by the front door.

"Joi made captain of her team," Jerome said, beaming and hugging her. "She's my basketball star."

"That's great," Junior mumbled as he rolled the hose up on its holder.

Sensing that Jerome's statement made Junior a little uneasy, Joi pulled slowly away from her father and said, "We're all good at sports, Pop. And it's all because of you."

Junior grunted playfully, and Joi smiled. Her comment had released some of the tension she initially felt. "That may be true," he said, "but you'll go a lot further than any of us. Any ideas about where you want to go to college?"

Though she'd already made up her mind, Joi told him, "I'm still doing my research."

"It sure would be nice if you interviewed your sister for your next column," Jerome mentioned proudly. "Maybe she'll even do an exclusive with you before she announces her college choice."

Junior pulled at a few weeds sprouting out of the hedges by the door. "That may be possible, but I'll have to check with my boss."

"Pop-pop, save me," Jerome III screamed from the backyard. "Uncle Josh keeps trying to tickle me!"

Hearing his grandchildren laughing in the backyard, Jerome ran to their rescue. Joi followed her father, leaving Junior to finish weeding the hedges. Once in the backyard, Joi leaned against the side of the house and observed the interaction between her new family members. Watching them, she wondered what her siblings in Philly were doing. She missed them. Much like Joshua's and Jerome's connection to the small children, Joi had a similar relationship with her stepfather and brothers and sister. As much as she pretended her Philly family bugged her, she really loved them more than her actions showed.

The screen door opened, and Grace came outside in cutoff jean shorts and a paint-stained cotton tank top. The splashes of color might have been the result of a messy art activity, but they added a touch of fashion to Grace's appearance. As a stay-at-home mom, Grace wore only clothes that she didn't mind getting dirty or torn.

"Hey, Joi," she said and waved for her to come inside. "Let's catch up while your brothers play with their new toys." As Grace finished her sentence, Junior appeared in the back alley and stood next to his fully loaded Lexus. "Maybe I'll graduate from my Honda Odyssey and get a luxury car, too, one day," she yelled, loud enough for her husband to hear. "I'm tired of driving the soccer mom car."

Junior looked up and smiled. "As soon as the kids are in college, you can get whatever you want, baby."

"C'mon, Joi," Grace said, playfully brushing off her husband. "That brother of yours is a mess."

Joi walked into the house and across the shiny hardwood floors and admired the decor. The walls were full of color, and the odd shapes and pieces of furniture throughout the house reflected Grace's upbeat and sometimes whimsical personality. If Joi's mother were to ever visit, she'd say the place looked like an indoor play center more than a home. Joi didn't mind the unique qualities of the home. Every time she was there, her mood brightened, and to her, that was the way everyone should feel when they walked into their home.

Grace walked into the open kitchen, and Joi hopped onto a lime green swivel stool in front of the breakfast bar. "How's the new school working out?" Grace said as she took a bag of carrots from the refrigerator.

"Coach Miller made me cocaptain today, after practice," Joi answered.

"Really?" Grace replied and began to chop a few carrot sticks.

"Yeah," Joi huffed. "The team wasn't too happy about that. Rocky's been the star player for Marshall for the last two years, so they didn't take too kindly to coach making *both* of us captain."

"They'll get over it. Once they see why you were chosen as an all-star, they'll understand why the coach made that decision," Grace said.

"I know," Joi sighed. "I just wish they liked me."

Grace placed the cut-up carrots on top of the tossed salad she'd dumped in a bowl earlier. "Have you made any friends?"

"Only one. Her name is Stacee," Joi said. "She's one of the point guards on the team."

Grace pushed a bag of cucumbers toward Joi and asked her to skin and slice them while she chopped the mushrooms. "More friends will come," she told Joi. "Just give it time. It's hard for some people to accept when things change. Take our family, for example." Grace put a few thinly sliced mushrooms into the salad bowl and continued to chop. "When you came into our lives, so many things changed. Instead of embracing the adjustment we all needed to make, some of us only concentrated on the hurt."

What took place at the family dinner instantly came to Joi's mind, and she stopped shaving the cucumbers.

"The dinner with Renee the other day is a prime example," Grace said, as if she'd read Joi's mind. "I hope you know that none of what's going on is your fault. It may be hard to believe at times, but it's true. No matter what the final outcome will be for Renee and Jerome, always remember that." Grace turned around and lowered the fire under a pot of hot dogs. "My husband went overboard," she continued. "He's a man of many opinions and talks way too much at times, but he has a heart of gold. He's also very protective of his family, especially Renee."

Grace finished with the mushrooms and then removed a tray of salmon patties from the oven. "I talked to Junior about what he said that night. He's so concerned about his mother that he can't see that you're hurting, too. Despite his allegiance to his mother, he's going to try and be more sensitive to your feelings. It may take a while for Renee to come around, but she will. She's a tough woman, but she loves Jerome. She's just hurting right now."

Joi almost cried. It felt good to know that someone other than Jerome and Joshua was concerned about her. "Everything happened so fast," she said as she finished shaving the cucumbers. "I found out about Jerome, then he had the heart attack, then I was visiting him for the summer, and now I'm living with him. Who would've ever thought?"

"It's overwhelming, I know, but we're happy you're a part of the family," Grace confirmed. "Zora and I need another female to talk to." Grace brushed the salmon patties with a clear yellow sauce and then sat on a polka-dot stool next to Joi. "Things will change soon. Junior told me Renee and Jerome are going to counseling."

"Wow," Joi said, surprised. Jerome hadn't mentioned that to her. "I hope they aren't considering divorce."

"I don't think so. They've been together forever," Grace said. "Renee's just hurt. Her man cheated on her and had a baby. Have you ever been hurt by someone you were in love with?"

"Unfortunately, yes," Joi said. Her ex-boyfriend, Markus, had fooled her into believing they were an exclusive couple. It pained her heart the day she ran into him and his college girlfriend at the mall.

"Then you can imagine how she feels. It's a good sign that they're going to counseling," replied Grace. "One day you'll have to tell me all about the guy that broke your heart."

The screen door slid open, and Joshua yelled inside the house, "C'mon, Joi! Let's go for a ride in my new whip."

Although Joi wanted to share in Joshua's excitement, she was enjoying her time alone with Grace.

"C'mon, c'mon, c'mon," Joshua repeated in a hurry.

"Go ahead," Grace said. "We have plenty of time to get to know each other."

Joi hopped off her stool and gave Grace a hug. She'd never been big on displays of affection, but something about Grace made her feel at ease. "Thanks for the talk," she said, and before she headed outside, Junior appeared at the door.

"I'm going with them, babe," he informed his wife. "They need big brother supervision, and I might start giving Joi some lessons while we're out."

A tear formed in the corner of Joi's eye, and she rubbed it before it could fall. Junior was actually reaching out to her and giving their relationship as brother and sister a chance.

Grace came up behind Joi and whispered in her ear. "Everything is going to be fine. Just give everyone time."

While Jerome met with his team in the Future Ballers program, Joi sat in his office at the Boys and Girls Club, stuffing envelopes for the new participants. Joshua was supposed to be helping, but he'd been talking on the phone for the last fifteen minutes.

"You again?" someone asked, and Joi looked toward the door. The guy that had bumped into her at school stepped into Jerome's office and stood next to her chair. "Are you here for the mentoring program?" he asked.

"I am," Joi replied, detecting his island accent for the first time.

Joshua ended his call and interrupted the conversation. "Hi, Denver. This is my sister, Joi."

"Mr. Thomas is your father?" Denver questioned. "Imagine that. It's a small world." Denver extended his right hand toward Joi. "I don't think we've met properly. My name is Denver McBride. I'm one of the assistants for Future Ballers."

"I'm Joi Belle," she answered bashfully and quickly released her hand from his.

"It's nice to meet you," Denver said and then pointed to Joi's box of envelopes. "Are these the packets for the meeting today? Jerome sent me to get them."

"Yes," Joi replied timidly. "I have a few more to do."

Denver picked up the box. "You can bring the rest when you come downstairs. People are starting to arrive, and I need to get them started on their paperwork."

Joi nodded, and before Denver left the room, he winked at her.

Joshua walked over to Joi and helped her finish the remaining envelopes. "Someone likes you," he teased.

Joi ignored her brother's comment. She hadn't come to Chicago to find a new love interest. That wasn't a part of her plan. "He's just being nice. Besides, he has a girlfriend."

"That may be," Joshua told her, "but I can tell that he has a thing for you."

~11~

Jerome

At 6:05 A.M. Jerome was jolted out of his sleep. He thought he'd had another bad dream, but when the house phone rang again, he opened his eyes and quickly answered it. "Yes," he said groggily.

"Sorry to wake you, Jerome, but I just got off the phone with Joi and thought you'd be up, too."

"Taylor?" Jerome asked, wondering why she was calling so early on a weekday morning.

"Yes, it's me," Taylor replied. "Good morning."

"Is everything okay?"

"I hope so," she answered snidely. "You promised to call me with updates about Joi on a regular basis. She's been with you for three weeks, and since it's now October and you've only called me twice, I guess I should be asking *you* if everything is okay."

Jerome lay flat on his back and covered his eyes with his left hand. He wished this was a dream. At least then he could control the outcome of the conversation. As it stood now, Jerome could tell things were heading in a negative direction. "Taylor," he sighed, "I know that you and Joi talk every day, so I didn't think you needed to hear from me as much."

"You've been around Joi long enough to know that she leaves out information," Taylor retorted. "I don't need to hear from you all the time, Jerome. But I do need to hear from you more than once a month. I want to know from a parent's point of view what's going on."

"Fine," Jerome replied, surrendering. He was willing to agree with anything if it would avoid conflict. "How often would you like me to call you?"

"I sense a little tension in your voice," Taylor said. "What I'm asking isn't far-fetched. Joi has been a part of my life for the past seventeen years. I'm missing out on her senior year in high school. That's pretty major, I think."

Jerome did understand, but he didn't know why Taylor couldn't talk to him at a more decent hour. "How often should I call?" he asked again.

"Twice a month. Every two weeks. I don't know, Jerome," Taylor replied snidely. "I just want to know how my daughter is adjusting to Chicago."

"I'll make sure I check in twice a month," he consented. "But I hope you know that if something major were to happen to our daughter, I wouldn't hesitate to call you."

"I appreciate hearing that," responded Taylor. "I really miss having her around."

Jerome sat up in bed and looked at the clock. It was 6:30, and there was no point in going back to sleep. "I know you do," he said with more sensitivity. "She's really doing well, so try not to worry."

"Well," Taylor added, "Thanksgiving is coming up. I guess I'll look forward to seeing her then."

Jerome didn't want to disappoint her, but he knew he had to be honest. "Joi has a tournament in Wisconsin that weekend."

"Tournament?" Taylor said and sighed deeply. "Okay . . . I suppose I can hold off until Christmas."

"Well—"

Taylor stopped Jerome before he could finish his sentence. "Don't tell me she has a tournament then, too."

"I know this is hard, but you know that Joi is here because of basketball."

"I didn't know that meant I'd never get to see her."

"Think of this as preparation for when she goes off to college," suggested Jerome. "There're going to be stretches of time when you don't see her."

"She's not in college yet," Taylor shot back. "But you're right. Basketball is important to her, so maybe I should come out there. I haven't been to one of her tournaments in a while."

"I'm sure Joi would like that."

"Okay," Taylor sighed. "I'll need to talk to my husband before confirming anything." It was clear she wasn't thrilled about having to compromise. "So, I guess I'll touch base next week sometime, but before I let you go . . . how are you and Renee?"

Jerome immediately thought about Taylor's last conversation with Renee. There was no way he was going to share more information than what was necessary. "We're fine," he responded.

That reply wasn't enough for Taylor. "Joi said she's not home yet. So *not* all is fine," she said.

Jerome chose his words carefully. He didn't want to set Taylor off, and he didn't want to risk Renee finding out about the conversation. "I don't think this is something you and I should discuss."

"She's been gone a long time," Taylor continued, as if she hadn't heard Jerome's reply.

"Let it be, Tay," he said firmly, but even that didn't stop her from probing further.

"You know, Lance and I hit a rough patch right after my daughter Leah was born," she shared.

"This isn't quite the same situation," Jerome said.

"Maybe not, but we surmounted it, and you and Renee will, too," Taylor assured him. "After all, she forgave you for our affair."

Jerome heard one of the kids run downstairs. It was time for him to get ready for work. "Thanks, Taylor, but I need to go," he said. Getting advice from his former lover was the last thing he needed. And before Taylor could ask any more questions, Jerome thought it best to end the call. "Let me know about Thanksgiving, okay?"

Taylor agreed and then said good-bye. When Jerome hung up the phone, he leaned on the wooden bedpost and stared at the ceiling. What if Renee had actually been home when Taylor called? Now he understood what Reverend Hampton meant by setting boundaries. Jerome wasn't sure how to address this with Taylor, but he knew at some point he would have to. Just thinking about having that discussion with Taylor unsettled him. Much like Renee, Taylor was a strong-minded woman.

Jerome stood up and then knelt by the side of the bed. The only way he could handle two strong women was with God's guidance. *God, you know what I'm dealing with. Please help me build positive relationships. Help Taylor realize that she has to respect my marriage. Show me what to do so that one day the three of us can be in the same room without tension. Help us work together as a unit to take care of and support Joi. And, Lord, please let Renee and me have a productive counseling session today.*

The light in the hallway turned on, and Jerome wrapped up his prayer. Joi and Joshua would be leaving the house soon. Now that Joshua was driving, he didn't have to drop them off at school or pick them up every day. It was still hard to believe that Joshua was driving. Before long, he'd be driving off to college. Once Joshua was away at college, he and Renee had plans to enjoy their empty nest. They would complete projects together and travel to countries they'd never seen. They'd take up new hobbies and take interesting classes at the local community center. *I miss my wife,* he sighed and then took the ironing board out of the hall closet. Jerome rummaged through a laundry basket on the floor and removed a pair of blue khakis and a button-down shirt. As he ironed his clothes, Jerome remembered something Reverend Hampton had said. "Doing the same thing will produce the same results. If you want a different result, sometimes, you have to try something outside of your comfort zone."

Jerome thought about the way he felt at the altar a few Sundays ago. The altar was a special place. A place where prayers were answered. A place where God's presence could be felt. Jerome laid his ironed clothes neatly on the bed and headed to the bathroom. While he undressed and prepared for his shower, something in his spirit told him that the answers he was searching for were waiting for him at the altar. "That's where I need to be," Jerome said and stepped into the shower. "I'll go to the altar every morning before work until Renee comes home."

"Let's start from the beginning," Mrs. Stroud said as she closed the door to her office. "We didn't get a chance to do that during our last session. Are you ready to share your earliest memories?"

Mrs. Stroud sat in her usual chair and opened her notepad. While she flipped to a clean page, Jerome began telling the story about the day he met his wife in a high school biology class. From time to time, Renee jumped in to correct the details of the day.

"As I remember it," Renee chimed in, "you invited yourself into my lab group. You kept telling corny jokes, and I tried to get everyone to give you the boot."

"It was love at first sight for me," Jerome said. "But after our first date, I couldn't keep her away from me."

Renee laughed aloud, and that made Jerome feel good. "Please, Jerome. I would come out of the house every morning, and you'd be waiting for me at the end of my block. You wanted to ride the bus to school together, you wanted me to stay and watch you practice after school, *and* you wanted to walk me home from the bus every day after school. After a while I just got used to your silly behind."

"Remember the first time I met your parents?" Jerome asked, recalling the lunch her mother had prepared. Jerome was so nervous that day, he accidentally dropped a ceramic sugar container on Renee's parents' newly carpeted dining-room floor. Weeks later, her mother was still finding small grains of sugar that the vacuum had missed in the carpet.

"How can I forget?" Renee said, recalling the mishap. "My mother asked you a million questions."

"From the twinkle in both of your eyes, it sounds like you had a wonderful courtship," Mrs. Stroud added and challenged the couple to talk about those times more often. "Tell me about the day you proposed, Jerome."

Thinking about that day, Jerome wished he had a more romantic story to tell. When he proposed to Renee, he was only eighteen and worked for an uncle who delivered bottled water to local grocery stores. Though he loved Renee, the proposal happened at such a young age because of selfish reasons. He didn't want her to go to college outside of Philadelphia. Jerome didn't have money for a real gold ring, but his uncle loaned him money to buy one from the jewelry department at T.J.Maxx. If Renee's parents hadn't paid for the entire wedding, Renee wouldn't have received the kind of ceremony she deserved. They would have instead been married by the justice of the peace.

Not many people approved of them marrying so young, but Jerome and Renee were determined to prove them wrong. They believed the love they shared could conquer anything. And for a while, love did. Their love was strong enough to overcome any problem that arose on their path. Their life wasn't perfect, but it was good. When the real trouble hit, neither Jerome nor Renee saw it coming. She was going to school and working full-time hours. Jerome was at home with their sons, while he looked for permanent work. Before they realized what was happening, Jerome had started staying out all night, just to get away from his nagging wife.

"This is a good place to pause," Mrs. Stroud said. "Next week we'll talk in detail about the problems that surfaced in your marriage. Should we reschedule for the same day and time next week?"

Jerome agreed to the time without hesitation, while Renee surfed through the calendar feature on her cell phone. "Can we meet after three next week? I have a meeting in the morning, and then I need to go look at an apartment."

Jerome's heart dropped. "You're moving?"

"Yes," Renee responded casually. "Darla will be in town for the next three months at least and—"

"You can't be serious. Don't you think getting an apartment is a waste?" Jerome questioned.

"It's a temporary lease, Jerome," Renee replied, like it was no big deal. "Darla made a couple comments about me staying in the suite, and before this becomes a problem for her, I think it's best I find a place . . . just for a few months."

Jerome wasn't satisfied with her response. There had to be something more than an overbearing boss to push Renee's buttons. Right away, he thought about Renee being at the mall with Everett, and although he knew they were friends, for some reason, their "friendship" didn't sit right with him today. "What is this move *really* about, Renee?"

Renee stared at him, confused.

"Are you sure this is about Darla, and not Everett?"

Renee rolled her eyes. "I said I needed to leave because of Darla. Let's not forget why we're here in the first place. Now, we had a good session today. Don't let us end on bad terms."

"I'm sorry, but I don't like this one bit," Jerome retorted. "You shouldn't be in some apartment. You should be back at home with me."

Renee put her phone inside her purse and then zipped it closed. "We're not ready for that."

"But we're ready for you to move into your own place?" Jerome snapped in disbelief. "Do you realize that you're abandoning me . . . and your son? How do you think this is affecting him?"

Renee ignored the question, but Jerome pressed harder for information. "I can't help but wonder if your friend Everett talked you into this."

"Why can't this just be about what's happened between us? Why do you have to bring Ev into this? He's my boss, and yes, my friend, but nothing more," Renee fired back. "He's been there for me. When you were sick, he came to the rescue."

"How exactly did *Ev* rescue you?" inquired Jerome. "And please, be honest with me."

Renee hesitated at first but then changed her mind. "After you had the heart attack, I wasn't in a good place mentally. Everett and I were working closely back then, and he could tell I needed someone to talk to," shared Renee. Jerome grabbed the arm of the sofa, hoping that Renee's story wouldn't get any more detailed. Jerome wouldn't be able to cope if Renee told him she'd slept with her boss. "I spent the holidays in California," Renee continued, and Jerome got off the sofa and walked to the window.

"We've gone over our time," Mrs. Stroud said softly. "Maybe we should . . ."

Jerome faced his wife before Mrs. Stroud finished her sentence. "Did anything else happen while you were there?" he asked. He had to know. "Was there a hug? Or a kiss? Did you spend the night with him?"

Renee's eyes fell to the floor. "We did kiss once," she confessed, "but that was a long time ago. We haven't kissed since then."

Jerome wanted to hit something, but he wasn't home. "How long ago, Renee?"

"Back when we lived in Philly," she answered.

"And you're sure nothing else has happened between you and *Ev?*" he asked.

"I'm not you," Renee snapped, offended that he'd asked.

"There seems to be some bottled-up emotions about this matter," Mrs. Stroud interjected. "We really need to save this discussion for next week. Jerome, can you meet after three next week?"

"Whatever she wants. She likes to control every-thing, anyway," Jerome replied with an attitude and then walked out of the office.

Without looking back or waiting for Renee to come out of the building, Jerome got in his car and drove to work. As he traveled along the expressway, he remembered that God had told him to stand. "Ahhhhh," Jerome screamed and hit the steering wheel. As angry as he was with Renee, he had to accept what happened and move on. The fact still remained that he had a two-year affair with Taylor. All Renee and Everett did was share a kiss many years ago. If they were going to mend their marriage, Jerome was going to have to trust his wife.

~12~

Renee

Like old times, Bianca helped Renee set up the main conference room for a meeting Darla had scheduled two days ago. "Where should we hang this?" she asked Renee as she held up a long poster of the Chicago skyline.

Renee centered a 1950s photograph of Mr. Kotlarczyk standing in front of the first Luxury Inn hotel and then scanned the Chicago-themed room. "How about the wall over the snack table?"

"That'll work," Bianca responded.

"Isn't the meeting supposed to start soon?" Renee questioned.

Bianca handed the poster to the hospitality team and told them where to hang it. "In fifteen minutes," she said as she looked at the clock on the wall.

Renee shook her head and continued to position various old pictures of the hotel around the room. As she'd learned last night at an impromptu meet and greet, today's meeting would include managers from the local branch hotels, as well as seasoned and new board members from California. Whenever visitors flew into Chicago for a meeting, Renee liked to decorate the room based on a specific theme. She found that incorporating interesting facts and foods broke up the monotony of long, tiring meetings. It provided opportunities for people to learn and share new experiences with their colleagues.

Everett stood at the doorway with a few of the board members. "Hey," he said, and Renee turned in his direction. "Can we come in?"

Renee put down the picture in her hand. "Sure," she said. "The meeting will be starting as soon as Darla gets here. Take a seat, or feel free to look around."

The board members strolled to the tables, and Everett inched close to Renee. "Where's Darla?" he inquired softly. "I've been trying to reach her all morning."

"I have no idea," Renee responded, then immediately greeted the next wave of guests entering the room.

When the guests were situated, Renee and Everett stood outside the double doors. They both prided themselves on starting meetings on time, so they were equally frustrated.

"What do you think Darla wants to talk about?" he asked idly.

"Your guess is as good as mine," Renee replied. "She mentioned something about presenting her ideas to everyone at one time."

"There's no telling what we're about to hear," he said, then changed the subject. "How's the apartment hunt going?"

"I saw one that I liked off of Madison last week, but before I sign anything, there are a few I'm set to see next week." Talking about apartments reminded Renee about her last counseling session with Jerome. Since that session, they hadn't been on the best of terms. Their conversations were short and to the point. Of all the things Jerome shouted at the session, Renee was most bothered by his comment concerning their son. In so many words, he'd accused her of being a bad mother. *What kind of a woman would choose to leave her children?* Jerome didn't say those exact words, but that was what registered in Renee's mind as he talked.

Though men often separated from their families without society's condemnation, when a woman chose to
leave without the children, it was highly frowned upon.
Renee prayed that God understood that she had to
leave, and that Joshua knew she still loved him.

Everett poked his head inside the conference room.
Although people didn't appear antsy, he wanted to respect their time. "Maybe I should go look for her," he
said, and Renee shook her head.

"Let me go," she said. "You stay here and keep them
entertained."

Renee walked down the long hallway and turned the
corner. Carmen was at her desk, typing fast on her keyboard. While Renee was in the meeting, she had asked
her faithful assistant to update her contact list and create a separate file for her personal records.

"Have you seen Darla?" she asked.

"No," Carmen replied without looking away from the
computer screen.

Renee continued down the hall to Darla's office and
knocked on the closed door. Impatient, she waited a
few seconds and then knocked again. Still, no one responded. Renee held her ear close to the door, hoping
to hear some sign of movement, but there was none.
Concerned, Renee headed back to Carmen's desk. "Can
you call Darla's suite for me?"

Carmen quickly dialed Darla's room extension as
Renee hovered over her. "There's no answer," she said
after five rings.

Renee looked at her watch. Through the years, Renee
had established a solid reputation for her professional-
ism. Though Darla had planned the meeting, people
knew that Renee ran the Illinois hotels. Not wanting to
tarnish her record, Renee decided to begin the meeting
without her. "Call her again, and this time leave a mes-

sage," she ordered. "Tell her that we're waiting for her in the conference room."

Though annoyed, Renee calmly returned to the conference room and closed the doors behind her. Almost everyone had claimed a seat, confirming that it was time for the meeting to begin. As she walked to the front of the room, Renee tugged on Everett's suit jacket sleeve and motioned for him to follow her.

Positioning herself behind the podium, Renee tapped the microphone to make sure it was on. "Good morning," she greeted, and the guests that were not yet sitting at one of the round tables rushed to an empty seat. "It's always good to meet with the Illinois managers and board members. I'm especially excited about meeting with the newest additions to the board. I hope that you'll enjoy your stay here in Chicago," Renee said. "As I briefly mentioned to the new members last night, my name is Renee Thomas, and I am the general manager of the Chicago, Northbrook, and Oak Brook hotels here in Illinois."

Everett eased behind Renee as she continued to share information about her background and the history of the Illinois hotels. Without her having to say it, he knew Renee was wasting time, and he was ready to jump in and say a few words. But he never had a chance to. In the middle of Renee's speech, the main doors swung open and Darla sauntered into the room, wearing a long emerald cocktail dress.

"Welcome," Darla said and beamed as Cybil trailed closely behind her.

Renee and Everett stared at one another. Darla's grand entrance had taken them by surprise.

"Okay," Renee continued. "Now that Darla is here, I'll turn the meeting over to her."

Renee sat down next to Everett, still dazed. Darla had entered the room like she was walking the red carpet for a Hollywood movie premiere. Cybil was dressed professionally, but as she walked to the front of the room, she waved as if she were on a beauty pageant float. The scene was ridiculous, and without looking at Everett, she knew they were both thinking the same thing. The day was going to be interesting and long.

As Cybil played around with the projector, Darla removed the microphone from the podium. "I'm so glad to see your smiling faces," she began. "I heard some of you were at karaoke night in the lounge last night."

Renee sat back and listened to Darla talk to the group as if they were longtime friends. There was no apology for her tardiness and no summary of what she planned to discuss. Instead of using the platform to conduct business, Darla used it to be the center of attention. It was hard to believe that she was the daughter of the man who had built the hotel chain.

Ten minutes after her arrival, Darla finally let the guests know what to expect. While Cybil operated the projector, Darla ran through the PowerPoint presentation without pausing for air. She glided across the room casually as she discussed her reasons for wanting to put a "new face" on the hotel.

Renee barely paid attention to her rambling. She'd already been sitting uncomfortably in her seat for an hour, and Darla had yet to get to the meat and bones of the meeting. When Darla was far enough away, Everett slid Renee a Post-it note.

When is the bathroom break?

Renee glanced around the room. She could tell by the drooping eyelids and the blank stares on some of the guests' faces that it was time for a break, and as Darla made her way back to the front of the room, Renee raised her hand.

"Question already?" Darla jokingly asked. "I was just about to go over my plans."

Finally, Renee thought but proceeded with her question. If Darla took nearly as long to share her plans as she did with her introduction, she'd talk straight through lunch. Renee doubted her bladder could hold out that long, and looking at some of the near-seventy-year-old board members, she was fairly certain their bladders couldn't, either. "Do you mind if we take a quick ten-minute break?" she asked.

Darla stared at Renee as if she'd done something wrong. "Well, I was hoping that I could share the details and then dismiss everyone for lunch. Is that all right with everyone?" Darla said. "I mean, I thought this would be something you'd like to talk about over lunch."

Renee squeezed her three middle fingers tightly with her hand. Lunch was over an hour away. Before she could comment, Everett spoke up.

"Why don't we take a five-minute break now?" he asked coolly. "That'll give people a chance to at least get a quick drink of water or use the restroom. Then we'll break for lunch whenever you finish outlining your plans. Does that sound fair?"

Darla agreed, and everyone jumped from their seats.

The break lasted longer than five minutes, and when Renee returned to her chair, she could tell Darla wasn't pleased. She had a feeling Darla was more bothered by the fact that she had asked the question than by the actual number of minutes it took for everyone to return to the room.

Once everyone was seated, Darla picked up where she left off, and as she talked, Cybil advanced the slides in the projector. "As you can see on the screen, I'd like to do a company makeover," she began. "The rooms look great, but I want to add more color. Our central theme will be a nice chocolate brown, but every floor will represent a different color." Darla walked to the screen and pointed to various pictures. "As you see here, the room is decorated with beautiful brown and blue accents. This is representative of how all the rooms would look on the fourth floor. Guests staying on the fifth floor would enjoy similar styles, but the colors would be brown and some shade of green. All the floor would have a signature color."

So far, Renee was all right with Darla's plans. It would cost more money to paint the walls and buy new linens, carpets, paintings, and fixtures for each room, but if that was all Darla had in mind, she wasn't going to challenge her.

"Now," Darla continued, "I want to do something dynamite for the second and third floors. There aren't many conference centers here in the city, so I was thinking we could renovate two floors to accommodate conferences and retreats. We'll keep the retail stores on the main level and the lounges for wedding accommodations on the ground level. I would like to add a courtyard for couples who'd like to hold outdoor ceremonies, but for the most part, the resources we currently use for weddings will remain the same."

That's actually not a bad idea, Renee thought as she jotted down questions to ask later.

Darla headed back to the podium and placed the microphone back in its base. "Let's talk about changes in staff and responsibilities."

Renee could feel the tension among the managers. For her, the moment was déjà vu. Before moving to Chicago, she sat in a conference with Mr. Kotlarczyk and listened as the top executives contemplated layoffs.

"Everett," Darla said and stretched her hand in his direction. "Can you please stand?"

Everett slowly stood to his feet. Whatever Darla was about to say would be news to him as well.

"As you all know, Everett has been with Luxury Inn for twenty-five years," Darla shared. "He worked with my father, and that's why I can confidently say that he would approve my nominating him as a future vice president."

"Is there a vacancy?" the Oak Brook manager questioned. This was news to everyone, especially Everett.

"Yes," replied Darla. "There will be an opening very soon. Mr. Donaldson is retiring this year."

For the first time today, Everett was speechless. The nomination couldn't have gone to a better candidate, but it was clear that he was caught off guard.

"I'm sure many of you have seen my wonderful new assistant walking the halls and in meetings," Darla said. "Well, Cybil has been hired as a general manager for the Illinois hotels. Her main duties will include supervising the accounting department. She worked in retail in Beverly Hills for almost fifteen years and has a wealth of knowledge to bring to this company. Who knows? She may even be the perfect replacement for Everett's current CFO position. She will be based here in Chicago and will report directly to Everett."

Confusion filled the room. How was this possible? Rather than address the apparent uneasiness in the room, Darla continued to speak about Everett. "It is my hope that Everett and Cybil will also work closely together on the London project. I haven't mentioned this yet, but it would be great if Everett could move to Chicago, at least until the project is finished. Interviews for the vice president position will take place through November, and an official decision will be made in February of next year."

Renee sat in her seat, paralyzed. How was Cybil the general manager of the Chicago hotels? And what did that mean for her? How could Darla make such drastic decisions without talking to the board members, investors, and executives first? She wondered if Darla's siblings knew about this. Was Darla grooming Cybil to take Everett's place? Renee was furious. If anyone at all the Luxury Inn hotels in the country was up for a major promotion, it was her. She thought about waiting until the meeting ended to confront Darla, but her spirit wouldn't rest.

"Did the board vote on these changes?" Renee blurted. "I like some of your ideas, but I have strong reservations about how this will affect the budget over the next couple years."

"I agree," Bianca added, and other managers chimed in as well.

Hearing the confirmation from the other managers let Renee know that she wasn't out of line. "I'm also unclear on the procedure for the promotions. I thought there was a set process for this sort of thing."

Darla stuttered as she tried to get her first words out. "I mentioned my thoughts to the members a few weeks ago."

"Was there a meeting?" asked Renee.

"I had an informal dinner meeting with—" Darla began, but she was cut off.

"Is this also informal?" Renee sarcastically questioned. "Everett and I should've been a part of any discussion regarding renovations or staff changes. I am extremely confused about the structure, as I'm sure others are, too."

"Darla, with all due respect," Everett said. "Changes affect everyone in this room and the future success of the hotel. Perhaps you, Renee, and I should meet to discuss a plan on how to better execute your ideas."

"Yes," Darla replied, visibly shaken. "And why don't we break for lunch now."

Before Darla officially dismissed the group, Renee grabbed her pen and notepad and then left the room. Inside her office, Renee paced the floor as she replayed what had happened. Was the way Darla handled things legal?

There was a light knock at the door, and Renee prayed it wasn't Darla. She was too furious to speak to her right now. "Come in," she said and walked to the chair behind her desk.

"Before you say anything," Everett said when he opened the door, "let's take a minute to regroup. I know you're mad, but we'll—"

"That's easy for you to say. You got a promotion, *and* the London deal wasn't stripped from you."

"Let's wait until we speak to Darla tomorrow. You and I both know she doesn't know much about this business, so let's be cool and wait," he said. "From now on, we're just going to have to pay more attention to her, that's all."

"That woman is going to ruin this hotel, and you know it." Renee was about to sit down when Darla burst into her office.

"If I didn't have thick skin, I'd be insulted," Darla remarked. "I want you to understand that Cybil and I thought carefully about these plans. I'm just trying to make our hotel branch a success."

"We're already a success, and we have been since the hotel was built." Renee tossed the notepad in her hand on her desk.

"What Renee means is that she's done a wonderful job as the leader of the hotels here in Illinois, as well as the one in Philadelphia. She's won numerous awards. This change seems sudden and—she's right—very costly," Everett said and shut the door so that no one passing by could hear them.

"It's not sudden," Darla said. "The financials have been reviewed thoroughly by a number of people, and—"

"You reviewed them without my input, and it affects the hotels I'm responsible for. Nor did you discuss this with Everett, who is still the CFO until he is offered the VP position. You did things backward," retorted Renee. "Cybil may be good at managing an upscale jewelry store, but this is a hotel. People go to college and earn degrees in hotel management," Renee stated. "And if this is some kind of competition between you and your siblings, I don't think it's fair to involve the people who work hard for this company every day. You cannot prove a point at the cost of people's careers."

"What Renee means," added Everett, "is that she has more than twenty years of experience in this business. Your father thought very highly of her."

"Thanks, Everett. But I can speak for myself," Renee told her friend. She appreciated his efforts at peace-making, but Darla had ignited an unnecessary war, and Renee was ready to do battle. "There's some shady stuff going on here, Darla. I've been demoted in front of a room full of people, some who I don't know, for a reason I have no clue about. You created a position for a friend, who, I suspect, is really being prepped for Everett's job, a position she may not be qualified for, and this is not going to fly with me." Renee finally sat down. "I know about the 'informal' meeting you had with the managers. They all felt like they were being interviewed. This all makes me wonder if you're trying to drive me out of this hotel. If that's the case, Darla, I want you to know that it's going to take a lot more than this to scare me away."

"Well," Darla said, and as she talked, her voice trembled, "you've been the general manager for three hotels. No one else has that responsibility."

"And that should tell you about my level of experience and competence for this job," snapped Renee. "Your father trusted me with these hotels without any complaints."

Darla walked backward to the door. "I didn't demote you. You've been complaining about your heavy load lately. I thought you'd appreciate less responsibility so that you'll have more time for your personal life."

"Excuse me?" Renee said. "When have I told you that I was so overwhelmed that I couldn't handle my job? I freely give plenty of time to this hotel because of the love I have for this business and the respect I have for your father. I've managed three hotels, designed and implemented company training, and developed concepts for the London hotel very successfully. My work is credible on many levels. Stripping me of my responsibilities is a foolish move."

"Considering the relationships that Renee and I have already established in London," Everett said, "it's definitely better for her to see this through to completion. We only have a few months to go."

Darla faced Everett. "You may be right."

"He *may* be right?" Renee was shocked. "Why didn't you think to speak to us before announcing this at your gala of a meeting? This is not the way to do business, and I'm not going to sit by and let you walk all over me or run this hotel into a hole. Your father would be ashamed of what you're doing."

"My father's not in charge anymore," Darla replied snidely.

"Look," Renee replied, "I should be the next in line for the COO position." Renee knew she sounded like a bratty schoolgirl, but she was right. No one in the company had matched her efforts. "I will not accept anything less than what I know I deserve."

"Is there a reason why Renee didn't get a promotion, too?" queried Everett.

Darla didn't respond.

"You know," Renee said blithely, "I have a *very* good lawyer, and I think—"

Everett moved close to Renee and touched her hand. "Let's not move too hastily," he blurted, and Renee shot him an evil glare. "Before we bring in any lawyers, is there a way we could sit down and iron out all the issues? Renee has done a lot for this company. She's a great talent, and we can't afford to lose that."

Darla's face flushed with fury. "I'm not going to discuss this anymore today. We'll finish this later."

"We'll definitely talk in the morning," Renee said sternly as Darla walked out the door.

Everett leaned against a tall file cabinet and placed his hands on his head. "What on earth happened today?"

"I don't know, but I'm not going to accept it," Renee told her friend.

"I know you're upset," Everett said. "But we'll get this straight . . . and without lawyers, okay?"

"I'll try to back off, but if she doesn't behave from this point on, I can't be held responsible for what will come next."

Renee stood outside her new apartment building and watched her sons and Jerome unload the moving truck. The apartment was furnished, but there were some things Renee didn't want to use, like the sofa and beds. She'd made arrangements for them to be put in storage, and she'd purchased new ones. Moving day was flowing better than she'd expected. The day after her dispute with Darla, Renee thought that she'd have to file a lawsuit and look for another job. Instead, Darla conveniently had to leave on a business trip, and while she was away, Darla agreed to place a hold on her new ideas until she returned and had a chance to discuss them in detail with Renee. In the interim, Renee continued to function as the general manager. Darla's timing couldn't be better. Three days after her departure, Renee found an apartment only one block outside of the Loop, and she didn't waste time moving in.

Ironically, Everett also found an apartment around the corner and made plans to move in at the end of the month. Renee didn't dare share this information with Jerome. It had been hard enough getting him to accept her need to live on her own for a while. He had ranted for days about Renee getting too comfortable on her own and had accused her of enjoying life as a single woman. As much as she wanted to go back to River Forest, Renee knew she wouldn't be happy. In the end, Jerome had softened his views and offered to help.

"Why not use the dolly?" she yelled to Jerome as he struggled to lift a box too heavy for one person to carry.

"I got it," he huffed and balanced the box in his arms.

Renee wanted to laugh as he wobbled from the street and up the stairs to the door. She shook her head as Jerome passed her. This wasn't the time to be a superhero, but she wasn't going to say that aloud and bruise his ego.

"Joshua's coming with the last box," Jerome said and stepped into a waiting elevator. "Junior will be up after he parks the truck."

"Okay," Renee replied, and when the elevator doors closed, she prayed Jerome wouldn't have another heart attack before he reached the third floor. While Renee waited for Joshua to get to the door, she looked up at the passing train. The constant sound and energy of the city were things she'd have to get used to. It had been a long time since she lived in a city. She couldn't believe Joshua was in his last year of high school. It seemed like yesterday that she'd walked him to kindergarten. He'd come a long way since then. As a child, Joshua was shy, until the day both of his brothers moved out of the house. Reggie moved into a tiny apartment with his new wife, and Junior moved into a college dorm. It seemed that Joshua morphed into an instant comedian the day they left. Where did all the time go? she thought as she watched Joshua climb the stairs with two small bags in his hands.

"Junior may be a while," Joshua said. "He said to go up without him."

Renee locked the side door and then rode the elevator up to her new temporary home. Inside the apartment, Jerome was in the kitchen, unpacking. Though he was putting things in the wrong place, Renee didn't interrupt him. Joshua went to the living room and watched television as he talked to someone on the phone.

"I'm going to set up my bedroom," Renee said.

"You know it's not too late to put everything back in the truck," Jerome responded. "All you have to do is say so. This place is too small for you."

"You just won't let it go, will you?" she laughed.

"I'll never let go of my one and only true love."

Renee shook her head. "Thanks for helping me, Jerome. I know this is hard for you to do."

"Well," Jerome answered, "I don't like it, but you know you can get me to do anything."

Almost anything, Renee thought. *I couldn't get you to not cheat on me.* "Whatever," she teased. "Junior should be up soon. The intercom to buzz him in is by the door."

Renee walked to her bedroom and started to put clothes in her dresser drawers. While she worked, she heard her cell phone vibrate against the kitchen table but didn't bother to answer it. Whoever it was could wait until she finished setting up her room.

When she was almost done, Joshua ran into her room. "Can Junior and I leave now? Joi and I want to go see a movie with some friends."

Renee refused to let the mention of Joi's name ruin her mood. "I thought you were going to stay for dinner? I was going to order your favorite deep-dish pizza."

"We can do that on Thursday," Joshua replied.

"So, you're going to leave me here all alone?" Renee half joked.

"I'll have dinner with you," Jerome shouted from the kitchen, and Renee sighed. If she didn't know any better, she'd think Jerome had planned this all along.

"Okay," she moaned and then kissed her sons as they walked out the door. Renee searched through a welcome packet and pulled out a pizza delivery menu. "Choose the kind of pizza you want," she told Jerome and tossed the menu on the table.

"So," Jerome said as he sat at the table, "what's new at work? I feel like I haven't talked to you about work in months."

"Darla's on some kind of warpath," Renee said and then poured herself a glass of water. "Would you like some water or tea?"

"Water is fine," he answered as he browsed the menu. "I hope Darla knows not to get in your way."

"If she's not careful, I'm going to have to give my lawyer a call."

"Wow!" Jerome exclaimed. "It must be pretty bad, huh?"

Renee poured water in a glass for Jerome and then handed it to him. "Yup, it's that bad."

"Since the kids aren't here," Jerome said, "do you want to order a veggie pizza?"

"That sounds good. Just make sure it's thin crust."

Jerome pulled out his cell phone and ordered the pizza. When he was done, he let Renee know that while she was in her room, she had missed a few calls.

Renee reached for her phone and checked the call log. Elise had called twice, and Everett had called once. There was one voice mail and two text messages from Everett. "Just the job and Elise," Renee said, although she didn't have to.

"Is Everett looking for you?" Jerome asked, slightly aggravated.

"Don't start, Jerome. We're having a good day. You always mess things up when you start asking questions you can't handle."

Jerome finished his glass of water and then put his glass in the sink. "If you and Everett did become more than friends while you're not living at home, would you tell me?"

"Jerome," Renee groaned, "please let this be the last time I have to say this. There is nothing going on with me and Everett. You need to get that into your head."

Jerome promised not to ask again and then went to use the restroom. Renee lowered her head when he left the room. She couldn't believe how easy it was for her to lie with a straight face. Although she and Everett were only friends, Renee knew that there was the potential for more to develop. But that was something she'd keep buried inside her heart until she was absolutely sure her marriage wasn't going to survive.

~13~

Joi

The cheering crowd boosted Joi's adrenaline as she ran down the court. With only twenty-two seconds left on the clock, she had to keep the other team from scoring and win the game. Guarding her opponent closely, she was careful not to draw a foul. Joi could tell the six-foot forward was itching for her to make a wrong move, but Joi had too much on the line to make a mistake. As she clung to the forward, Joi also had her eye on the basketball. As time winded down, the other team suddenly lost possession of the ball, and without hesitation Joi charged for the loose ball and dribbled down court. She could sense players running behind her, and she picked up speed. As she approached the basket, Joi subtly looked left and right. No one had caught up with her yet. Not wanting to make too much of a statement, Joi decided to save her fancy moves for a different game. Coolly, she lifted the ball in the air and tossed it into the net. The forward ran up on her, but it was too late. The basketball was safely inside the net, and with only three seconds left on the clock, it was clear that Marshall had won the game.

When the buzzer sounded, the players on the bench raced to the center of the court, excited about their victory. Stacee lightly punched Joi's shoulder. "That's what I'm talking about."

Kiana, Marshall's flamboyant center, taunted the other team with a chant and then gathered her team together in a huddle. Swaying from side to side, the girls sang a short verse of Jill Scott's "Hate on Me." Joi was overjoyed, and if no one was looking directly at her, she might have cried.

After the team huddle, Joi ran over to the bleachers. It wasn't hard to find her family. Jerome had ordered special bright yellow T-shirts with Joi's face on the front. Though she found them embarrassing, Joi appreciated the support.

"Good game, sis," Joshua shouted as he leaped from the bleachers.

Jerome jumped down behind him and gave Joi a congratulatory hug. "You did your thing today, boss. I'm proud of you."

"Thanks, Pop," Joi replied and blushed.

"I'm proud, too, little lady," Melanie added as she smoothed a few loose strands of Joi's hair into place.

Behind Jerome, Grace and Junior stood arm in arm, waiting for their turn to say hello. Junior wasn't wearing his yellow T-shirt, but Joi knew that was a lot to ask. She was just happy he'd made time to be at her game. "Thanks for coming," she said, resisting the urge to hug him.

Junior let go of his wife and shoved his hands into his jean pockets. "Guess I better interview you before all the scouts and other reporters start to hound you."

Joi looked at Grace, and she winked. Grace had told her Junior would come around in time. "You'll always have first dibs," Joi assured him.

That made Junior smile. "A Syracuse scout was here. I'm surprised he didn't say anything to you."

"That scout doesn't have a chance," Jerome said, butting in. "I'm scaring away everyone, 'cause she's going to U of I."

Joi shook her head. It was no secret that Jerome wanted her to attend college in Illinois, but Joi had her own plans. When she was a freshman in high school, she mapped out her career path. Just as she'd set her mind on becoming an all-star, she was going to college in Connecticut, and from there she was going to play in the WNBA.

Joi was about to head to the locker room when she noticed Denver walking toward them. "Our girl did good today," he said and put his hand on Jerome's shoulder.

"Yes," Jerome agreed. "I'm proud of her." Melanie tapped her watch, and Jerome nodded. "I hate to run, but we have a meeting in thirty minutes. I need to run back to the office, so you and Josh go home and start dinner without me."

"We have time to hit the club down south," Joshua teased, and Jerome cut his eyes in his direction.

"Just be home before I get there," he told his jovial son.

Joi caught Denver staring at her and quickly turned away. "I better get to the locker room," she said and thanked everyone for coming.

"That was smart playing," Denver said as she walked away. "Only great players think in the heat of the moment."

Joi hadn't realized he was following her. "You're saying I'm great," she replied nonchalantly.

"Not exactly," Denver replied." I'm saying you have the *potential* to be great. You'd have to beat me in a game to be classified as great."

Intrigued by his accent, Joi asked another question just to hear him speak again. "Is that a challenge I hear?"

"Not a challenge. I just want to see what you *really* got on the court. I'm told I'm the best around these parts," he bragged. "No one from this school has beat my record since I graduated *two* years ago."

"Well, in case you haven't noticed," Joi said and stopped at the locker room door, "there's a new sheriff in town."

"Ah, the gal has moxie, does she?" Denver replied. "I guess we'll have to settle this on the court."

For some reason, Joi felt comfortable with him. "Anytime. Just name the day and the place."

Stacee came out of the locker room and giggled when she saw Joi talking to Denver. She coughed lightly to get their attention. "Coach wants to have a meeting right now."

Denver smiled, and Joi admired his straight white teeth. "I need to go, too. Your dad will be looking for me," he said. As he turned away, he shouted, "I'll be thinking about our match."

"Mmm," Stacee moaned as she grabbed Joi's arm and pulled her inside the locker room.

"What's that for?" Joi asked. "There's nothing going on between us except basketball."

"Mmm," Stacee moaned louder.

"I'm serious," Joi stressed. "This year is too impor-tant for me to be distracted by some boy . . . no matter how fine he is."

Joi loaded her backpack with a couple of thick text-books and then closed her locker.

"There goes the boss!" a student announced as he passed Joi in the hall. Since yesterday's game, Joi had been the talk of the school. Somehow, the name she earned in Philadelphia had been resurrected.

The warning bell rang, and Joi secured the padlock. As much as she wanted to meet new people, she couldn't be late for English class. With a new bounce in her stride, Joi strolled down the hall in the new ankle boots Melanie had picked out for her one day at the mall. Not used to heels higher than two inches, Joi prayed she wouldn't slip and fall. When she reached the end of the hallway, Joi turned the corner and saw Jamila and her crew standing by the stairwell. If luck was truly on her side today, Jamila would have a change of heart about her, just like the other students had.

Joi strut by Jamila, and as she passed her, the grimace on Jamila's face let Joi know that she did not share the same feelings the other students had. Joi had no idea why Jamila didn't like her, and she didn't have time to make peace. Mrs. Bryant was standing at the classroom door.

"She thinks she's so cute," Joi heard Jamila grumble. "But look at those bony arms. They're thinner than a giraffe's leg. I don't see how she can even dribble a ball."

Joi ignored the insults and walked faster. It was only a matter of seconds before Mrs. Bryant closed the door.

"Spaghetti arms," Jamila teased as she followed Joi down the hall.

Is that the best you can come up with? Joi thought and rolled her eyes. Yes, her arms were skinny, but they were also strong. And she could dribble and make a basket from the center of a court.

Two doors away from her destination, Jamila and her friends rushed in front of Joi, forcing her to stand still. She wanted to yell Mrs. Bryant's name, but it was too late. Mrs. Bryant's back was turned, and she didn't see Joi coming, so she shut the door.

"Excuse me," Joi said with authority. "I have to get to class." Joi tried to get around the small female mob, but they wouldn't let her get by.

"You're no boss! Giraffe is a better name for you," taunted Jamila, and her friends giggled in agreement.

Joi rolled her eyes and tried to walk in a different direction, but was blocked. "What is your problem?" Joi asked with attitude.

Jamila gritted her teeth, then bumped Joi's shoulder as she circled her space. "I don't like the way you look at my man," she said in Joi's ear.

Confused, Joi stepped to her right so she could face Jamila. "What are you talking about?"

"Denver, the Jamaican king," Jamila sang as she danced to a reggae beat only she could hear. "Don't act like you wasn't flirting with him, 'cause I saw you."

"I wasn't *flirting* with Denver," Joi said, hoping that would ease her mind. "He asked me about basketball."

"Do I look stupid to you?" questioned Jamila.

Joi didn't answer. Jamila was a nice-looking girl, but it was *stupid* to pick a fight with someone who didn't do anything to her.

"I think she wants your man, Mila," said the shortest member of the three-woman gang, instigating.

"I don't want him. Now, can I please get to class?" Joi snapped and forced herself through the girls guarding her. She thought she was home free until a tug on her hooded sweater yanked her backward. Stumbling, Joi almost dropped her backpack. Before she could compose herself, Joi felt a punch in her back. There wasn't time to ask questions or think about what to do. It was clear Jamila wanted to fight. Ready for battle, Joi dropped her backpack and turned around, just in time for Jamila's fist to land on her shoulder blade. The hits after that one came too fast, and Joi fell onto the hard floor. Not wanting Jamila to pounce on top of her, Joi cried out to God for help and bounced back to her feet. Throwing jabs randomly, Joi was able to slow Jamila down. *Where are the guards when you need them?* Joi thought as she defended herself. She couldn't believe someone hadn't called them by now.

Using what felt like superhuman strength, Jamila picked Joi up by the waist and threw her into the lockers along the wall.

Jesus, help me! Joi moaned, and with all the strength she had left, Joi lifted her leg and shoved Jamila away. A sharp pain shot up Joi's back, but she knew she couldn't stop swinging. Jamila was clearly out for blood.

Separated only briefly, the two girls lunged at each other and bumped heads. Joi blacked out for a second but then continued to hit her enemy.

"Get to class!" Joi vaguely heard someone shout and prayed help had arrived. A whistle soon followed, and then someone wrapped their arms around her and pulled her away.

One of the school guards whisked her a few feet down the hall and told her to stay put. Little did he know how happy Joi was to see him. The guard went back to the scene and helped his colleagues clear the area. Joi had had no idea a crowd had formed.

"Here you go," the guard said when he returned.

Joi took the brown scrunchie from his hand and then fingered through her hair. As she'd suspected, her natural ponytail was loose and her hair was now a full, tangled bush. Quickly, Joi tied the scrunchie around her hair.

When she lowered her arms, Joi noticed a tear in her sweater and faint blood stains. Inspecting her body carefully, Joi found a thin, long scratch running down her left arm. It wasn't painful to the touch and would probably heal in a few days, so she didn't let it upset her. If a hairline fracture was the worst that had happened, she considered herself lucky.

She didn't see Jamila, but Joi wondered if she'd received any bruises, too. Selfishly, Joi prayed she'd given her at least one.

A balding guard walked over to Joi and handed her the backpack she'd thrown down.

"Thanks," she said. "Can you give me a note so I can get into Mrs. Bryant's class?"

"You're not going anywhere but to the principal's office," the older guard informed her.

"I'm going to miss English?"

"You've got bigger problems than that," he told her. "Our policy here at Marshall is to suspend students who like to fight. Now, let's go. I have lunch duty in ten minutes."

Joi followed the two guards downstairs. *I can't get suspended,* she thought. *I have a game on Thursday, and Junior's going to interview me.* How was she going to explain this to her brother, or to any scout that showed up for the game?

Joi prayed that God was on her side as she walked into the main office. Aside from missing a game, it dawned on her that Jerome had to be called, and she wasn't sure how he'd handle the news.

Dr. Whitmire, the school principal, was standing by her door when Joi reached her office. "Jamila's not far behind," one of the guards said. "This here is the new girl."

With little expression, Dr. Whitmire replied, "Thanks, Mr. Davis. Have Jamila wait in the counselor's office."

Dr. Whitmire invited Joi inside. "Have a seat," she said as she sat behind her desk. "What's your full name?"

The principal's tone was frightening, but Joi spoke firmly. "Joi Belle. Belle has an *e* on the end."

This was the third time Joi had been sent to the principal's office. The first time, she was in second grade, and a boy had called her a bucktoothed beaver. He'd made Joi so mad, she delivered a mighty blow to the boy's stomach. The second time happened years later, when Joi made the all-star team. The principal at her old school wanted to personally applaud her academic and athletic accomplishments.

While Dr. Whitmire pulled up her records, Joi studied her. She wasn't like any principal Joi had ever seen. Dr. Whitmire's high-fashion pantsuit and silky brown hair, which wrapped around her round face, made her look more like a high-powered attorney.

"You're Jerome Thomas's daughter?" Dr. Whitmire asked insipidly, and Joi nodded. "Your father donates sports tickets to the school every year. He's a nice man." Dr. Whitmire moved away from her screen and stared at Joi. "So, do you want to tell me what happened?"

Feeling the stiffness in her back, Joi shifted in the wooden chair. The large room suddenly felt small and stuffy. Joi took a deep breath and, as best she could, told Dr. Whitmire her version of what had happened.

Unmoved by the scattered tears, Dr. Whitmire leaned forward and folded her hands atop her desk. "We have a nonviolence policy here," she stated when Joi was done. "However, you are new, and I didn't see anything in your records that leads me to believe this is a habit, so I'm inclined to bypass the suspension."

Joi was relieved but sensed there was a catch.

"I will need someone to come get you today," Dr. Whitmore continued and looked back at the computer. "You're on the basketball team?"

"Yes, ma'am," Joi replied politely.

"Well, I'm going to share this with Coach Miller. Maybe she can bench you for one game."

"Sit out *one* game?" Joi wanted to shout. She'd rather Dr. Whitmire call her mother.

As the principal dialed a number on her phone, Joi tried to come up with an alternative to suggest. She just couldn't miss a game. Sitting on the bench for any athlete was mild torture.

Dr. Whitmire pressed the receiver on the phone and looked at the computer screen again. "Guess I'll try your mother."

"My mother lives in Philly," Joi said.

"Then who is Renee Thomas?"

"My stepmother," mumbled Joi.

If Dr. Whitmire contacted Renee, she would punish Joi more than she would ever realize. Suddenly, calling her mother or being benched for one game didn't sound so bad, after all.

~14~

Renee

"Mrs. Thomas," Carmen called from Renee's office door. "Sorry to interrupt your meeting, but there's a call from a principal Whitmire."

Whitmire? That must be a new principal at Josh's school, Renee thought as she excused herself from an informal meeting with Darla and Cybil. "Thanks, Carmen. I'll take the call." Renee walked to her desk. Turning her back to the two women, Renee picked up the phone receiver and pushed the button for line one. "This is Mrs. Thomas," she said, wondering why the principal was calling. Unlike her older sons, Joshua was a good student.

"Hi, Mrs. Thomas. This is Dr. Whitmire, the principal at Marshall High School. I'm calling in reference to Joi Belle."

"Joi?" Renee answered, confused.

"I wanted to let you know that Joi was involved in an altercation today. I tried Mr. Thomas, but he didn't answer," Dr. Whitmire informed her. "We're not going to suspend her, but someone needs to pick her up from school today."

Renee faced the window and lowered her voice. "I'm in the middle of a meeting right now. What time does she need to be picked up?"

"I understand that this is sudden," said Dr. Whit-mire. "I can keep her busy in the office until about five thirty."

Renee didn't know where Jerome was, but she was going to track him down. "I'll see that her father gets there before then," Renee said and then hung up. She had no intention of leaving work early to pick up Je-rome's daughter.

Back at the table, Renee sat down, and Darla stopped reading a pamphlet in her hand. "Is everything okay?"

Renee picked up her pen, ready to continue where they had left off. "One of the kids needs a ride."

"Do you need to leave now?" Darla asked.

Though she should've said yes, Renee didn't want to postpone the meeting. They were in the middle of redefining job titles and responsibilities. When Darla returned from her long business trip, Renee had made it clear that she would apply for the CFO position when it became available. Darla did not discourage her from doing so. Nor did she take Renee off of the interna-tional project.

"We should be done by four, so I think I'm good," Renee told Darla.

At 4:06 P.M. Darla ended the meeting. They should have been done over an hour ago, but Darla had chal-lenged most of Renee's suggestions and opinions. Though they didn't agree on several of Renee's job responsibilities, Darla added a clause in the job de-scription that would allow her to revisit Renee's perfor-mance in six months.

Exhausted, all Renee wanted to do was go to her apartment, but first she needed to make sure Joi was picked up from school. As soon as the ladies cleared the room, Renee called Jerome's cell phone but got his voice mail. She tried his work phone, but Melanie was away from her desk each time she called. Renee called Jerome's cell again and this time left a message. "Joi was in a fight at school, and I'm going to pick her up. Please make this the last time I have to step in for you."

Just like old times, Renee thought when she disconnected the call. When the boys were young, she often dropped her plans to handle important emergencies. She didn't mind, because they were her children. But this time, the child wasn't hers.

Before putting on her coat, Renee considered calling Grace. But it would take more time for Grace to get three kids out the door. Renee looked at the clock on her desk. It was 4:11 P.M., and she was wasting time. By the time she made it through traffic, she'd be lucky if she reached the west side by six o'clock.

"Hello," Renee called when she walked into Marshall's main office. Everyone must've gone home for the day. There wasn't one person within view.

Seconds later a well-dressed woman about her age surfaced. "You must be Joi's stepmother," she said.

Renee tried to mask her displeasure in hearing that label. "Yes, I'm Mrs. Thomas."

"Nice to meet you," the woman said and shook Renee's hand. "I'm Dr. Whitmire.

C'mon back to my office. Joi's working on her homework."

Renee apologized for her tardiness as she walked to the principal's office and settled in a chair in front of her desk. Joi sat behind her at a smaller table, reading from a science textbook. Unable to look Joi in the eyes, Renee talked to Dr. Whitmire as if they were the only two people in the room.

Dr. Whitmire summarized the incident as told by both girls. When she was done, she shared the solution and then asked if there were any questions. Renee turned her head slightly toward Joi. If this sort of situation happened often, Jerome needed to consider enrolling Joi in a different school. Basketball was not worth her safety, happiness, or chance to receive a solid education. Didn't Jerome know that his daughter wasn't used to the inner-city lifestyle? Was he *that* blinded by the fact that he wanted her to live closer to him?

"I was defending myself," uttered Joi, and Renee looked back at the principal.

"What measures are in place to prevent this from happening again?" Renee asked.

"Jamila has been suspended. We're also working on a modification program for her," Dr. Whitmire responded.

Though Renee liked the principal's style, her response wasn't satisfactory. Had Joi been her biological child, she would've demanded to meet with Jamila's parents to find a reasonable solution. "Okay," Renee said and stood up. "Her father will be in touch if he has any other concerns."

Renee said good-bye and then walked to her car in silence as Joi trailed behind her. Once they were inside the car, faint sniffles caught Renee's attention, and from the corner of her eye, she saw Joi wipe her cheek. Renee put both hands on the steering wheel. Having raised three boys, she wasn't sure how to handle an upset teenage girl. It had to be frightening being in a new city and establishing new friends. An unfriendly stepmother didn't help make Joi's transition any better.

"I'm sorry this happened to you," Renee said sincerely.

Hearing those words, Joi burst into tears and buried her face in the palms of her hands. Renee couldn't bear to see her in this state and looked out her window. What would she say? Should she hug her? Renee stretched her arm toward Joi and rubbed her shoulder. "Should I take you to the house or to Jerome's office?"

"Home," Joi sniffed.

Renee turned on the car and drove to River Forest. The drive was quiet, but her mind was racing with the words she'd say when she saw Jerome. Renee replayed those words until she reached River Forest and pulled into the driveway.

"Thank you," Joi said when Renee turned off the ignition.

Before they could get out of the car, Jerome came out of the house and walked to the car. Like a small child, Joi ran into her father's arms. Renee couldn't hear the words Jerome whispered in his daughter's ear as he rubbed the back of her head. Whatever they were soothed her, and she immediately stopped crying.

Renee had intended to go inside the house, but watching Jerome comfort his daughter, she changed her mind and started the car. Every time she saw them together, Renee couldn't stop thinking about her husband's deception. At some point, Renee knew that she'd have to forgive Jerome, but today she couldn't. Her heart was numb.

Jerome escorted his daughter to the front door and then walked to Renee's car. They'd been apart only a short time, but it looked like Jerome had picked up a few pounds. Renee couldn't complain. As a result of eating too many carryout dinners and fast-food lunches, her clothes were fitting a little more snugly than usual, too.

"Thanks, babe," Jerome said when Renee rolled down her window. "I really appreciate the way you stepped in for me. I was meeting with some folks in Itasca and left my cell in the car by accident."

Renee stared at the dashboard. All the words she'd rehearsed escaped her memory. "I don't want to have to do this again," she said coldly.

"I know," Jerome said. "I'm sorry I inconvenienced you."

Renee wished he'd stop apologizing. Words couldn't change things of the past, nor could they change the way she felt. "You need to find another emergency contact. Maybe Junior or Grace," she ordered. Her cell phone rang, and she reached inside her handbag as she continued to fuss. "You know I'm busy in meetings all day. I can't have these kinds of interruptions, especially now." By the time Renee located her cell phone inside her cluttered bag, it had stopped ringing.

"If that's what you want," Jerome replied, clearly trying to avoid an argument. "I'll make sure the school takes your name off the list. I just thought you'd be there for Joi if there were ever an emergency . . . despite what you may feel right now about her."

"I don't want anything bad to happen to her, Jerome. I just don't want to be the *first* person called if you're unable to be reached." Renee looked at her call log. She actually had three missed calls. One was from Everett, probably reminding her about their business dinner tonight. The other calls were from Elise, and Renee remembered that she owed her a return call. "I better go. I have a lot of work to do," she said and shifted the gear from park to reverse. "When you call the school," Renee said as she slowly rolled down the driveway, "make sure you follow up with the principal."

***

Holding a double-bagged plastic bag, Renee walked into her apartment building. She was supposed to buy only dessert and a jug of tea but couldn't pass up the sale on blackberry wine. The sweet alcoholic liquid had become her drink of choice every night before bed. With the problems at work and the tension between her and Jerome escalating, Renee's stress level was at an all-time high. She'd tried prayer. She'd tried exercise. She'd tried listening to smooth jazz. But none of those stress relievers seemed to relax her the way wine did. After one glass, the problems she encountered all day didn't feel so urgent and overwhelming.

When Renee walked into the lobby, Everett was waiting for her by the elevator. He must've come straight from the office, because he was still dressed in a suit. *What a way to come home,* she thought as she stepped into the elevator. Just looking at Everett was enough to make her forget about her problems. Unfortunately, Renee couldn't let her mind linger on his appeal. That would certainly get her into more trouble. So, as they walked out of the elevator and into her apartment, Renee told Everett about her evening.

"You do realize that as long as Jerome is your husband," Everett said as he emptied the bag of food in his hand on the kitchen table, "you'll have to be Joi's mother whenever Taylor isn't around."

"I think that's too much to ask," Renee replied. "I don't even think that's something Taylor is expecting. We're not exactly friends."

Everett threw the empty bag in the trash can under the sink. "What does that say for the future of your marriage? Even though he messed up, I'm sure Jerome wants his wife to accept his child."

That was a question Renee asked herself every night before going to bed. "Enough about Jerome," she said and put her wine in the refrigerator. "We've got other things to handle tonight. Any word from the bank in London yet?" Renee closed the refrigerator door and suddenly felt Everett's hands on her shoulders. *Jesus,* she said to herself. Renee should've immediately pushed away, but it'd been a while since she'd felt a man's touch.

"You're tense," he said and kneaded her shoulder blades.

Renee closed her eyes and, for a moment, pretended she wasn't married. That way, what she was feeling wouldn't be a sin. Rolling her head back, Renee let the gentle pressure soothe her. "I have a lot going on," she replied softly.

"You haven't had a vacation in a long time," Everett reminded her. "Maybe you should think about spending a few extra days in Wisconsin after the company retreat." Everett's hands lowered to Renee's biceps, and as he massaged her upper arms, her body tingled. "It would be nice if you could get something in before the holidays, but I think February is a better time. No one can truly relax around the holidays."

Renee needed to make him stop but was afraid to turn around. With the way he made her feel, her lips might have a mind of their own and find their way to his. Renee held the handle of the refrigerator door tight and answered weakly, "That's a possibility."

"Make it happen," Everett playfully demanded as he removed his hands. "In the meantime, let me at least help get dinner ready."

"Paper plates are in the third cabinet," Renee told him and then removed a small ice cube from the freezer. Her body temperature had risen, and she needed to cool down. *Lord,* she said to herself, *please don't let that man touch me that way again. Next time*

I may not be so strong. Renee walked to the living room to get her laptop, and when she returned to the kitchen, Everett had made her a plate of food.

It wasn't unusual for them to talk about work over dinner. In the past few months, it had actually become a standard thing to do at least three times a week. This was, however, the first time they'd had dinner in her apartment. Every now and then Renee caught herself gazing at her boss while he talked.

"Once we get this approved, we can move forward with the . . ." Everett stopped talking when Renee's cell phone rang. "Renee," he said and stopped typing on his computer. "You need to take a break and answer your phone."

Renee quickly looked away and down at her phone. Elise was calling again. "It's just my friend," she said. "I'll call her back when we're done."

"We're done for tonight," he said and shut down his computer. "I'll send Darla an update in the morning, and then all we need to do is wait for the bank to send the check."

"Okay," Renee answered. "Then I guess we'll touch base in the morning. What time are you leaving again?"

"My flight departs at two o'clock."

For the first time since she'd known him, Renee felt a sense of sadness. She didn't want him to go back to California. She stood up and covered the partially eaten cake she'd purchased from the store. "Shall we meet for breakfast?"

Everett must've felt the same way. "Soon we'll be able to eat all our meals together," he said as he loaded his computer into the case. "I'll be right around the corner in a few weeks."

"That'll be nice," Renee said and leaned against the sink. For a while, Renee and Everett stared at one another. She didn't know what was happening, but she liked the way Everett made her feel tonight.

Renee's cell phone rang, and Everett picked it up. "Do you need to take this?" he asked and walked over to Renee.

When he was close enough, Renee grabbed his hand, and instead of taking her cell phone, she pulled him close. Without a word, Renee kissed him and almost immediately pulled back. "I'm sorry," she said and took her phone. "I don't know why I did that."

"I do," he replied and wrapped his arms around her waist. "The chemistry between us is strong." Everett gently kissed her lips and then lightly kissed the side of her neck. "One day, you'll realize that," he said and then walked away.

Speechless, Renee stayed in front of the sink and watched him leave. When the front door closed, Renee exhaled. She couldn't explain what had happened, but she knew that Everett, her friend and boss, would soon become her lover if he continued to touch and kiss her the way he did tonight.

~15~

Jerome

"Tell Joi to pack her bags," Taylor shouted through the phone.

Jerome put his cell phone on speaker and dropped it on the passenger seat. He'd planned to call Taylor when he got home last night, but Joi must've called her mother before he had a chance to. He knew it was his job to protect his daughter. The school was tougher than any other, but if Joi wanted to stay, he would be more vigilant to see that she was not harmed again. More than anything, he wanted to be a good parent. "It's all under control, Taylor. Joi is tough, and she wants to stay, so let her stay. I wouldn't do anything to put our daughter in harm's way. So, trust me on this one."

"Even if I were to agree with you . . . why did it take Renee so long to go get her? She wouldn't leave one of her children sitting in school after hours," Taylor griped. "I can't have my child there if Renee isn't going to look out for her."

Although Jerome agreed, he couldn't let Taylor know. "She was in a meeting," he said, defending his wife. "I'm glad she was able to get her at all."

"I don't like this one bit, Jerome. You're lucky Lance calmed me down. I was ready to fly out there tonight."

Jerome could only imagine what her husband had to do to hold her back. Renee was feisty at times, but Taylor could be well out of control if not handled correctly. "I'm going to enroll her in self-defense classes," he said and hoped that would make Taylor feel better.

"Oh, please. Is that the best you can come up with?" Taylor snapped. "Look, if this happens again, that school will have to deal with me."

Jerome told Taylor not to worry and then hung up the phone. For the school's sake, he prayed there wouldn't be another incident.

As usual, Joshua was sitting in the kitchen, talking on the phone, when Jerome walked into the house. "Where's Joi?" Jerome asked.

"At the salon," Joshua said quickly and resumed his conversation.

"She's *still* there?" Jerome joked and then grabbed a warm bottled water from the pantry. Melanie had taken Joi to get her hair done after she learned about the school fight. That was almost three hours ago. Jerome didn't understand how women could sit in any salon for over three hours just to get their hair washed and curled. It seemed insane to him, but for a woman, it was routine.

Jerome opened the water bottle and headed to the family room. Before sitting down, he searched the room for the remote control for the television. It was supposed to be kept on the end table, but since Renee had left, things weren't quite where they were supposed to be. Unable to find it, he hit the power button on the television and then sat down. As he settled in the seat, Jerome put the water on the end table and felt a sharp object in his side. Looking down, he located the remote wedged between the cushion and armrest.

Getting comfortable, Jerome flipped through the channels, looking for the sports channels. The doorbell rang, and he thought he was hearing things. He wasn't expecting a visitor. When the bell rang a second time, he stood, walked to the door, and peeked through the window. At first, he saw a yellow taxicab. Then he recognized Renee's best friend standing off to the side. Before she turned to leave, Jerome quickly opened the door. "Elise?" he said, confused. What was she doing in Illinois?

"Hi, Jerome," Elise said. "Is Renee home?"

"No," he said, studying her troubled face. "Was she supposed to meet you *here?*"

"We had plans this weekend. I tried calling her cell a few times, but she hasn't returned any of my calls," explained Elise. "I called the hotel, and she wasn't there. I left a message with her secretary, but it's after seven now, so I took a cab over here, hoping to find her. . . . Is she all right?"

"She's fine, Elise," Jerome said.

"Do you know where I can find her?"

It was clear that Renee hadn't talked to her best friend in a while. Jerome offered to pay for her cab and then invited her inside the house. "When is the last time you spoke to Renee?" he asked and turned the television off.

"We touched base a few times last month," Elise said and sat down. "We were confirmed for this week. . . . Are you sure she's all right? I'm getting worried."

Jerome sighed. "Um, I don't know how much Renee has told you about us, but we're having some problems."

Elise crossed her legs at the ankles and sat her hands in her lap. "Renee mentioned something about that."

"Has she told you about Joi?"

"The daughter you have with Taylor?" Elise questioned. "Yes, she did."

"She could tell you about my daughter, but she failed to tell you she moved out in August?" Jerome said in a frustrated tone.

"Renee moved out?" Elise asked. "I don't understand."

"I'm surprised she didn't tell you."

"Well . . . do you know where she's staying?"

"Yes, in an apartment in the Loop."

"Jerome . . . I don't know what to make of all this. Why didn't she tell me?" Elise said, more to herself than to Jerome. "How could she forget that I was coming this weekend?"

"I'm afraid we're both preoccupied with all that is happening in our lives. Her job is stressful. I started my mentoring program. . . . It's easy to forget some details. We're not in our twenties anymore," he joked. "I know this is shock. I'm still in shock, too, but we're seeing a counselor."

"I'm glad to hear that," Elise said, still concerned. "You guys have been together for so long. I pray you'll be back together soon."

"I've been going to church to pray every morning, too," Jerome told her. For some reason, he wanted her to know that he was serious about restoring his marriage.

"If you believe God can, then He will mend the marriage," Elise said and stood up. "I hate to run out on you, but I really need to find Renee. Do you have a number where I can reach her?"

"Sure. I'll give her a call now," Jerome said and pulled out his cell phone. He dialed Renee's number, and when she didn't answer, he left a message.

Worried, Elise picked up her purse. "I guess I'll go back to the hotel. Do you mind calling me a cab?"

"Don't be silly," Jerome said. "I can drive you downtown. And maybe we should stop by Renee's apartment first."

Jerome double-parked in front of Renee's building and offered to go inside to ring the buzzer, but Elise insisted that she'd be all right. Through the glass doors, Jerome watched Elise and waited for her signal before he could leave. He was glad that Elise was in town. She'd always given Renee unbiased, good advice. Maybe she could help Renee see that she needed to be home with her family.

Elise waved at Jerome to let him know that Renee was home. He wanted to go upstairs, too, but thought it best to let Renee and her best friend catch up. Jerome was about to pull off when the elevator doors opened, and a tall, bald man stepped out. Either Jerome's eyes were playing tricks on him or the man was Everett. Jerome leaned across the passenger seat to get a better look, but when Elise gave the man a hug, he was certain it was Everett.

Everett walked out of the building and ran down the steps with a swagger that annoyed Jerome. Jerome opened his car door. His instinct was to jump out of the car and follow him down the street. He needed to know why Everett was coming out of his wife's apartment building at this hour, but he'd seem silly confronting him. His wife shouldn't be living in her own place. Jerome closed the car door and slowly counted to ten, a technique he hadn't used in months. As he breathed deeply, Jerome remembered the text messages he'd read on Renee's cell phone, without her permission, the day she moved into her apartment. Thoughts of the kiss they'd shared also came across his mind. Instead of calming down, Jerome's heart raced even faster.

As he tried to control his thoughts, a quiet voice whispered in his ear, "Be still."

I'm not sure I can be still, he thought to himself. He'd been faithful in his prayers and his visits to the altar each morning. But at the moment, it was hard for him to believe that God was working on his prayer requests. Was God listening to him?

A policeman pulled alongside Jerome's car and motioned for him to move. Jerome waved to acknowledge his presence and then drove off. "God, I'm trusting in you," he said as he turned down Randolph Street.

~16~

Renee

Renee stood at her apartment door, wondering how she forgot about the mini vacation she'd planned with Elise. There was a lot going on in her life, but how could this have slipped her mind? Renee's hand trembled on the doorknob. Not only would she have to explain why she forgot about their girls' weekend, but she'd also have to explain why she was living in an apartment. Renee heard the elevator doors open across the hall and opened her door.

"It sure has been something trying to find you," Elise said when she stepped out of the elevator.

"I'm so sorry," Renee replied. "I've been so busy with work, and—"

"Just give me a hug," Elise interjected. "We can talk about what's going on with you later."

Renee embraced her friend and then welcomed her inside. "Time must've gotten away from me," Renee said as the women settled inside the kitchen.

"No need to tell me you're sorry," Elise answered. "I just need to know what's going on. I've been calling you for the past two weeks now, and when I get here, I discover that you and Jerome have separated. *And* on the way up here I ran into Everett. It seems a lot has happened since we last talked."

"Everett and I were working," she said and took out two glasses and placed them on the table. "As for Jerome and me," she continued, "we've temporarily separated."

"Are you sure about that?" Elise questioned.

"I'm not sure about anything anymore," Renee replied as she opened the refrigerator. "Would you like something to drink?" Elise declined, and without realizing it, Renee took out a bottle of red wine and poured herself a glass.

Elise stared at her friend strangely. "You drink wine now?"

Drinking wine had become routine for her, but for those who knew her, it was a surprise. "I don't drink often," she fibbed.

"Are you sure?" Elise asked. "I've never known you to keep any kind of alcohol in the house. Should I be worried?"

Renee took a small sip and then sat down. "No, I have this under control. It's the other areas in my life that are a little troubling right now."

"Well," Elise said. "This is why we planned this weekend. Let's talk about the things that are bothering you, and see if we can figure out some solutions. As I told you before, you're like my sister. There's no need for you to hide things from me or go through rough times alone. So . . . start talking."

Renee took a deep breath and then shared her concerns with her friend. She talked about the pressures at work, what drove her to leave the River Forest home, her feelings about Joi, and the rising emotional connection between her and Everett.

When she was done, Elise sat back in her chair. "Wow, that is a mouthful," she said, "but the beauty in all this is that these are things you can get control of one step at a time. For instance . . . it may be best that you and Everett maintain a strictly business relationship. You probably shouldn't have any more working dinners in this apartment."

"Everett and I have discussed this, and I think we'll be fine. It was just one kiss," Renee said defensively.

"You say that now, but that's how the enemy creeps in," replied Elise. "Right now, you're stressed and vulnerable. It only takes one cozy 'work' night in your apartment for other thoughts to birth. One thing leads to another, and the next thing you know, you've committed adultery."

Renee poured herself another glass of wine. "With all that I've been through, would it really be wrong if Everett and I had an affair?" Renee wasn't really looking for an answer to her question.

"That's crazy talk, Renee. Trust me, Jerome is being punished right now for what he's done."

"It's not punishment enough, if you ask me."

Elise looked at her friend as if she were a stranger. "Renee, don't go getting any ideas. You're still married to Jerome. And after talking to him tonight, I know he still loves you and wants—"

"Love?" Renee responded, feeling some effects from the wine. "What does he really know about love?"

"I understand that you're hurting. But wait until you've finished the counseling sessions before you make any rash decisions," said Elise. "Everett is only going to complicate and cloud your true feelings and judgment."

"You have all the answers, don't you?" Renee remarked and finished her glass of wine.

"What do you mean?"

"I mean, you told me not to move out, and now you're telling me to stay away from Everett," Renee replied. "Whose side are you on? You know better than anyone else what Jerome has put me through."

Elise stared at her friend, baffled by her comments. "I'm not the enemy," she said calmly. "I think the wine has you a little confused."

"You're the one that's confused," Renee snapped. "Your husband didn't cheat on you because he felt substandard. He didn't lie to you about having a child, a daughter no less, who plays basketball better than all three of the sons I gave him. You didn't have to spend the summer with that child and be reminded of that affair daily. So, don't tell me about love, about counseling, and or about letting go of a friendship with a man who has done nothing but care for me since the day I met him."

Elise tried to maintain her cool demeanor. "You're taking this out of context, and I think we need to table this until tomorrow. You've been drinking, and now you're a little emotional."

Though she'd had two glasses of wine, Renee said, "This has nothing to do with one glass of wine. This is about everybody disregarding my feelings."

Elise stood up. "We just need to talk about this later. I don't like what I'm seeing, and I think you need to take a long look in the mirror. The Renee I know never talked to me like this. She'd never forget about a planned vacation with her friend. She wouldn't entertain the thought of having an affair, and she certainly wouldn't be drinking wine." Elise walked out of the kitchen.

Renee dropped her head on the table. She didn't mean for the conversation to get out of control. In her heart she knew Elise was right, and Renee had no one to blame but herself for falling behind at work and forgetting important details. She got up from the table and walked into the living room. Elise was standing by the window. "Why don't we call it a night? I'll have Carmen cancel the reservation at the hotel. You can stay here, in the second bedroom," she told her friend, glad that the extra bedroom would be put to use. At the time she signed the lease, Renee pictured the second room being used by Joshua. But with his busy schedule, he could sleep over only once every other week.

"I don't want to rehash anything, but I have to tell you that your behavior is scaring me," Elise said. "If I'm going to stay here, we're going to work on ways to rebuild you. I sense that you're losing yourself in all of this."

"I can't argue with that," replied Renee. "I'm stressed and I'm tired. I don't know what I'm doing anymore."

"That's what this weekend is for, and that's why I'm here," Elise responded. "We're going to work on getting you back to being the woman God created you to be."

"Thank you for being my friend," Renee said, and she meant it. There weren't any friends in Illinois that she confided in, and if Elise lived closer, maybe she'd have a stronger support system and be in a better place.

Elise grabbed Renee and gave her a hug, and then the two friends mapped out their plans for the weekend.

~17~

Joi

At the end of the day, Joi walked out of the school building, excited about the weekend. Who knew that leading the basketball team to a victory and defending herself against the school bully would instantly change her social life? She now had friends to eat lunch with and talk to throughout the day. Life at Marshall High School was beginning to fall into place, just as she had planned.

As Joi walked out of the building, Stacee and Kiana ran up to her. "Do you think Josh will mind taking us to the Boys and Girls Club?" Stacee asked.

"Not at all," Joi said.

The girls turned the corner, and Joi spotted Joshua's car near the end of the block. As they walked toward the car, Joi heard an unfriendly, familiar voice. Was she really hearing Jamila, or was her mind playing tricks on her? After the fight yesterday, Dr. Whitmire said Jamila had been suspended for three days, so Joi hadn't expected to run into her again until later in the week.

"There she is," Joi heard someone say from inside a dark blue Buick. Before Joi could see who made the statement, the passenger door opened and Jamila got out of the car.

"There's the giraffe," Jamila taunted, and two other girls got out of the same car.

Joi's heart beat faster, but she continued to walk straight ahead. At least this time, if Jamila started a fight, Joi wouldn't be alone. She only hoped her teammates wouldn't let Jamila and her crew beat her to a pulp.

Sensing Joi's stress, Kiana mumbled low, "Don't worry. She's not gonna do anything."

As they passed the Buick, Joi was still on guard. "Are you sure about that?" Joi asked.

"We're not exactly cool, but she promised to leave you alone until we win the championship," Kiana told her. "I wouldn't go starting trouble, but you should be safe at least until April."

Stacee laughed aloud. "If you're lucky, she'll forget about you after then."

"Or you better make sure we get that championship trophy," Kiana teased.

A little more at ease, Joi took a deep breath and opened Joshua's car door. She poked her head inside and asked him if her new friends could ride to the club with them. As she suspected, Joshua welcomed the girls into his car.

The girls piled into the car, and before Joshua pulled out of his space, Denver ran to the driver's side of the car.

"Hey, man," he said to Joshua and then greeted the girls. "Are you on your way to the club?" Though the question was directed to Joshua, Denver stared at Joi.

The light blue sweater he was wearing complemented his brown skin. Joi found it hard to pull her eyes away, but knew she had to. Jamila was only a few cars away.

Joshua answered Denver's question, but Denver wasn't interested in the reply. "I'm sorry about the disagreement you had with Jamila," he told Joi. "She can be very possessive at times."

Joi stared at the glove compartment. "No problem. I'm sure we just had a misunderstanding."

Denver wanted to say more, but Jamila approached the car and leaned on his side. "All right, D. That's enough chitchat. We need to go," she barked and tugged his arm.

Denver seemed bothered by her orders but didn't put up any resistance. "I'll see you in a few," he told everyone in the car and then walked away with his girlfriend.

"Now I see why Jamila doesn't like you," Stacee said as Joshua drove away from the school. "I think Denver has his eye on you."

Joi didn't understand Denver's attraction to the school bully, but that, too, wasn't her concern. "I don't think so. We both like basketball, that's all."

"Whatever. There's clearly more than basketball between you two," Stacee replied.

"Let's not forget that the island boy is fine, too," Kiana said in her best imitation Caribbean accent.

"That's Denver's girl?" Joshua asked, surprised. "They seemed like an odd couple."

Joi agreed. Denver seemed calm and reserved. Jamila, on the other hand, was feisty and difficult to talk to.

"They are quite the couple," Stacee confirmed. "Jamila played volleyball and ran track for a while. She was good, too. That's kind of how they met."

"She was kicked off both teams, though," Kiana added. "The coaches couldn't control her temper tantrums."

"And that's when she started fighting *all* the time," said Stacee.

For the duration of the ride, Joi listened to her team-mates' stories about Jamila and Denver, each more dramatic than the last. She understood that they had once been a couple everyone envied, but once Jamila changed, why didn't Denver cut his losses and break up with her? Either he truly loved her, was blind to her evil ways, or for some reason felt trapped. Whatever the reason, Joi almost felt sorry for him.

"Is she the reason he's working at the school?" Joi wanted to know.

"He stopped playing ball after his Pop messed up at the church they went to," Stacee said. "Coach Brown is trying to help him get back on his feet."

"Well," Joi said as Joshua pulled into the Boys and Girls Club parking lot, "I'm not interested in Denver McBride."

"Not yet," Stacee sang.

"Not at all," Joi said firmly, but no one in the car was convinced by her reply.

Denver strolled into the Boys and Girls Club over an hour late, as Joi played a noncompetitive game of basketball with a mixture of friends. When she noticed him approach the court, she lost control of the ball.

"I make you nervous?" Denver teased as he tossed his jacket on the side of the court.

"Not at all," Joi said and ran up the court. To make up for her mistake, she tightened up her guard on her opponent, forcing him to shoot the ball from an odd angle and miss.

Denver jogged alongside Joi, surprising her, and told one of the players to exit the game. Though Friday night was coed night, mentors didn't typically play against the participants.

Joi was tired but suddenly gained a boost of energy. There were five other players on the court, but in Joi's mind it was only her and Denver. She could tell he was rusty, but Joi had no sympathy. She played against him fiercely. At some point the battle between them became evident, and the other players cleared the floor, leaving Denver and Joi alone on the court. They dribbled up and down the court several times, but neither was able to make a basket. The longer they played, the stronger Denver became, but Joi was just as tough. Determined not to let him score, Joi successfully blocked every shot.

"That girl is bananas!" Joi heard someone cheer from the sideline.

Hearing the cheers boosted her ego, and when Joi regained possession of the ball, she pushed her body against Denver's with what seemed like superhuman force and drove the ball through the basket.

"That challenging enough for you?" Joi asked an out-of-breath Denver.

"That was just a test," he huffed and headed toward the water fountain. "We'll have a rematch in two weeks."

Joi laughed. "You need two weeks to recuperate, huh?"

While Denver was at the water fountain, Stacee walked over to her friend. "Still not interested in him, right?"

Joi ignored Stacee's comment and concentrated on gathering her belongings from a corner of the gym. There wasn't much time left before the program ended for the day. While all the participants waited for the mentors to recap the evening, Denver walked to the bench to talk to Joi.

"I have two tickets to a women's game at DePaul on Saturday. You interested?" he asked her.

Joi looked around and zipped her duffel bag. Was he serious? Was he *really* asking her out on a date? "I don't think Jamila would approve," she said.

Denver flashed a semi-crooked smile. "We broke up."

"When?" questioned Joi. "You were just with her."

"About an hour ago. We've grown apart," he said. "I need to be with someone a little more mature."

"Oh," Joi said, without realizing she had a huge grin on her face. "I'm not so sure—"

"Joi, I just thought you'd enjoy the game," he said. "I don't know any other female who would *really* appreciate watching the game. It's just a game, and . . . we're just friends."

Against her better judgment, Joi spoke before her mind fully comprehended her reply. "I better ask my dad," she said and headed to Jerome's office.

Skipping up a flight of stairs, Joi couldn't believe her excitement. *What if he's lying about him and Jamila?* she thought, but as quickly as the thought came to her mind, it left twice as fast. Denver just didn't seem like the type to lie. Besides, it was just a basketball game. And if Jamila did find out, she couldn't be mad, because Denver was, in his words, no longer her boyfriend.

As Joi walked into her father's office, she prayed the risk she was taking wouldn't lead her to the principal's office again.

"Hey, sweetheart," Jerome said when he saw his daughter. "Did they send you up here to get me? I'll be down in a minute, okay?"

"Okay, but I have a question," Joi said, out of breath.

"Shoot," Jerome said as he helped Melanie organize a bunch of index cards on his desk.

"Can I go to a game at DePaul on Saturday?"

"Sure," he answered.

Joi was about to leave but figured she should be honest. "Um . . . it's with a guy."

Jerome stopped working. "A guy?"

Melanie smiled as she put a stack of index cards inside a small box.

"Yes, Denver, to be exact," Joi said and hoped Jerome wouldn't change his mind.

"Denver McBride, the mentor?" Jerome asked sternly.

Joi had never seen him look so serious. "Yes," she mumbled.

"Sounds like it should be fun," Melanie said to lighten the mood. Joi was glad Melanie was on her side, otherwise she would be out of luck.

Jerome ignored Melanie's input. "I don't think it's a good idea, Joi. Tell him no."

"But why can't I go?" Joi questioned. "It's not a date, Pop."

"Just trust me on this, sweetheart," Jerome said matter-of-factly. "Now, go back downstairs. I'll be down soon."

Joi looked at Melanie, pleading for backup with her eyes. But what could Melanie really say to change Jerome's mind? She wasn't Joi's mother, nor was she a relative. Why would Jerome give her input any consideration?

If Joi were back in Philly, she would take matters into her own hands and figured out a way to go to the game, anyway. But Joi had changed, and she didn't want to give Jerome the same attitude and defiance she would've given her mother. Rather than stand at the door, disappointed, Joi went back downstairs to the gym to let Denver know she wouldn't be able to go.

~18~

Jerome

"You might want to reconsider," Melanie told Jerome after Joi left the office. "She seemed a little upset."

"She'll get over it," Jerome replied and grabbed a set of keys from his desk. "He's too old for her, anyway."

"It's a three-year difference. That's not so bad."

It wasn't a surprise that Melanie didn't understand Jerome's concerns. Age gaps weren't a problem for her, and if Joi wasn't his daughter, the difference wouldn't be a problem for him, either. But Joi was child, and though Denver seemed like a good man, he was too old for his only daughter.

"Nothing you say is going to change my mind, so you might as well drop it," he said and walked to the door. "You ready?"

Melanie picked up the box of index cards and followed her boss. "If it were me," Melanie said as they walked down the stairs, "I'd trust Joi. It's *only* an afternoon ball game."

Sometimes Melanie couldn't leave well enough alone. She had no idea that Denver was the second older man Joi had been attracted to. Or that Joi had lied to her mother on several occasions just so that she could be with her college boyfriend. Jerome refused to let Joi repeat that pattern.

Melanie and Jerome separated once they walked into the gym. The young athletes were all seated in the bleachers, patiently waiting for Jerome to dismiss them. While Melanie passed out the index cards, Jerome gained everyone's attention with a fancy whistle. The murmurs throughout the gym ceased, and Jerome gave the group instructions for the weekend. In the morning Jerome was taking them to the Chicago Bulls training facility to work out with some of the NBA players. "If you fail to bring the items listed on the cards Melanie gave you, you won't be allowed on the bus," explained Jerome, and as he ran down the agenda for the Saturday trip, he noticed that Joi wasn't paying attention. "The bus will leave promptly at six A.M.," he continued and looked away from his daughter, "and we'll be back by noon."

Some of the athletes moaned, but Jerome ignored them. One of the goals of the program was to provide a taste of an NBA player's life. Waking up early to work out was a major part of a professional athlete's day.

Jerome dismissed the group, and as they exited the building, he watched Denver interact with the other mentors. As much as he liked Denver, he didn't trust him with his daughter. Ashamed, Jerome had to admit that most of his reservations stemmed from who Denver's father was. *Like father, like son,* he thought, fearing Denver would eventually succumb to his father's demons and ultimately hurt Joi.

Having those thoughts, Jerome felt like a hypocrite. How could he condemn a man for cheating on his wife when he was once an adulterer himself? And how could he accuse Denver of following in his father's footsteps? Especially since his own sons had proved to be an exception. Though the thoughts raced back and forth in Jerome's mind, he still didn't want to take a chance and give Denver the benefit of the doubt.

Melanie stood next to Jerome and stared straight ahead as she talked. "I'll just say one more thing about the situation," she whispered. "If Joi does like him and you keep fighting her feelings, she's going to resent you. I know she's your little girl, but you've got to let her grow up and experience life. That includes puppy love and heartache."

"I don't want him to distract her," he replied. "I need her to focus on basketball. I know what's best for her."

"Well," Melanie replied, "I'm sure you'll keep her on track. Just give her a little room to enjoy life the way she wants to. You don't want her to go sneaking around behind your back, do you?"

"No real man would sneak around with my daughter," stated Jerome.

"C'mon, we hear about this kind of stuff all the time from these kids," Melanie said. "Don't be naïve. Joi is an attractive and smart girl. If not Denver, it's going to be someone else."

"Then let it be someone else," Jerome retorted. "Someone whose father isn't known for impregnating a young girl."

"He's not his father. You know that," Melanie responded. "Remember he stepped up to take care of his family when his father left the house. *And* it's just a basketball game . . . in the afternoon . . . in a very crowded gymnasium."

Jerome stared at Melanie and shook his head. He knew she was right.

"Maybe you should talk to him," she said and patted his back. "That might ease your mind a bit."

"Thanks, Mel," he replied, and as Melanie walked away, he thought about Renee. It would be nice if she were around to give that kind of advice.

"Hey, Denver!" Jerome yelled. "Do you have a few minutes?"

Denver nodded.

For added privacy, Jerome had Denver follow him back to his office. If Denver was nervous, he hid it well. Jerome closed the door and then asked him to take a seat. "Joi talked to me about going to DePaul tomorrow," Jerome said and sat down across from him. "I'm going to be honest. I used to be young once, so forgive me for questioning your intentions."

"I have no intentions, Mr. Thomas," Denver said. "I came across tickets to the game and thought she'd like to go."

"You can't ask someone your own age?"

"I don't know anyone who loves the sport the way Joi does," Denver answered. "I wouldn't take advantage of your daughter. She's a nice girl."

Jerome knew Joi had a passion for basketball that couldn't be matched by an average teenager. A stranger could pick that up after talking to her for just five minutes.

"Does my age bother you?" Denver asked.

"Honestly, she's my only daughter," Jerome replied. "If anything happened to her that I disapproved of, I'd be willing to go to jail."

"If it would make you feel better, I could get an extra ticket for you. She's lucky to have you as a father," Denver said.

Jerome leaned back in his chair and folded his hands across his chest. He was impressed that Denver had offered, but he had a different idea. "Why don't you give that extra ticket to Josh? He's free Saturday afternoon."

***

Sitting in an empty house on a Saturday night was not something Jerome was used to. Having four children and three grandchildren, there was always something going on in his household. His house was the hub for the family. But since Renee moved out, all of that had changed. The grandchildren used to spend nights at the house, and he would drop them off on his way to work at least once a week. Now he was lucky if he saw them twice a month. He had confronted Grace about it, and she'd assured him that things were fine between them. She and Junior were not taking sides. As convincing as she'd tried to appear, Jerome knew his son viewed his mother leaving as his fault. Junior always took his mother's side.

Jerome walked to the kitchen and surveyed the freezer. Sunday dinner was supposed to be at his house this week, but everyone had other plans. Since Elise was in town, Joshua would spend the night with his mother tonight, and tomorrow Renee would take the family to dinner. Though he wanted a full, active house, spending quality Daddy-daughter time with Joi was a good alternative. He would use the time to question her about the outing with Denver.

Jerome took pork chops out of the freezer. Smothered pork chops, the way his grandmother used to make them, mashed potatoes, and steamed broccoli would make a good Sunday meal. He'd been good on his new diet when Renee was around, but since she'd been gone, he'd been craving fried chicken, cold cuts, and warm rhubarb pies. If he wasn't careful, he would clog his arteries and gain weight and be at risk for another heart attack.

The house phone rang, and Jerome answered without looking at the caller ID. Since Joshua had started driving on his own, he'd get nervous whenever the phone rang.

"Hey, Thomas," Melanie said when he answered the phone. "What are you up to?"

"Just thinking about Sunday dinner," Jerome replied, curious why Melanie was calling on a weekend. Unless there was a big project they were working on, there was no need for her to call. "What's up?"

"Well, I was on my way to grab a bite to eat by myself when I remembered that your kids were going to a game today. No sense in being alone," Melanie said. "Care to join me for an early dinner?"

Melanie had asked Jerome to have dinner with her on several occasions, but tonight was the first time he actually considered saying yes. "Maybe next time. I should be here in case the kids call or need me."

"You do have a cell phone, right?" Melanie said. "If Joi and Josh need to reach you, I'm sure they know to call your cell. So no excuses. You need to get out of the house."

"Not tonight," he repeated. "I really want to stay home and watch television."

Melanie didn't press the issue further. "Okay . . . but next weekend, I won't take no for an answer."

Jerome hung up the phone and then placed the pork chops back in the freezer. He knew not to go out with Melanie, but if he didn't do something, he was going to lose his mind. Most of his friends were married and with their families. There was one neighbor across the street that he had played cards with a few times. Maybe he'd be up for a game of poker tonight. A night with the neighbors would definitely help take his mind off the fact that he was lonely and missed his wife. Even if it were a temporary fix.

***

On Monday Jerome showed up at the counseling session ten minutes later than scheduled. He'd lost track of time during prayer at the altar, but if traffic hadn't been delayed on the Dan Ryan Expressway, he would've made it there on time.

When he finally made it to Mrs. Stroud's office, he thought Renee would already be there. He had prepared himself for the attitude she might have about his being late, but she, too, was running late. Jerome knew that Renee had had a long weekend, because her friend was in town, but Renee was rarely late for anything. Since she didn't need to take the Dan Ryan, Jerome wondered if something else had gone wrong. They had barely spoken to one another all weekend, and he hated not knowing what was going on with his wife.

"Renee's on her way," Mrs. Stroud said when Jerome sat down. "She had to drop a friend off at the airport."

Jerome was relieved to know that she hadn't blown him off, but wondered why Renee hadn't thought to call and inform him. He didn't like the way he felt. Instead of the separation bringing them closer, he felt Renee slowly slipping away from him.

Mrs. Stroud sat in her usual chair. "Renee should be here soon. In the meantime," she said, "tell me about your weekend."

Jerome talked about how difficult it was to let Joi go on a date with a young man who was older than her, and how hard it had been for him to be alone all weekend. "I think I'm losing Renee," Jerome said.

"Sometimes," Mrs. Stroud said smoothly, "the tighter you hold on to someone, the more uncomfortable it feels for that person. I'm sure you've heard the expression 'Let go and let God.'" Jerome nodded in agreement. "Well, you may need to stop asking Renee to come home. Let go, and let God work His miracle. I often remind patients that God does answer our prayers, but what if He doesn't answer them the way we think is best? Certainly, you want your marriage to work. That's why you and Renee are here. But what if, in the end, it's God's plan to help you see that it's time for divorce? I'm not trying to discourage you, but I am asking that you prepare yourself for whatever the outcome will be."

Jerome was silent. He'd never considered that God wouldn't mend his relationship with his wife. He knew Mrs. Stroud meant well and she was probably right, but Jerome refused to think that way. Renee was coming back home. She just had to.

"Sorry I'm late," Renee said as she entered the room.

Jerome mumbled hello and then moved to the end of the sofa. Renee seemed to be in a great mood, and that was suspect to him. In his mind, there was no way she should be so carefree and high-spirited. Either someone else had already taken his place or Renee had fallen out of love with him.

Mrs. Stroud began the session with a recap of important points from previous sessions. Jerome was paying attention, but if the session was going to be productive, he needed to say what was on his mind. "I'm sorry to interrupt," he said and then faced Renee, "but I have to get something off my chest. It bothered me all weekend."

While Mrs. Stroud gave him permission to speak, Renee's face filled with puzzlement.

"When I dropped Elise off the other day, I saw Everett coming from your apartment," he began. "I know you're going to tell me that the two of you are friends, but I have to let you know that I'm bothered by him being there."

Renee subtly rolled her eyes. "Jerome," she said, avoiding eye contact, "how many times do I have to tell you that Everett and I are friends? I'm really getting tired of sounding like a broken record."

"I just don't understand why he had to be there."

"We were working," Renee stressed.

Jerome's frustration increased. "Why don't you understand how this makes me feel? I can't stand to see him coming from your apartment."

"You're only annoyed by it because I told you we kissed," Renee retorted.

"Am I really being unreasonable here?" Jerome asked Mrs. Stroud.

Mrs. Stroud closed her notepad. "Well, you have to understand that the trust in the marriage has been broken, and that opens the door for suspicion on many levels. Regaining trust is going to be a slow process. Both of you have to understand that, and more importantly, you both have to want it."

"I want to do whatever is needed to fix all that has been broken," Jerome asserted. "I know I messed up, but how long is my mistake going to be held against me? How long do I have to *patiently* stand by while another man is using our separation to his advantage?"

"You have to trust your wife, Jerome," Mrs. Stroud said.

"I'm trying to," Jerome replied. "But it's a real challenge. I feel like the relationship with Everett is getting stronger. Meanwhile, there's no effort to get to know my daughter. How long is she going to be treated like a disease? She's my blood, and I can no longer pretend that she doesn't exist."

The upbeat mood that Renee had been in when she entered the office had disappeared. "I'm just curious, Jerome," Renee said sarcastically. "How exactly do you want me to treat your daughter? Do you really believe I'm supposed to welcome her with open arms? Am I supposed to allow her to call me Mom?"

"You're missing the point, Renee," countered Jerome.

"Am I?" questioned Renee. "I'm sorry that you feel like Joi is being treated like a disease, but you can't force me to feel something that I don't, and right now I don't feel like I have to accept her."

"But when are you going to at least make an effort? Don't make Joi pay for my mistake," urged Jerome. Renee shook her head and faced the window, signaling that she was done with the conversation, but Jerome wasn't. "And what about you and Everett?"

Renee faced Jerome. "What about Everett?" she snapped. "Let's not forget that you kept your affair a secret. You didn't tell me about your daughter for several years. Don't you dare sit here and chastise me because you *think* Everett and I are having an affair. For the last time, Everett and I have been working together for years. If our working relationship or friendship becomes something more, I'll let you know. Right now, I don't know what I want," she said. "And I don't want to feel pressured about my relationship with you or with him anymore."

"So . . . what are you saying?" Jerome asked, clearly upset.

"I'm saying, I need space," Renee replied.

Both Renee and Jerome stared at opposite sides of the room. Jerome had a decision to make. Either he was going to pray harder or he was going to start thinking about plan B, a plan that didn't include Renee.

"Renee," Mrs. Stroud said softly. "I think you need to decide what you want to do about your marriage. Jerome has clearly told you that he wants to try. If you really want your marriage to survive, it can, and I can help you with that. But . . . you've got to want it. Jerome will have to be patient, but you've got to make a decision. Do you want your marriage to survive?"

Jerome continued to stare at the wall and prepared himself for Renee's response. If Renee wasn't willing to try, God would have to give him the strength to move on.

"I love Jerome," Renee replied. "I would love for us to get past this, but I also need to be honest with myself. I am angry, hurt, and disappointed by all that happened, and I really don't know if I can truly get over it this time. All I can do is pray."

Though Jerome didn't like Renee's reply, there was some hope in her words. The fact that she mentioned prayer was enough for Jerome to hold on to his faith that they'd be together again like a true husband and wife should.

~19~

Renee

"That's enough, Darla," Everett said in a tone Renee had never heard before.

In disbelief, Renee stared at the documents in front of her. How did she mess up last month's budget report? It didn't seem like her. She was always so careful and accurate. Though it was true that Darla had been out to get her since the meeting with the board members, she actually had just cause this time to question her. As she sat in Darla's office, listening to her outline the details of the incomplete budget report, Renee tried to figure out how she could've made such a massive mistake.

"Everett," Darla continued, despite his request, as she flipped through the five-page document, "look at this. Cybil and I stayed up all night trying to understand it. There are tons of mistakes. How could you submit such an important document without reviewing it first?"

Renee studied the pages in front of her in more detail. Darla had taken the liberty to highlight all the errors in a bright pink marker. Pages were missing, departments weren't represented, and formulas were incorrect.

Everett pushed his copy of the report in Darla's direction. "I'm not going to let you poison her name.

Renee has been a vital part of Luxury Inn, with major contributions to both the Philadelphia and Illinois hotels. She is fully competent and knows a great deal about this business."

"I never said she wasn't competent. I just have concerns based on her recent family problems and all," replied Darla.

"Wait a minute," interrupted Renee. "What goes on in my personal life has nothing to do with this job."

"Well, Renee," Darla said, "you've been coming in to work late some days, and your grandchildren have been here a few times during work hours. This isn't a day care—"

Renee couldn't believe her ears. Her grandchildren had been to her office only twice this month. Grace had two dentist appointments, and Renee offered to watch them for a couple of hours. They were so quiet, Renee was surprised Darla even knew they'd been there at all. "Who do you think—"

Everett touched Renee's hand, and she stopped talking. "At this point, I think you need to let Renee and me review this and resubmit a more accurate report. There's no point in wasting any more time."

"Well, Everett," Darla said in a professional tone, "if you work with her, that's fine. I would appreciate that."

Renee wanted to reach across the table and shake Darla.

"Are you done? I have a meeting in ten minutes," Everett said and stood up. "We'll take care of this."

Without waiting for Darla to reply, Renee picked up the document, then left the room and headed to her office. It boggled her mind that she had made mistakes, especially ones that reflected on her job performance. She knew there were issues in her life. She knew she was drinking more, but none of that should compromise her career. She was almost positive of that.

As soon as Renee got into her office, she turned on her computer. It was possible that she'd sent the wrong file. Or maybe Darla was trying to sabotage her in retaliation for Renee embarrassing her. Renee found it hard to believe that she'd submitted a budget analysis with so many mistakes. She clearly remembered inserting the necessary information. Renee searched through all the files on her computer but couldn't find the one she needed. That was weird. "Maybe I didn't save the file?" Renee questioned aloud. "But I know I didn't leave out so much information."

Renee pushed the keyboard aside and sighed. It was her fault for not making sure the file she sent was complete, but Renee still felt like Darla was up to something. In case her suspicions were correct, she started a file to document the daily interactions in the office. Renee felt the need to protect herself, and for added assurance, she made a note to call Connie, her lawyer.

There was a knock at the door, and Renee looked up from her desk.

"Hey, Renee," Cybil said. "Do you have a minute?"

Renee didn't have anything personal against Cybil, but she didn't trust her, either. "I was about to go to lunch," she said.

"I'll only be a minute," Cybil replied as she entered the room. She closed the door behind her but remained at the threshold. "I thought I should clear the air. I'm not here to step on your toes. I respect what you've done here. Darla and I may be friends, but I have a mind of my own. Whatever is going on between you and Darla, I want you to know I have nothing to do with it. She asked me to help her understand the budget. I had no idea it was something you created."

"I appreciate your coming to me," Renee said. "However, and this is no offense to you, but . . . I don't want to discuss this any more today. As a matter of fact, I think I'm done for the day here." Renee logged off of her computer and then stood up. "I'm going to work from home for the rest of the day."

"No offense taken. I completely understand."

Renee recalled the comment about her weird hours. "In case Darla wants to know, no one has ever questioned my hours. I work around the clock. Some days I come in late, but I work well into the evening almost every day."

"We know how hard you work, Renee. Really, go ahead. I'll talk to you tomorrow."

When Cybil left, Renee stopped by Everett's office to apologize, but he was on a conference call. She tiptoed into his office and wrote a message on a sticky note on his desk.

Sorry for putting you in a tough position earlier.

Everett continued to conduct business on the phone as he wrote Renee a reply.

No worries. Dinner and jazz tonight? We'll deal with the budget in the morning.

Renee didn't know how to respond. Before the last counseling session with Jerome and the talk with Elise, she would've said yes without hesitation. It also didn't help that she and Everett had shared that second kiss, a kiss that she'd initiated. She looked at Everett and nodded, although she wanted to say no. *It's just dinner between two friends,* she convinced herself. But just in case, Renee was going to ask Bianca to join them. That way, she could be sure that the dinner wouldn't lead to something more.

***

Renee stumbled down the street, next to Everett. For the first time in her life, she was officially drunk. She could barely hold her own weight, but she did her best to camouflage how she really felt inside. There was only two blocks left to go, and Renee prayed she could keep up the charade and make it to her apartment. Renee wasn't sure how this had happened. She had only one Long Island Iced Tea. The bartender must've given her a double shot of rum. There was just no way one drink could make her feel this way.

Bianca had never made it downtown to join them, but Renee felt she could keep things under control. Everett had tried to talk about his feelings twice, but each time Renee had changed the subject. Eventually, he'd caught on and kept the topics of discussion platonic. As Renee carefully strutted down State Street, she passed Garrett's and contemplated waiting in the short line to buy a warm bag of caramel popcorn. She was hoping the popcorn would coat her stomach and take away some of her queasiness. "Do you have a minute?" she asked Everett.

"Sure," he replied and followed Renee inside.

As Renee walked into the tiny store, she stumbled over the welcome mat and fell back into Everett's arms. "Guess I'm getting too old for heels," she joked, and the people around her laughed.

Everett held on to Renee's arm and whispered in her ear. "Or maybe it's that Long Island Iced Tea."

"I am a little tipsy," she confessed softly. "But I am still aware of my surroundings."

Renee and Everett exchanged funny stories about Darla as they waited in line. When it was her turn to order, Renee caught a glimpse of a young couple walking inside. When she recognized Joi, she backed away from Everett and stopped smiling. What was she doing downtown with a guy that had to be at least twenty-five? Renee tried to hide, but the store was too small.

There was no way she could leave the building without saying hello.

Everett ordered and paid for two bags of popcorn and then reached for Renee's hand. "Do I need to help you out of the store?" he teased.

Renee didn't smile. "I think I can make it," she said and pulled her hand away.

"Hi, Renee," Joi called from her place in line.

Renee pretended that she was seeing her for the first time. "Hi, Joi," she said, trying not to sound too phony. Strictly out of kindness, Renee reintroduced Everett, and Joi introduced her to Denver. Denver and Everett talked for a few minutes, while the two ladies pretended to be interested in the conversation.

"Well," Renee finally said, "I guess I'll see you later." Joi nodded, and as Renee walked out of the store, she prayed Joi wouldn't run home to her father and exaggerate the interaction she'd witnessed between her and Everett. Jerome was already going to be upset when he found out that they were together.

When Renee opened her eyes, the bedroom lights were out and she was under the covers in her nightgown, with a splitting headache. "No more Long Island Iced Teas," she grumbled and closed her eyes. The last thing she remembered when she made it to her apartment was hanging up on Jerome.

Before she made it home, he had called her cell phone, but she hadn't been in the mood to pacify him. Jerome had a reason to be upset because of what they'd discussed in their last counseling session, but she couldn't talk about it tonight.

Renee stretched her legs and kicked someone's arm and realized that she wasn't alone. Frightened, she slowly sat up and turned on the lamp. Who else would be in her bed? She distinctly recalled saying good-bye to Everett after he walked her home, so who could it be? Still feeling dizzy, she pushed herself forward and was surprised to see Jerome, fully dressed and curled up in the left corner of her bed.

Jerome jumped when the light came on and rolled onto his back. "You okay?"

"I'm fine," she said, trying to remember how he'd ended up in her apartment. "I must've been half asleep when you got here. I don't remember letting you upstairs."

"I'm not surprised. You had a few drinks last night," Jerome replied and turned back on his side. "You agreed to let me come over to talk, but when I got here, you were too tired."

Renee grabbed her head and then lay back down. "I thought you meant you were coming over tomorrow. Not tonight," she retorted. "I can't talk now, Jerome. I have a headache."

Jerome chuckled lightly. "When I came in, you could barely make it to the bedroom. That was the first time I saw you drunk."

"I wasn't drunk," Renee mumbled, slightly embarrassed, then looked at the clock. It was almost midnight. A flashback of the days she used to get him ready for bed when he was drunk crossed her mind. There were even times when he fell asleep on the floor or knelt by the side of the bed and she left him there. "I probably should've had more than a salad for lunch. Anyway . . . you can sleep in the guest room if you want to be more comfortable."

"I'm not going to the guest room, Renee. I am still your husband."

"Humph," Renee moaned and turned off the lights.

The room was silent. The cars traveling down the street and the periodic trains that passed by reminded Renee of her childhood days in West Philadelphia.

"I need to admit something," Jerome said, breaking Renee's nostalgic moment.

"What is it, Jerome?" she asked nonchalantly.

"I read a text Everett sent you the day I helped you move in," he said and paused briefly before continuing. "When Joi told me she saw you with Everett tonight, I was jealous. I know you told me there is no need to be, but I can't stand that the two of you are so close. If only you'd come back home—"

"I'm not ready for that. It wouldn't be fair to Joi if I moved back now." Renee sat up. "Besides . . . how did you see Everett's text?"

"Your phone was ringing while you were fixing up this bedroom. I looked at the screen and saw his name, because I wanted to know who was calling so much and couldn't help myself. I'm sorry, but curiosity got the best of me that day."

"Everett and I have been friends for a long time. You never had a reason to snoop through my belongings or not to trust me. Why question the friendship now?" Renee queried. "Is my word no longer good enough?"

"You two may be friends now," Jerome told her, "but you're not a man. I know he's enjoying the fact that we're not living together."

"He's just as happy as I'm sure Melanie is," Renee said sarcastically.

"Melanie knows I want my wife to come home. Does Everett know that you still want to be with me?"

"It's after midnight, Jerome. I have to go to work in the morning." Renee turned on her side. "Good-night."

"When did you start drinking?"

"It was *one* drink. I haven't started drinking," she fibbed. There was no need to tell Jerome that she enjoyed a glass of wine every night. "No big deal."

Jerome crawled up to Renee's side and lay on top of the comforter.

"C'mon, Jerome. You know better than to lie all over my expensive comforter," fussed Renee. "I haven't been out of the house that long."

"I'll only be a minute," he said and put his arm around her. "I'm worried about us."

Renee didn't push him away. "I miss you, too, but what I'm feeling is bigger than our love. Please understand that I'm doing this to get myself together as well. We shouldn't rush this. I'm not in a mental place to handle everything right now."

Jerome started to rub Renee's back, and again, she didn't stop him. "This is hard, but okay," he whispered in her ear. "Just make sure when you're ready, you'll come back to me."

Renee turned around and cuddled even closer to her husband. She missed sleeping next to him. Sensing her warm up to him, he kissed her neck, and when Renee looked up, her lips brushed against his. In the heat of that moment, Renee and Jerome caressed one another passionately. Soon, Renee forgot about the separation, the affair with Taylor, and Joi and found herself touching him back.

A few hours later, Renee woke up wrapped in Jerome's arms. As silly as it sounded, she couldn't believe that she had had sex with her husband. Instead of feeling happy and secure, she felt the opposite and questioned whether or not that was God's way of telling her that there was nothing left between them. Renee tried to move to her side of the bed, but Jerome held her tight.

"Are you all right?" he asked.

"Yes," Renee moaned, although her spirit was troubled. There was no question that she missed him, but she prayed this wouldn't become a habit. Sex almost always complicated things. Renee needed to separate herself so that she could clearly consider her options.

Jerome lightly stroked Renee's leg. "Thanksgiving is coming up," he said. "I'd hoped you'd be back home by now, but since that's not the case . . . Will you be joining us?"

By "us," Renee assumed Jerome was subtly trying to say that his daughter would be spending the holiday in Illinois. She didn't know how to respond without making him upset, especially after their recent act of intimacy.

"Please," Jerome playfully begged, sensing his wife's resistance. "Grace offered to cook, but she's a vegetarian. We can't have an imitation turkey."

"Grace knows how to cook a real turkey," Renee responded.

"But not as good as you."

Remembering a conversation she'd had with Elise, Renee did as her friend had asked and let her guard down. Thanksgiving was only *one* day. She could tolerate being around Joi for a *few* hours. "All right, Jerome," she said. "I'll give Grace a call in the morning. We'll work something out together."

"Good," Jerome said and then sat up. "I just remembered something. I really hope this won't change your mind . . . but . . ."

Curious, Renee faced him. "Just spit it out. What's wrong now?"

"Taylor and her family are coming."

"Coming where?" Renee questioned with an attitude. Jerome couldn't possibly mean that his former lover and her family would be joining them for Thanks-giving.

"She wants to be with Joi," he said softly.

Renee couldn't even formulate the right words to say. She barely wanted to be there with Joi. What made Jerome think that she'd want to spend the holiday with Taylor? "And explain to me why she has to do that in Chicago."

"Joi is playing in a tournament, and—"

"I don't think I feel like dealing with that," Renee interrupted. Again, Jerome was giving out more than Renee was ready and willing to handle. "Don't you think that's a bit much?"

"I know and I'm sorry, but please . . . The day won't be the same without you," Jerome pleaded.

"You're really pushing my limits," Renee said and rolled away from him. "I'm going only because I don't want to disappoint the boys."

Jerome left well enough alone and turned on his side. When he started to snore, Renee faced the op-posite wall and prayed. Thanksgiving was a day to be thankful for God's blessings, but she was finding it painfully hard to see the blessing in inviting Taylor and her family.

Renee removed the top of her flask filled with Peach Schnapps. Wine was usually her drink of choice, but she decided to try something a little stronger for the holidays. Renee swallowed a few mouthfuls. The only way she was going to make it through Thanksgiving was with the help of a little alcohol. The sweet mixture would definitely keep her in a mellow, stable mood.

Through the bedroom door, Renee heard Taylor laughing downstairs and rolled her eyes. Although

Renee had agreed to share Thanksgiving with Taylor and thought she could handle it, she was having second thoughts. She was also having second thoughts about staying at the house overnight. Since she had slept with Jerome, he was overly optimistic that their situation had changed. That was far from the truth, and last night Renee had to remind him of their reality.

Jerome had been under the impression that Renee was going to sleep in their bedroom, and when she placed her luggage in the guest room, an argument occurred. "I don't want to confuse the children," he had said in anger. Renee gently reminded him that they had been separated for a while now. She didn't have plans to move back in the house before the end of the year, so it was best, in her eyes, that they sleep in separate rooms. Of course, Jerome didn't agree, and he went to bed angry.

Renee took another quick swig of her drink and then pushed the closed flask between the mattress and the box spring. When she finally made it downstairs, Taylor's twin boys were in the family room, playing with her grandson's toy trucks.

"These are my new friends, Gama!" her grandson said and beamed as he watched the twins play.

Renee rubbed the top of his head. "Make sure you put away your toys when you're done with them," she said, and as she turned to leave the room, she nearly stepped on her youngest grandchild. She reached down to pick him up and then kissed his plump cheeks. "You need to be in your walker," Renee cooed. "Where's your mommy?"

Joi emerged from the kitchen with a training cup in her hand. "I'm keeping an eye on him," she said. "He must've crawled out here while I was refilling his cup."

Reluctant to hand over her grandson, Renee placed him in Joi's arms. "Did you meet my sister, Leah?" Joi asked as a younger version of Taylor walked toward them.

"Nice to meet you, Leah. Make yourself at home." Renee felt that was the polite thing to say. "I better go check on the status of the appetizers," she said and walked to the kitchen.

Taylor was cutting up a bowl of yams at the counter when Renee walked in, and she paused. Taylor had, at one point, taken possession of her husband. She didn't like that she'd claimed ownership of the small space on the counter.

"Pretty sweater," Zora said as she arranged cold shrimp on a serving tray.

Renee thanked her and then took an apron hanging on the back of a kitchen chair to cover her new cashmere sweater.

Taylor turned around and said, "Happy Thanksgiving, Renee."

Normally, Renee would be a gracious host and welcome her guests with a friendly hug. She couldn't do that with Taylor. It would be insincere and fake. "Same to you," Renee replied and walked to the oven to check on the turkey.

It was more than halfway done, and Renee reached above the stove and grabbed a utensil so that she could baste the turkey. As she poured juices over the twenty-pound bird, she heard Jerome sharing an old basketball story with all the male guests in the small cottage in the backyard through the slightly open windows. This year Jerome had set up a big-screen television in the cottage for all the males to enjoy the football games without interruptions. *He can be so loud and animated at times,* Renee thought, recalling the days when they would hold parties in Philadelphia. After he had three drinks, everything that came out of Jerome's mouth was full of drama. When he stopped drinking, Renee thought his exaggerated behavior would, too, but she was wrong.

Renee closed the oven and walked over to the table and sat down. Grace was whipping together ingredients for corn bread. Renee opened a bag of onions and peppers and prepared to chop them. Once the greens were close to being done, she'd dump the onions and peppers inside the pot and let them simmer.

"I haven't seen all of Chicago, but I can see why my daughter wants to live here," Taylor said as she placed the yams into a large skillet.

"This is a beautiful city," Zora added. "How long are you staying?"

"Our flight leaves at six A.M. Monday morning," Taylor answered. "I wish I could stay longer."

"You'll have to come when the weather is nicer," Grace said, and Renee cut her eyes in her direction. How dare she encourage Jerome's ex-lover to come back for another visit? Whose side was she on? *Sorry,* Grace mouthed and continued to work on the corn bread.

Sensing Renee's uneasiness, Zora initiated a discussion about the latest episode of *The Game.*

As the women talked, Renee snuck a few glances at Taylor. For a woman who had had four babies, she looked good for her age. If Renee's memory hadn't failed her, Taylor even looked slimmer than she was the last time they talked in Philly. Renee subtly searched for gray hairs but didn't spot one. A fashionable woman like Taylor had to have dyed them. Maybe that was why she looked younger that she actually was. Though Renee spent a couple hours in a salon twice a month, she didn't bother with dyeing her grays. There was no point in disguising what was destined to take place. By the time her mother was sixty, she had a head full of dusty white hair. Renee was positive she would follow in her mother's footsteps.

"I brought some dip and a vegetable tray," Taylor said when she was finished with the yams. "Would you like me to set them out in the dining room?"

"You can put the appetizers out on the—" Zora began but was cut off by Renee.

"I think the ladies and I have it covered. There isn't much left to do here, so why don't you go and relax?"

Taylor didn't push the issue. "Okay. I'll go and keep the kids company."

"I'm proud of you," Zora remarked after Taylor left the room.

"I'm glad *someone* noticed my effort," Renee said and chuckled.

Grace poured batter into muffin trays. "Yes, I noticed, too. However, we can't leave her alone in the family room with all the children. That would be rude, don't you think?"

Renee ignored the question, and Grace focused on her task, afraid to go against her mother-in-law.

"Well," Zora said and picked up her shrimp platter. "I'm going to take her a glass of tea when I'm done and then chill with her for a while. Is that allowed?" she laughed.

"It's not that deep," replied Renee, although the thought of Taylor getting to know her daughter-in-law did bother her. "Better you than me."

After the dinner, Taylor and Joi offered to wash the dishes. Renee didn't like the idea of mother and daugh-

ter working together in the kitchen, but she was tired
and gave them permission to help. Shockingly, dinner
wasn't as painful as she thought it would be. Taylor's
husband seemed like a very nice man, and together
they appeared to be a happy couple. Selfishly, Renee
resented the fact that an adulterer could fall in love
with a good man and live happily ever after.

When the dining room was empty and everyone had
retired to different rooms in the house, Renee and Zora
went to the living room to relax. It had been a while
since they had a chance to talk, and for the next hour
Renee questioned Zora about her career and the possibility of giving her another grandchild. Zora never let
on that she was bothered by Renee's probing. If only
Renee had practiced that much restraint with her own
mother-in-law in the beginning of her marriage.

"Is that the door?" Renee asked and stood up. She
walked a few feet to the front door and opened it,
expecting to see one of the neighbors. But, to her surprise, it wasn't one of the neighbors at all. Shivering in
a dark gray wool miniskirt and thigh-high black boots,
Melanie stood on the small porch, holding a cake container.

"Happy Turkey Day," Melanie said cheerfully.

Renee stared at Melanie's fancy chinchilla fur, which
stopped at her waist, and wondered why she was there.
Surely, Jerome hadn't bumped his head and invited
her, too. She could understand why Taylor had been
invited, but Melanie?

Tired of waiting for Renee to reply, Melanie held up
the cake container in her hands. "I brought dessert for
the family. Jerome wanted to taste my gram's famous
rum cake."

Rum cake? Renee silently questioned. Jerome wanted
to taste a rum cake? He was a recovering alcoholic. That
just didn't make sense.

"Hi, Mel," Zora said as she walked to the front door. "Come on in. You can take the cake to the kitchen."

"No worries. She's not staying," Zora whispered in Renee's ear before escorting Melanie down the hall.

Renee stood lifeless at the door and looked toward heaven. *God, you've got to be kidding. Isn't one woman enough for me to bear?*

"Who was at the door?" Jerome questioned as he carried his infant grandson down the stairs. Renee raised her left brow, and Jerome stopped walking, clearly confused. "What's wrong?"

Before Renee could answer, Melanie walked out of the kitchen. "Hey, Thomas. Happy Thanksgiving. I just stopped by to bring that cake I promised."

"I forgot about that," Jerome said as he continued down the stairs. "How much do I owe you?"

"Don't worry about it, Thomas," Melanie said. "This one's on me. You can pay for the next one."

Jerome carefully placed his grandson on the floor, and he crawled into the family room, where his siblings were playing. "Thanks," Jerome said, concerned about the no-nonsense look on Renee's face.

Before Jerome extended an invitation for her to stay, Renee opened the front door wide. "Thanks for stopping by," she said and forced herself to smile. "Enjoy the rest of your evening."

Melanie zipped her jacket and then said her goodbyes. As soon as Melanie set foot outside of the house, Renee shut the door, careful not to slam it.

"Did you have to be so mean?" Jerome asked as he watched Renee climb the stairs.

"Not today, Jerome. It's Thanksgiving."

Renee went into the guest room and slammed the door. She needed some time alone. She waited a few minutes before getting her flask of alcohol to be sure no one had followed her upstairs. When she felt certain that no one had, Renee sat on the bed and drank the rest of her liquor.

Renee heard herself snore and jumped up. For a moment, she thought she was dreaming. How long had she been asleep? She jumped off the bed and looked in the mirror. Her hair was still in place, but she was afraid remnants of the peach schnapps lingered on her breath. After returning the empty flask to its hiding place, Renee unzipped a pocket on her suitcase and took out a small tin of mints. She popped a few inside her mouth and then headed downstairs.

When she walked into the family room, she discovered that Taylor and her family had left and the house was filled with the people Renee loved most. Like old times, Joshua suggested they play a game called Taboo. Game night was something the family had always enjoyed.

"Let's get more dessert before we start," Junior shouted, and everyone shifted to the kitchen. Renee stayed behind. She'd eaten enough for one day.

"You don't want anything, Mom?" Joshua asked when he returned to the room with a huge chunk of carrot cake.

Renee shook her head and rubbed her full belly. "Stick a fork in me, baby, 'cause I'm done," she joked. "So . . ." Renee began after Joshua sat next to her, "how's Dannette?"

"She's been hanging with a cornball, but I can tell he won't last too much longer," Joshua replied.

Joshua had many friends, but Dannette was the only girl that he spent time with. They'd been friends since middle school.

"You know I like Dannette," Renee said, "but don't hold out for one young lady. Sometimes girls date several men that are no good for them, and that's not necessarily a bad thing, because when the right man comes along, they'll really appreciate him."

"Was it like that with you and Pop?"

"No," Renee answered and grinned. "Your father was my first real boyfriend. My mother told me to date other people before getting serious, and sometimes I wish I had listened." Renee took a deep breath as she thought about her regrets.

"I won't rush into anything, Mom," Joshua assured her. "I have a plan, and I'm sticking to it. It's funny. That's one of the things Joi and I have in common. We're driven to succeed."

"You really like her, huh?" she asked.

"I do," Joshua answered with pride. "She's a cool person, and I'm really glad she's my sister. I hope one day you'll learn to like her, too."

Listening to her son, Renee wished she could look past Jerome's infidelity and see Joi as an individual. While Renee believed Joi was different from her mother, it was hard to separate her from her parents' mistakes. "Who knows," Renee said as her family filed back into the room. "Maybe one day I will."

Every time Renee was summoned to Darla's office, she didn't know what to expect. The last time, Darla reprimanded her for submitting an incomplete budget report. Though it was Renee's fault, she and Everett corrected the mistakes and sent an accurate file the next day.

Bianca was already in Darla's office by the time Renee made it down the hall. "Do you know what she wants?" Bianca asked as soon as Renee entered.

"Not a clue. I thought you were just here for the managers' meeting this afternoon."

"Me, too," Bianca whispered. "I think she's out to get me."

"I wouldn't worry," Renee assured her. "I'll let her stress me, but I won't dare let her bother you."

"I don't like what she's doing to you, either," Bianca stated and sat down. "This place is not the same anymore."

"I don't think it will ever be again," Renee solemnly replied.

"I've got some exciting news to share," Darla announced as she bounced into her office.

Renee and Bianca remained silent until Darla told them what was on her mind. There was always a motive behind her excitement, so the ladies had learned to save their responses until they had all the facts.

"I'm sure you've heard about the 'situation' at the New York hotel," Darla began. What happened at the New York hotel was no secret. One of the managers had embezzled money from one of the holiday project funds. "I'm glad that's my sister's hotel and not mine. And to think," Darla said, "I thought *we* had troubles."

Renee and Bianca glanced at each other. "We do have troubles," Renee wanted to shout. "You!"

"My sister is in a tizzy about an immediate replacement," Darla continued. "She mentioned that you two started the holiday projects a few years ago, so I had great idea." Darla beamed with pride. "I thought Bianca could go down to New York and help them figure out how to save the project. Renee, I thought you could stand in for Bianca in Northbrook while she is in New York." Darla waited for a reply, but the women were confused. "New York is a lovely city at Christmastime. This is a good plan, right?"

"Actually," Bianca replied, "I'll be on vacation next week. I've been planning this for at least a month now. . . . How many days do you want me to stay in New York?"

The grin on Darla's face slowly disappeared. "My sister would need you at least until Christmas Eve. She's looking for a replacement, but someone will need to train them. Is that okay?" Darla queried. "I hope I didn't mess up again."

How inconsiderate, Renee thought. Darla knew Bianca had made plans to be away next week.

Bianca hesitantly replied, "Yes, it's okay."

"Good. I was afraid I put my foot in my mouth once again," Darla responded with a weak chuckle. "I told my sister this was a good plan. She asked for Renee, but I told her that she had family obligations here."

"Why do you always feel that you have to speak for me?" Renee spouted and prayed God would keep her temper in check. She had been in a great place lately and didn't want Darla to change that. What Darla had decided wasn't such a big deal, but did she have to bring her personal life into it?

Darla's hands dropped on the desk, and she pouted. "Why does *everything* have to be a problem for you?" she groaned. "I was thinking of your best interests."

"I highly doubt that, but it's okay," Renee told her. "Are we done here?"

"When is your sister expecting me?" Bianca asked.

"Tomorrow," Darla answered.

Renee couldn't keep silent. "You do realize that Christmas is next week, and that Bianca already had plans. It might have been better to send me so that she could spend time with her family. I see my family all the time, despite what you may think," Renee said sarcastically. "My husband can handle the days I'll be gone. Besides, although Bianca can execute any of the holiday projects, I'm the one with all the main connections."

Darla turned red. It pained her to admit that Renee was right, but after hearing her speak, she had no choice but to send Renee instead. "Okay. If Bianca doesn't want to go, you should. I just thought it was a great opportunity."

"Thank you," Bianca said, "but I'd really like to spend this time with my family."

Renee got up to leave, and before she and Bianca made it out of the office, Darla made another sly remark. "I'm sure you know Everett will be there in a few days."

Renee almost shared a few unpleasant words with her boss but held her tongue. She was beginning to sound like Jerome. Of course she knew Everett would be traveling to New York on his way back from London. He was needed to help with the reorganization. She and Everett were partners and worked together on a regular basis. Darla would understand that if she were a true businesswoman. There was no need for the implications.

"Enjoy the holidays," Renee said and walked away. In a way, she was looking forward to being out of the office. Any time away from Darla was considered a blessing. Prayerfully, Jerome would see it her way, too. They had plans to spend the week together—decorating the Christmas tree, baking cookies, wrapping gifts, and shopping. Thanksgiving had been enough for Renee, but Mrs. Stroud had convinced her to give Christmas a try. Joi would be around only until the day after Christmas. Then she'd be on a plane to Philadelphia to see her mother.

"It would be good for the family," Mrs. Stroud had said during their last session. Renee had her reservations, but she was willing to give it a try.

~20~

Jerome

Jerome hated going to the mall, but Renee had given him a list of the last-minute gifts she needed for their grandchildren. The parking lot was just as hectic as the mall, but at least he was done, and it was only three o'clock. He still had the rest of the day to relax before picking Renee up at the airport.

"Hey, Mr. Thomas," Jerome heard someone say, and he turned around.

"Carmen!" Jerome sang as he shoved the bags in his hands into the trunk of his car. "I see you had a lot of gifts to buy at the last minute," he joked and closed the trunk.

Carmen rearranged the bags in her hands and laughed. "Today was the only day I could leave work early," she said. "With Mrs. Thomas *and* Mr. Coleman stranded in New York, there was no reason for me to stay in the office."

Jerome looked as if he'd seen a ghost. He knew that Renee's flight was delayed, but he didn't know that she had gone to New York with Everett. Why didn't she mention that? "I hope they make it out before the blizzard gets too bad," he said, trying to mask the sting of the news.

"Don't worry," Carmen replied. "Your wife will be home in time to read stories to your grandchildren tonight."

"I hope you're right," he responded. "That's one of the only traditions we commit to every year."

Carmen wished Jerome a happy holiday and then proceeded down the parking lot. Jerome got inside of his car and started the engine. "This is no big deal," Jerome said aloud, trying to convince himself. Renee and Everett traveled together all the time. There was no reason to be alarmed. This was a last-minute trip, and it was possible that Renee forgot to mention it.

By the time Jerome made it home, his house was full of children. Grace had dropped off the grandchildren, like she did every year, so that she could do her last-minute shopping and wrap gifts without interruptions. Joshua and Joi were watching them and had also been joined by their friends Denver and Dannette. The house smelled like peanut butter cookies, and he hoped they hadn't made too much of a mess. Renee was going to be home in a few hours, and he didn't have the energy to clean up before she arrived. It had taken a lot for her to agree to stay at the house tonight, so he wanted to be sure everything met her expectations.

When he walked into the kitchen, Jerome was relieved to see Dannette washing dishes. He was also pleased to see his grandchildren sitting at the table, quietly coloring and eating hot dogs. Everything was under control.

"Hey, Pop," Joshua said and then tossed Jerome the cordless phone in his hand. "Mom's stuck at the airport."

Jerome waved to everyone and then walked into the family room. He wanted to speak to his wife in private. "Hey, babe," he said. "I just got back from the mall, and I got everything on the list." He did his best to hide his suspicions.

"Good," Renee answered. "I was hoping to be there by seven, but my flight got canceled again. Apparently, the blizzard is heading toward Chicago."

Jerome took a deep breath. "So . . . when will you be home?"

"As of now, my flight is set to land at one forty tomorrow afternoon."

Anger crept into Jerome's spirit, and he wondered if Renee was telling the truth. The last time he listened to weather reports, Chicago wasn't expecting snow until Christmas night. "I saw Carmen today," he blurted, eager to hear Renee's response. Any delay in her reply would raise even more suspicion for him.

"Really?" Renee answered. "You stopped by the office?"

"No, she was leaving the mall," he replied. "She mentioned that Everett was in New York with you."

"He came in from London yesterday," Renee said. "I'm glad he came, too. This New York crew can be tough." Jerome was at a loss for words, and Renee picked up on his mood change. "Is everything all right?"

In their last counseling session, Mrs. Stroud had instructed Jerome and Renee to be honest about their feelings. So, at the risk of him sounding like a spoiled child, he confessed his uneasiness. "I guess I'm wondering why you didn't mention that he was there when I spoke to you last night."

"Oh, Jerome, don't tell me you're bummed about that," Renee responded. "Don't make something this small a huge problem."

"I'm not. . . . It's just that . . . you'll be with him for Christmas Eve."

"Are you kidding me, Jerome?" questioned Renee. "You *have* to be joking."

"I'm not upset, but it does seem like Everett is always around. He gets in the middle of us a little too frequently lately."

"In the middle of us?" Renee asked in a high-pitched tone. Jerome knew then that the conversation was about to take a turn for the worse.

For the next ten minutes, Jerome and Renee went back and forth about her relationship with Everett. At some point, Renee became fed up and brought up Jerome's affair and emerging relationship with Melanie.

"This has gotten out of hand, Renee," Jerome said. "The bottom line is that I miss you. Melanie is my assistant. She spends more time with Joi than she does with me, really. Trust me."

"Stop asking me to trust you," Renee snapped. "Where was the trust when you went through my cell phone?"

Jerome sighed. "It's no secret that we have trust issues, but I'm trying to start anew by being honest and understanding your feelings, and I hope you'll do the same," he said. "I mean, I get frustrated by the way you treat my daughter. I feel like what's done is done. We're either going to move on or give up."

"Really, Jerome," replied Renee. "That sounds like an ultimatum."

"You're taking what I said the wrong way."

"I don't think I am, and I'm not ready to accept Joi, so I guess we need to move on."

"C'mon, Renee. Let's not ruin Christmas this year."

"Why not?" she retorted. "You ruined the holidays last year. Guess we're even."

"This is unbelievable," Jerome replied and prayed the children were too busy in the kitchen to realize he and Renee were arguing. "Is there any hope for you and Joi?"

"Not now," Renee answered with an attitude.

"Well," Jerome said, "we're both aggravated, so why don't we revisit this later?"

Renee agreed and then hung up the phone. Jerome put the phone on the coffee table and then used the remote control to turn on the television. "That didn't go as planned," he moaned as he surfed through the channels. A small part of him wished he had kept his cool. He and Renee had been getting along well until he bumped into Carmen at the mall. Maybe he'd overreacted slightly, but he had to say what was on his mind. He just prayed he hadn't made matters worse.

~21~

Renee

Renee dropped her cell phone on the hotel bed and closed her eyes. It had been almost a year since Joi had entered her life, and it seemed like no progress had been made. She and Jerome were no longer living together, and they couldn't seem to go longer than a week without arguing. This wasn't the way she wanted to live the rest of her life. Renee opened her eyes and walked into the next room, where Everett was waiting for her.

"You ready?" Renee said and removed her coat from the hall closet. "I made reservations for seven."

Renee put on her coat and then leaned against the wall. Holidays were supposed to be filled with peace and joy, yet her heart was heavy. As she leaned on the wall, she covered her eyes with her hands and cried. She couldn't continue to go through waves of emotions when it came to her husband. Renee felt Everett grab her arm, and without resistance, she fell into his arms.

"Once trust is broken, it's almost impossible to gain it back," Everett said. "You can't keep putting yourself through this."

"I know," Renee cried.

"You need to be honest with yourself," he continued as he gently stroked the side of her head. "Do you *really* want to save your marriage? Do you *really* want to deal with all the changes?"

Though Renee knew the answers to his questions, she couldn't bring herself to say the words aloud.

"Renee," Everett said softly, "do you still love your husband?"

Renee remained silent. She wasn't ready to admit the truth, that although she loved Jerome, she was no longer in love with him.

"Okay," Everett said and wiped Renee's tears. "It's time to put a smile back on your face. How about ice-skating in the park? Are you up for a challenge?"

Renee appreciated Everett's attempt to cheer her up and nodded yes. "Not sure two fifty-year-olds should do anything challenging on ice, but I could use a laugh. Just give me a minute to check my makeup," she said and headed back to the bedroom.

Renee made sure Everett couldn't see her from where he was standing and quietly took her flask from inside her purse. As Renee took a few sips of her favorite wine, she couldn't believe that she was seriously considering divorce. Any doubt that she had before today had been put to rest. Her marriage was over, and if she wanted to experience real happiness again, she would need to put the past behind her and move on . . . without her husband.

Renee closed the flask and returned it to her purse. Before the night was over, she'd need to refill the container. Thinking about returning to Chicago made her uneasy. There was no way she wanted to pretend to be happy around Jerome and her children. She hated to be away from them during the holidays, but Renee needed space. She decided to call Reggie and Zora in the morning. This Christmas, and possibly New Year's, would be spent with her oldest son and his wife.

***

After spending an unexpected week in New York with her son, Renee returned to Chicago in better spirits and ready to begin the New Year as a brand-new woman. While she was in New York, she had time to put a plan into motion. She wanted to expedite the divorce, but her lawyer and friend, Connie Shaw, convinced Renee to wait until the second week of January to serve Jerome papers. Though the wait weighed on her heart, there was no need to make Jerome's holiday miserable. It was already bad enough that she had decided to remain in New York over the holidays.

Renee strolled into Luxury Inn around 11:30 A.M. with a smile on her face, determined not to let Darla or anyone else alter her current state of mind. Before going up to her office, she stopped by the front desk and caught up with some of the employees. It had been a long time since she had conversed with them about matters outside of work. The relationship she'd established with the employees was part of the reason the Chicago branch was so successful. The workers respected and liked Renee, and often put in extra hours to make sure the hotel met her high expectations. With so much going on in her personal life, Renee had lost touch with many of them. But that was about to change.

As she listened to one of the interns share the details of her performance in a Christmas play, she noticed Jerome walk into the hotel. From his brisk, wide steps, Renee could tell that something was wrong. The divorce papers weren't going to be served for another two days, so she had no idea why he was charging toward her.

Without speaking to anyone, Jerome walked up to Renee and barked, "Can I talk to you in private?"

Renee excused herself and then walked to an empty conference room on the far end of the building. Worried, she wondered if something bad had happened with his mentoring program or one of the children.

"How could you do this, Renee?" Jerome asked and tossed a set of papers on the table. "Divorce? You can't really be serious about this."

Renee was taken by surprise. Maybe she had her dates mixed up. Though she wasn't prepared for his outburst, she was surprised by Jerome's reaction. "Jerome, when we last talked, I told you—"

"Don't give me that, Renee," he snapped. "We were both angry the last time we talked. I thought we were going to discuss this when you got back into town."

"Lower your voice," Renee said and pulled the door closed. "Let's be honest. Neither of us is happy anymore. We're trying to fix something that is broken into too many fragile pieces."

"Says who? Everett?" Jerome demanded to know.

"Will you please lay off the Everett angle?" Renee said, louder than she realized. "This is about *you* and *me*. No one else!"

"I'm not going to let you do this," Jerome charged. "We haven't even finished counseling. Can't we at least get through that?"

Renee sighed. "No, Jerome. Let's just put an end to our misery. I'm tired of—"

"Misery?" Jerome said, alarmed. "I knew you were upset, but *misery?* That's how you feel, Renee?"

"How can you be so shocked?" Renee replied. "I've been miserable for months, and I'm sick and tired of feeling miserable around the man I married."

"I didn't know you were *this* unhappy," he confessed. "But now that I know, I can either pray harder or give up on what I believe God told me. And, Renee, I choose to stand on God's word."

Everett tapped on the window, and Jerome groaned. "What does *he* want?"

Ignoring her husband, Renee opened the door.

"Is everything all right?" Everett asked Renee, and Jerome walked across the room to the door.

"She's fine," he shouted, and Renee begged him to lower his voice. She didn't want an argument to ensue, as it had over a year ago in the Northbrook office.

Everett disregarded Jerome's statement. "You might want to go to your office or lower your voices. We can hear you down the hall," he told Renee. Renee nodded and attempted to close the door, but Everett wasn't finished. "If you need me, I'll be in the atrium."

Jerome forced his way forward. "This is the last time I want to tell you to mind your business."

"Cut it out, Jerome," Renee pleaded, but Jerome was on a mission.

"Don't think I don't know about you and my wife," he fired at Everett. "You have everyone believing you're such a upstanding man, but I'm not fooled. I know you've been pursuing my wife. You may have convinced her to get a divorce, but I've got news for you, partner. What Renee and I have is greater than your friendship. A divorce will never happen."

"Your wife lives in an apartment," Everett replied and smirked. "I'd say a divorce has already happened. Those papers will just make it legal."

"C'mon, guys," Renee said quickly and stood between the two men. "Let's not have a repeat of what happened last year, please. Everett, I'll handle this. Now please leave me alone with Jerome."

Renee could hear Jerome breathing heavier and became concerned. There wasn't an easier way to ask for a divorce. Jerome would've countered no matter how Renee presented her need to be free. "Jerome," she said and closed the door, "why don't we go to lunch and discuss this calmly."

"Calm?" Jerome huffed. "How can I be calm? You're leaving me for another man."

"I'm not going to argue anymore. I'm supposed to be working," Renee retorted. "But for the millionth time, this is *not* about Everett. This is about the affair you had with Taylor."

Renee could tell Jerome had more to say, but he refrained. He stood next to her in silence for several minutes and then abruptly walked out of the room. He charged down the hallway so fast that he accidentally knocked over a glass vase, causing it to shatter into huge chunks across the tiled floor.

As luck would have it, Darla was coming out of a different conference room as Jerome zoomed by her. Looking confused, she turned in Renee's direction. "What happened here?"

The last thing Renee wanted to do was share her personal business with Darla, but now that Jerome had left an obvious mess that needed to be cleaned up, she felt like she had no choice. "Do you have a free minute?" Renee asked.

Darla stepped around the pool of water that had gathered in the middle of the floor. "Yes, Renee," she said. "I think we need to talk. Can you come to my office in thirty minutes?"

"Sure," Renee replied, and when Darla walked away, she went to find someone to help her clean up the water and broken glass.

Exactly thirty minutes later, Renee walked into Darla's office and was surprised to see Cybil sitting at a small meeting table in the corner. While Darla sat behind her desk, fidgeting on the computer, Cybil invited Renee to have a seat at the table with her. As Cybil tried to entertain Renee with stories about her children, she watched Darla from the corner of her eye. When Carmen entered the office and immediately left after giving Darla a folder, Renee sensed that something bad was about to happen.

"So," Darla began as she made her way to the table, holding the folder in her hand, "I'm sure you're wondering why I asked Cybil to join us."

"I am curious," Renee said in a controlled manner.

"Well, it's no secret that I've been concerned about your performance as of late," Darla mentioned. With trembling hands, she placed the folder on the table. "I've been thinking about this for some time now, but after the incident today, I think it's clear that we need to let you go. Effective immediately."

Renee thought she was dreaming. Did Darla just terminate her?

"You devoted many good years to Luxury Inn," Cybil added, "and that is something you can always be proud of."

"Yes," Darla asserted with a mild smirk, "you can be proud of the work you did. But with your *recent* behavior . . . The company needs someone a little more stable." Darla pushed the folder toward Renee and opened it. "I've taken the liberty to print out a record of concerns. As you will see, you made major mistakes on a budget report, you missed an important meeting, you conducted personal affairs during business hours, you set your own work hours, you used the Governor's Suite for your own personal pleasure . . . I could go on, but you can take a look at all the areas of concern when you have more time."

Cybil directed Renee's attention to the left side of the folder. "The company is prepared to give you a severance package," she said, and Renee almost snapped.

After her thirty-plus years of extraordinary service, Luxury Inn owed her that.

"You'll find the severance very generous," noted Darla.

Renee stared at the letter in the folder until the words all jumbled together as one. She couldn't believe that she'd been fired. Without losing her cool, Renee closed the folder. "Your father would be appalled."

"My father isn't in charge anymore," Darla snarled.

"You're right," Renee said and stood up. There was no point in arguing any further. Luxury Inn had a new boss, and unless she was willing to conform to Darla's regime, it was time to move on. Maybe this was a part of God's plan. Renee grabbed the folder and, before leaving the office, looked Cybil in the eyes. "Good luck to you. You're going to need it."

Fighting back the tears, Renee walked to her office for the last time. Although this wasn't a total surprise, she wasn't prepared for it today. As she approached Carmen's desk, she could tell that she'd been crying.

"I'm so sorry, Mrs. Thomas," Carmen said. "I didn't know what she was up to until ten minutes ago."

"I know, Carmen," Renee said without stopping. She wanted to get her most important belongings, including the laptop she had yet to be reimbursed for, and leave the building as soon as possible. She didn't want to engage in any long, sorrow-filled good-byes. At a later date, she would send everyone a card or treat them to a nice lunch.

Closing the door behind her, Renee walked to the large windows overlooking Lake Michigan. She remembered how blessed she felt on the day she moved into her office. *I guess nothing lasts forever,* she thought. *But why, God? Why can't the good moments last a lifetime?* Renee rubbed her damp eyes. God had every right not to answer her cries. She hadn't exactly been obedient to His word in the last year. And though she had fought to stay in tune with God, she had slowly drifted away from the solid relationship she once had with Him. "God, you said you'd never leave me," Renee moaned. "You said when one door closes, another one opens." Today two doors had closed, and Renee prayed that the doors that opened would revive her soul, because right now she felt depleted of all strength.

Renee took a deep breath then stuffed a few pictures into her briefcase and grabbed her laptop. There wasn't much else that she wanted to hold on to. If she was going to move forward, she wanted to leave all the unpleasant reminders and memories in the past.

Renee walked out of her office with an air of confidence, but inside, her heart ached as she realized the relationships she'd helped to nurture over the years had abruptly come to an end. With the exception of Everett, it was highly possible that she would never see the people that worked in the hotel again.

Renee exited the hotel through a back door and took a taxi to her apartment. As soon as she entered her place, she went into the kitchen and poured herself a glass of wine. The first glass went down easy and fast. Halfway through her second glass, Renee realized that she hadn't spoken to Everett. By now, he had to know that she'd been fired.

Renee took her cell phone from the purse she threw on one of the kitchen chairs and sent him a text. Before he worried about her, she wanted him to know that she was home and doing all right . . . at least for now. Before she put the phone down, an incoming call from Jerome caught her attention. Renee considered letting the call go to voice mail, but when Jerome left the hotel, he'd been breathing hard. In case his health had relapsed, Renee answered.

Renee barely had a chance to say hello before Jerome began another tirade. "Look, Jerome," Renee interrupted before her temper took over, "thanks to you, I got fired today." She realized that she'd stretched the truth by blaming him, but it was too late to take her words back. "Now do you see why I want a divorce? My life is falling apart, and I need to regain control before I lose something else that matters."

Jerome lowered his tone. "I'm sorry that you lost your job, but this is happening because you're out of line with God. Just come back home, Renee. We can work through this," Jerome pleaded. "Just trust me. Everett isn't the man for you."

After all that had happened, how could he seriously ask her to trust him? "It's been a long day," Renee replied. "Why don't we touch base in a few days? You're very upset, and I don't want to be the reason you have another heart attack."

"Renee—" Jerome began, but Renee cut him off again.

"Good-bye, Jerome," she said and disconnected the call. The phone rang again, and this time Renee hit the ignore button, then turned the ringer off.

After finishing her second glass of wine, Renee poured a third glass and then went to the living room and sat down. She was well aware that she'd disconnected herself from God, but she didn't need to hear that from Jerome. He didn't have the right to judge her. She sipped a little of her wine and then placed the glass on a coaster on the end table next to her. *I can't believe my career and marriage ended within the same hour,* she thought and sighed. What on earth was she going to do now?

Someone banged on her front door and then called her name. Renee was almost positive the voice be-

longed to Everett, but how did he get inside the building? "Renee," he called again and knocked a little
harder.

Renee rushed to the door and let him inside. "Hey,"
she said. "How did—"

Everett threw his arms around her. "You had me
worried. I called your cell a dozen times," he said. "I
left the office as soon as Darla told me what happened.
Are you okay?"

"I'm fine," Renee replied and then walked back to the
living room. She picked up her glass of wine and swallowed a mouthful. "I can't say I didn't see this coming."

Everett took the glass from Renee's hand and sat it
back down. "You know I don't agree with Darla. However . . . I have to say that you're not the same woman
who could run the hotels blindfolded. I kept quiet because I knew what you were going through. Maybe I
should've been more active in helping you stay on top
of things, but . . . Renee, you have been slipping up a
lot lately. Your problems with Jerome have really taken
a toll on you. I mean . . . look at you. You're drinking
more than I've ever seen you do. What happened to
the good Christian woman that didn't drink anything
stronger than a virgin daiquiri twice a year?"

Renee turned her back to her friend. There was nothing she could say to defend herself. She was, as many
people had told her in so many words, out of order. She
stared at the bottom shelf of the end table and noticed
a Bible, which she hadn't opened in weeks. God was
surely giving her a wake-up call. Renee just prayed
she was strong enough to respond to Him. "God has to
be angry with me," she mumbled. "I haven't been the
woman He created me to be for quite some time."

"Don't be silly, love," Everett said tenderly and
grabbed Renee from behind. "God isn't like man. For

whatever reason, your season with the hotel is done. It's time for you to bless another company."

Renee turned around and caressed Everett's shoulders. "Thanks for being my friend," she said. "I needed to hear that."

"You know I have your back," he replied.

Without thinking about what she was doing, Renee gently kissed his lips. That one peck led to three others, and soon their lips locked for the next two minutes. It felt natural, and Renee slowly backed toward the sofa. With their lips still connected, she lowered herself onto the cushion and tenderly pulled him on top of her. Either she was longing for affection after such an emotional day or the moment was just right. Lying on the sofa, intertwined, Everett eased his hand up her shirt and Renee held tight to his back. Her mind was in a different place. A place where her problems had disappeared and she was in love with a man that loved her back wholeheartedly.

"I can't do this," Everett said and stood to his feet. "Not today and not under these circumstances."

Still on her back, Renee stared up at him with pleading eyes. She needed him to soothe her with more than his encouraging words.

"As long as I've waited for this moment to come, I can't go through with it," he said. "You're vulnerable right now. I don't want this to be something you regret in the morning."

Renee exhaled and then sat up straight. Everett was right, and in her longing, she was actually glad that he didn't follow through. "Can you at least hold me?" Renee asked, and without hesitation, Everett sat down next to her and let her lie in his arms.

~22~

Joi

Uneasy, Joi sat in the passenger seat, gnawing at a hangnail on her pointer finger. This was the first time she was leery about Joshua's novice driving skills. He was usually a careful driver, but at the present time his mind was in another place.

"Why wouldn't she tell us she lost her job?" Joshua asked.

"That's not exactly something to be proud of," Joi told him and gripped the door handle as he darted around a curb. Telling Joshua what she'd overheard Jerome tell Renee on the phone the other day was turning out to be a bad idea. She should've announced herself when she walked into the house last week, but Jerome was upset and she didn't want him to know that she'd heard the conversation. "What are you going to say to her when we get to her apartment?" Joi questioned.

"I need to know the truth," Joshua said.

"I shouldn't have told you what Pop said on the phone, or that I saw her at Garrett's," replied Joi. "If she gets mad at you, I'm going to feel guilty."

"Why should you feel guilty? Mom is the one to blame. If Mr. Everett is the reason she's leaving Pop, I should know. I'm almost an adult. I can handle the truth," he said and turned onto Randolph Street. "If it is true, I don't understand why she lied to me."

An eerie feeling formed in Joi's stomach, and her leg started to shake. "Maybe we should go home," Joi suggested. She knew her presence would only agitate Renee. "This may be something you want to ask her when I'm not around."

"There she is," Joshua shouted and suddenly tapped the brakes, stopping inches behind the car in front of them.

Joshua's eyesight was sharp. Renee was shorter than the average woman, making it difficult to locate her in the crowd of commuters traveling up and down the street.

"There's nowhere to park," he said, scanning for an empty space.

Joi was glad and prayed he wouldn't find one. "I'm not sure about this," Joi stated, trying to convince her brother to drive back home. "Renee is still pretty upset. You didn't hear her and Pop arguing last week. You can't just spring questions on her. Have you thought about what you're going to say when she asks why we're here?"

"Relax, Joi," Joshua said calmly. "We had a half day of school and decided to surprise her. Maybe she'll take us to lunch."

Joshua has to be a blind optimist. There is no way Renee's taking me to lunch, Joi thought as she stared straight ahead.

Renee's back was facing the street, so she didn't see them drive by. *Good,* Joi thought and sighed with relief. Then, just as she was about to pull her eyes away from Renee, Joi saw a tall, well-dressed man come out of the building. What was Everett doing there in the middle of the day? Joi's leg bounced harder and knocked against the door. If Renee was involved with Everett romantically, Joshua was going to be devastated. Rather than point out Renee and Everett, Joi closed her eyes and pretended she didn't see a thing.

Determined to speak to his mother, Joshua looked at the growing number of cars on the street and said, "I'll circle the block one time, and if we're not lucky, I'll park in a lot."

They dodged through the traffic, and Joi said a prayer as she trembled in her seat. By the time Joshua pulled the car around the block, the traffic was bumper to bumper. The light at the corner of Randolph Street turned red before Joshua could turn, and although there were a number of people walking up and down the street, Joi had a clear view of Renee and Everett. She glanced at them out of the corner of her eyes, hoping that Joshua wasn't watching them, too. It seemed like the longer the light stayed red, the more intense their conversation became. At one point Everett grabbed Renee's hands, and when he leaned down and kissed her on the lips, Joi's heart beat fast.

"Is Mr. Everett kissing my mom?" asked Joshua.

"I'm not getting a good vibe, Josh. Let's just leave," she said. Joi wasn't aware that he was looking at them, too. She'd never seen his caramel-colored skin turn a deep shade of red before.

"It's too late now," he answered.

The light turned green, but traffic was still at a standstill, and an impatient driver persistently honked his horn. Flustered, Joshua slammed on the gas pedal. As the car lunged forward, he tried to swerve away from the vehicles in front of him but lost control of the car. In a matter of seconds, the car ran up onto the sidewalk and into the side of the corner building. Instantly, the passenger air bag burst through the dashboard and forced Joi's body to jerk back into the seat.

The impact had given her an instant headache, and Joi automatically touched her forehead. "Josh?" she groaned and tried to turn her head, but her neck was stiff and sore. "Josh?" she called a little louder.

There was a tug on the passenger door, and around the air bag she could see that the door was slightly detached from the car. "Josh?" Joi said again. When she didn't get a response, she strained to turn her head, but before she could see her brother, she was whisked away from inside the car.

Once out of the car, Joi heard screams and frenzied voices and was suddenly filled with fear. "Where's my brother?" she asked the man carrying her to the sidewalk.

"How do you feel?" the stranger asked as he gently laid her down.

He was polite, but too loud for Joi's sensitive ears. Besides a few pains, she felt fine. "Can you go get my brother?" she asked the kind man.

"Calm down, honey," a gentle voice said as the man ran back to the car.

Joi didn't understand the statement. She was calm, but as she looked around her, she noticed people running around in confusion. Then, out of nowhere, someone screamed Joshua's name. Joi attempted to stand but was stopped. "I need to get my brother," she explained to the elderly woman beside her.

"Don't move, baby," the woman replied in tears as she rubbed Joi's back.

The screams grew louder, and the sound of sirens was rapidly approaching the scene. "Josh!" someone screeched, and Joi grabbed her head. The memory of what had happened finally registered. There had been an accident, and there was the strong possibility that Joshua had been seriously injured.

"I've got to get to my brother," Joi said firmly and pushed herself away from the woman holding her. In slight pain, she limped toward the ambulance.

There was a small crowd, but Joi pressed her way through. When she was close enough, Joi could see the mangled car against the side of the building. "Oh, God," Joi moaned and limped around all the people. As she inched closer, Joi feared what she was about to see. With each step, she took a deep breath and prepared herself. But nothing could've made her ready for what lay on the other side of the car.

"*No!*" Joi yelled when she saw Joshua lying on the ground. Renee was hunched over him, rocking back and forth, while Everett knelt by her side. Joi's legs went numb, but the woman was there to keep her from falling. She stepped forward, now crying hysterically. As she approached her brother's bloodied body, her heart sank. No longer feeling pain in her own body, she dropped to the ground and rubbed Joshua's face. Joi placed her hand under his nose, and then over his slightly opened mouth, but it was clear that he wasn't breathing.

Renee looked up, and when she saw Joi, a puzzled look crossed her face. "Joi? What happened?" she cried. "Please, tell me what happened. Why was Josh driving here?"

Joi looked at Renee's blouse, stained with the blood from Joshua's wounded chest. Joi's bottom lip trembled as Renee pressed for an answer; she couldn't tell her the truth.

"That's enough, babe," Everett said. "Let's just get to the hospital. The ambulance is—"

Renee looked at Everett with fire in her eyes. "Don't tell me what's enough!" she shouted as the EMTs jumped out of the ambulance. "This is *my* son lying on the ground! Not yours. So, don't tell me that something is enough!"

Like Everett, the EMTs tried to calm Renee, but she was heated. Ignoring everyone, she gently touched Joshua's chest and begged him to breathe. "Please," she wailed over and over, but it was too late.

"Ma'am," a young EMT whispered in Renee's ear. "We really need to get him to the hospital."

Not wanting to let go, Renee slowly moved aside. She remained on the ground, and her sobs escalated to shrieks each time an EMT touched Joshua's body. And when he was rolled into the ambulance, Renee jumped up and ran around frantically. Everett tried to grab hold of her, but Renee didn't want to be touched.

Watching her pained Joi. *This is all my fault,* she thought as she fell to the ground. *If I didn't tell Josh what I knew about his mother, he'd still be alive.*

~23~

Jerome

Staring at his son's lifeless body on the cold metal table almost took Jerome's breath away and he nearly buckled, but Dr. Ruberg helped him maintain his balance. "He didn't suffer," the doctor told him, and Jerome studied his son. Was that supposed to make him feel better? Maybe somewhere down the line he could accept that, but at the moment it didn't matter. Jerome touched the table to keep his balance. It was hard to believe that Joshua was gone. "He was gone before the EMTs arrived, but your wife asked us to try and revive him." Dr. Ruberg slowly covered Joshua's body. "I am very sorry for your loss. Your wife is in a room down the hall. We had to give her a mild sedative."

Jerome said a quick prayer over his son's body and then faced the door. "What about my daughter? Is she all right?"

"She's fine," Dr. Ruberg stated. "She has a few minor bruises, and we stitched a cut coming from her ear, but she is all right. She's in the room next to your wife."

Jerome walked out of the room and followed Dr. Ruberg down the hall. He reached Joi's room first, and when he walked inside, his teenage daughter immediately burst into tears.

"This is my fault," she cried and leaned into her father's side. "I heard you talking to Renee and say she got fired and—"

"Hush now, sweetheart. It was an accident," he said and rubbed the top of her head. "I'm just glad you're all right. Were you able to reach your mother?" Jerome asked, regretting making the call himself.

"One of the nurses called her. I think my cell phone is still in the car," Joi replied.

"Okay," he said, trying to stay strong. Now wasn't the time for him to break down. He kissed Joi's head, and a nurse entered the room to check her vitals. "I need to check on Renee," he said, "but I'll be back in a little while, okay?"

Teary-eyed, Joi nodded yes and then watched her father leave the room.

Next door, Jerome was a little disappointed to see that Everett was sitting in a chair next to Renee's hospital bed, but this wasn't the time for him to express his displeasure.

Renee's face was partially hidden in a fluffy white pillow as she rocked back and forth, whimpering quietly.

Everett stood up as Jerome approached the hospital bed. "Jerome . . . if there's anything you need," Everett said, "please give me a call." Without waiting for a response or saying good-bye to Renee, Everett left the room.

Jerome hopped in the bed next to his wife and hugged her tight. Without saying a word, she rested in his arms. Through tears, she asked, "What are we going to do?"

"I don't know. But we'll figure this out together," replied Jerome. "And just for a short while, I think it would be best if you stayed at the house. It's not good for you to be alone at a time like this."

Renee didn't put up a fight, and that comforted Jerome. As much as he didn't want her to be alone, he couldn't bear the thought of being without her, either.

He laid his head on top of hers, and for the next hour, they lay together in silence.

Finding it hard to sleep, Jerome decided to go downstairs and make a cup of tea. Renee was always more of a tea drinker, but from time to time he'd make a cup to settle his stomach or to help him fall asleep. It had been five days since Joshua died, yet every time he closed his eyes, the image of his son lying on the table surfaced.

As Jerome tiptoed down the hall, he noticed that the guest room door was open. He poked his head inside and saw that Renee wasn't there. She'd been having trouble sleeping, too. In fact, every night around midnight he'd hear her making noise in the kitchen. Jerome never bothered her at night. He figured she needed the time to herself. If she wanted to talk, she knew where to find him.

Jerome walked downstairs, and as he suspected, Renee was in the kitchen, watching the late-night news and drinking from one of her favorite mugs.

"Hey," she said quietly without turning away from the television screen.

"I guess you couldn't sleep, either," Jerome responded. Assuming Renee was drinking tea, he touched the teapot to see if the water she'd used was still warm, but it was cold as ice. Maybe she put water in the microwave, Jerome thought. Planning to do the same, he took a cup from the cabinet. As he passed Renee to get to the microwave, he smelled faint traces of alcohol. At first, he thought his nose was playing tricks on him. But as a former alcoholic, that was a scent he could never forget. Jerome sniffed a little harder, and this time he was certain Renee was drinking something stronger than hot tea.

Jerome searched the trash can and then the refrigerator for evidence, but he didn't see any liquor bottles.
Unaware of his actions, Renee continued to sip the
liquid in her cup. Before Jerome confronted her, he
needed to find out what she was drinking. He stood in
the middle of the floor and stared at the back of Renee's
head. That was when he spotted a plastic bag under
her chair. Jerome walked over to the table and reached
for the bag. He thought Renee would stop him, but instead, she looked at him, daring him to speak.

"What's this?" Jerome asked, though he already
knew the answer.

"Wine, Jerome. It's wine," Renee slurred. "I needed
something to help me sleep. I don't want to take those
pills the doctor gave me anymore."

"Don't do this, Renee," begged Jerome as he held up
a half-full bottle of Moscato. "This is just as bad as the
pills. Let's talk about—"

"I don't want to talk," she snapped.

"Renee, you know God wouldn't want you to do this.
What if someone from church or one of the kids sees
you?"

"My children are grown. They'd understand," Renee grumbled. "And I really don't believe I'm the only
woman in church who consumes a drink from time to
time."

Jerome sighed but couldn't be quiet. "You know
what drinking can do, babe. It separates you from God.
You taught me that. Don't you remember what I went
through? Remember how I would show up to church,
reeking of alcohol?"

"I'm not you, and I said I need it for tonight. Just
tonight!"

"I know you're nervous about the funeral tomorrow,
but this isn't—"

"My God, Jerome!" exclaimed Renee, holding on to her mug of wine. "Please, just leave me be! I'm going to my son's funeral in the morning. What else do you expect me to do?"

Jerome wanted to tell her to pray, but Renee's hurt was too great for her to think rationally. She was probably questioning God, just as he had the day of the accident. Jerome decided not to push the envelope and went upstairs. Before getting into bed, he fell on his knees and prayed for his wife.

~24~

Renee

"No mother should have to bury her son," Renee heard as she walked down the center aisle of the church. Renee was surprised at the turnout. Every seat in the building was filled. There were even a few people standing in the back, against the wall. Joshua was a family-oriented young man. He had a few close friends but socialized with everyone. The seniors of the church loved him, families in the community adored him, and the deacons wanted to groom him for leadership. He touched everyone he came into contact with in a special way. Joshua had many ambitions, but his greatest purpose was to make people happy through laughter.

Renee clung tight to Jerome's arm, afraid that if he wasn't there to hold her up, she'd fall. Every part of her body felt numb. She still hadn't accepted the fact that her son was gone, and she definitely wasn't ready to say her final good-bye.

Following Jerome's lead, Renee spotted Everett in the second row in the left section of the sanctuary, seated next to Bianca, and subtly eyed him as she passed by.

Jerome stopped at the first row and waited for Renee to sit down. As the family piled into the reserved seats around her, Renee stared at the slide show on the big screen. Pictures of Joshua faded in and out, and she reminisced about her son. Joshua had been a good kid. Unlike Reggie and Junior, he'd brought home good grades. His heart was pure, and he brought out the best in others. Though Joshua went on a few dates, he didn't have a steady girlfriend. Dannette, his science lab partner and friend, was the girl Renee had hoped he'd marry one day. But that day would never come to pass. Joshua would never bring a girl home for Renee to reject. He would never be a husband or a father. He would never be the accountant he longed to be. *I can't believe my baby's gone,* Renee thought as she picked at the handkerchief in her hand.

In honor of Joshua's home going, all the church choirs united as one. When the last person finished viewing his body, the choir stood up and began to sing Renee's favorite version of "I'll Fly Away." Deacon Arrington walked to the family section and in a soft voice said, "The family can come to the casket for a final viewing now."

Everyone but Renee stood up. She didn't want to participate in this part of the service. The images of Joshua being carried from the crushed car and then lying on the cold street had scarred her. She'd watched him lay motionless on the stretcher in the ambulance and then again on a hospital table. All those memories would remain etched in her mind forever. She didn't want to remember her son with a bruised forehead and scarred lip. She wanted to remember the child she gave birth to that was full of life, hope, and love. Not a lifeless corpse with faded skin and stilled features.

Jerome tugged at Renee's arm, but she yanked it back. Seeing that she was serious, he let go of her arm and walked to the front with the rest of the family. The first lady noticed Renee was still seated, and left the pulpit to talk to her. "I know you're hurting, honey . . .

but the casket can't be opened once we close it. Go and say good-bye to your son. You don't want to have any regrets about this day later."

Renee groaned aloud and then took a deep breath. The first lady was right. Giving in, she slowly joined her family. Junior tried to push her forward, but Renee opted to stand in the back between him and Joi. As Jerome prayed for the family, Renee squeezed Junior's hand tight. So that she wouldn't stare into the casket, Renee focused on her leather pumps.

Jerome finished the prayer; then each member of the immediate family said their personal good-byes. After all the children were done, Jerome stood in front of the casket alone. Renee wanted to join him, but her feet wouldn't move. The choir belted out a powerful verse of "I Love the Lord," and Renee's legs trembled. Junior and Joi ran to her side, and Renee unconsciously pulled away from her stepdaughter and grabbed her son's hand. She didn't mean to look up, but when she did, she caught a glimpse of Joshua's hands folded on his chest and, without warning, let out a scream that could have shattered glass.

Junior placed his arm around his mother and whispered in her ear, "It'll be all right, Mom."

Unable to take any more, Renee turned around. "I need to sit down," she sniffed, and Junior escorted her back to the front row. From her seat, Renee watched Jerome touch Joshua's hand and then nod at the deacons. It was time to close the casket. Someone bellowed from behind, and Renee shrieked as the deacons covered Joshua's face. She felt as if her heart had been ripped to shreds.

Minutes later, Reverend Hampton's voice filled the temple. As he prayed, Renee slowly sat up. The slide-show tribute had disappeared, and a beautiful winter floral arrangement now covered Joshua's casket. Before Reverend Hampton preached, he told a couple stories about Joshua, stories that Renee had never heard. As she listened to him speak, Renee's mind wandered. She thought about the last time she saw Joshua, their last conversation, his first day of kindergarten, and the first time he rode a bike on his own.

Instead of listening to Reverend Hampton preach, Renee tried to remember every important occasion in Joshua's life. She didn't want to forget anything about him. As she ran through each year of his life, Renee pretended to be attentive to the pastor's words. She tuned out completely several times, but by the end of the sermon, people were standing on their feet and shouting to the Lord. Reverend Hampton had successfully turned a solemn occasion into a celebration of the life Joshua had lived.

Jerome had insisted the repast be at their River Forest home. "It's more personable," he'd told Renee after she complained about cleaning up after everyone. Cleaning up wasn't the real reason why she didn't want people to come back to the house. After the service, all she wanted to do was gather her belongings and go back to her apartment. She didn't want to listen to any more stories about her son or pretend to be interested in what was happening in anyone else's life.

While people moseyed around the house, eating catered food and socializing, Renee sat at the kitchen table, holding her granddaughter, while Elise rubbed her back. Every now and then someone would ask if she needed anything, and each time, Renee would politely reply, "No."

The house had been filled with guests for at least two hours now, and Renee wondered when they'd all go home. She considered leaving but didn't want to appear ungrateful in any way. All the guests, including Elise and Taylor, were there because of the love they had for Joshua. Renee didn't know that Taylor knew her son well enough to fly in for the funeral, but figured she was there to comfort her daughter. Still, the moment was overwhelming, and she shuddered at the thought of attending the burial service in Philadelphia in two days. A long time ago, Renee and Jerome had purchased two adjacent grave sites at a Philadelphia cemetery, because they wanted to be buried near their parents. Not once had they considered they'd outlive any of their children.

Joi walked into the kitchen with a long-haired, bearded young man. The young man had to be at least twenty years old. Though he seemed polite enough, he was a little too mature in age for Renee's taste, but that wasn't any of her concern. Joi wasn't her daughter. After pouring him a glass of lemonade, Joi followed him out of the kitchen.

From where Renee was seated, she could see into the hallway. Melanie was standing there, holding a tray of puff pastries she'd baked in the oven a half hour ago. "No, Renee hasn't moved back home yet," Renee heard Melanie tell a few of her colleagues. "She lives in an apartment in the city. Josh was on his way to see her the day of the accident."

Why is she telling Jerome's colleagues my business? Renee thought, highly annoyed.

One of the women mumbled something Renee couldn't comprehend, but Melanie's response was clear. "When I went to see Joi in the hospital, she told me that was the reason they were going over there,"

Melanie tried to whisper. "If I saw my mother kissing another man, I might lose it, too."

Knowing that Joshua had witnessed the kiss between her and Everett minutes before he died suddenly made it difficult for Renee to breathe. Without thinking, she jumped up and handed her granddaughter to Elise. "How dare you?" Renee snapped as she charged toward Jerome's faithful assistant. "How dare you come into *my* home and disrespect me and my family on the day of my son's funeral?" Renee snatched the tray from Melanie's hand. "Are you lobbying to be the new woman in Jerome's life? Are you trying to move into my home? Well, I've got news for you, Melanie . . . I'm *still* the woman of this house. I *still* pay the mortgage here, and Jerome is still *my* husband, so give it up. You can't have my life!"

"Renee," called Elise, attempting to stop her friend, but her voice faded into space.

Renee marched into the kitchen and threw the tray, with the few pastries on it, in the trash can. "Now, get out of *my* house!" Renee screamed.

Jerome ran into the kitchen and looked at Melanie, who was on the verge of tears. "What's going on in here?" he asked, confused.

"It seems your daughter is the reason Josh drove to my apartment," Renee declared. "And your *assistant* feels it's appropriate to share our personal business with her friends."

"I—I'm sorry, Jerome. I didn't mean any harm by—"

Jerome cut Melanie off. "It's all right, Mel. We're just a little anxious, that's all."

"A little anxious?" Renee interjected. "Is that *all* you can say? Melanie just shared information that wasn't hers to share with people I barely know at a *very* insensitive time, and all you can say is that *I'm* a little anxious?" Renee advanced toward them, and Melanie backed out of the kitchen. In anger, Renee blamed Joi again, instead of the role she played on that day, too. "I just told you that Joi may be the reason Josh rammed into a building, and—"

"All right. This has gone far enough," Taylor blurted as she charged into the kitchen. "I know you're upset, but I'm not going to let you make my child feel guilty about what happened." Taylor's husband attempted to pull his wife away, but Taylor wouldn't budge. "Joi didn't tell you to move out, and she definitely didn't tell you to lie to Josh about your relationship with Everett."

Stricken with guilt, Renee couldn't let Taylor embarrass her in front of the guests. "You're the last person in here that should scold me about lying. Do I need to run down what started all this mess in the first place?"

"Why don't you all just stop!" Joi yelled from the hallway before she ran upstairs. Renee saw a few people follow behind her and, for a brief moment, felt a bit of remorse. Behind the people gathering in the hallway, Renee could also see Everett leaving the house. They hadn't talked all day, but she knew that he, too, felt a sense of guilt about what Joshua might have seen the day of his accident.

"I'm going to take the high road here and walk away," Taylor stressed as she backed out of the kitchen. "This isn't godly."

Renee began to follow her, but Jerome gripped her arm tight. "Was it godly to sleep with my husband, Taylor?" Renee remarked, and Taylor stopped walking. "Maybe this is all *your* fault."

"That's enough, Renee," Jerome said and pulled her close to him. "This isn't the time or the place to air our business."

Renee laid her head on Jerome's chest and took several deep breaths. From behind, she could hear people leaving the house and was glad. This wasn't the way she wanted them to go, but she was finally glad they were heading to their own homes.

"Renee," someone said, and she turned her head. Reverend Hampton had come into the kitchen.

Great, Renee thought. Not only had she shown an ugly side of her, but now her pastor was coming to remind her that God wasn't pleased with her actions.

Jerome let Renee go and left them alone. The pastor gently guided Renee to the table, and they each sat down. Shaky and mildly out of breath, Renee prepared to listen.

"I won't lie to you by saying I understand what you're feeling. The bond between a mother and her child is unique and special," Reverend Hampton began carefully. "So, while I understand loss, I'll never be able to understand what a mother must go through after losing a child. I do know," the pastor continued, "that God places specific people in our lives for a reason. They remain in our lives for an appointed time, and when that time is over, they move on or they return back to God. As difficult as this may be, one day you'll understand what I'm saying, and instead of experiencing sorrow, you'll thank God for the precious gift he gave you, even if it was for a small moment in time."

Though Renee knew he was right, she was having a tough time convincing her heart to believe it. Why would God give her such a beautiful child and then take him away before he had a chance to become a man? Did God choose to take Joshua's life to punish her?

"Until you reach that place, let's reflect on the love Joshua spread. He wouldn't want this, Renee."

"I know everyone is appalled by my behavior earlier," Renee responded and started to cry. "Josh wouldn't be proud of me, but I miss him so much."

"Everyone here knows that," Reverend Hampton said, "but you've got to take control of *your* feelings. Don't let the enemy win. You've got a great support system. Lean on those who love you for a while. Let them ease some of the pain you're carrying."

Though Renee couldn't feel God's presence, she asked Reverend Hampton to pray with her. Realizing her weakness, she needed the covering of God and all His angels.

After the talk with Reverend Hampton, Elise drove Renee back to her apartment. Renee didn't care that her best friend was with her. As soon as she changed her clothes, Renee poured herself a tall glass of blackberry wine. The day had drained her physically and emotionally, and if she didn't relax soon, she was liable to snap at someone else.

"Jerome told me that he caught you drinking the other day," Elise said as she put her coat in the closet. "Should I be worried?"

Without facing her friend, Renee gulped a considerable amount of wine. "One glass of wine before bed isn't anything to worry about."

"Maybe," Elise replied and sat down. "But when you have to sneak out of the house in the middle of the night because you need a drink, that is somewhat of a concern."

Renee finished the wine in two gulps and then refilled her glass. "As I told Jerome, I don't have a problem. I'm in mourning."

"God gives us other alternatives to heal our hurts. Alcohol isn't one of them."

"I know that, Elise," Renee replied as she leaned against the counter. "But as you can see, God isn't too happy with me, because I turned away from Him. Now . . . He's turned His back on me."

"That's ridiculous. It may not seemlike it right now, but God does love you."

"There used to be a time when I really believed that. But not so much anymore. I mean . . . I messed up. I knew I was messing up and didn't want to change. So, God let me go."

"I'm not going to sit here and let you feel sorry for yourself," Elise said with bass in her voice. "You're human, and no matter how you try, you can't be perfect or in control *all* the time. God is not built like us. People may let us down or shun us when we make mistakes, but not God. He may teach some hard lessons, but He'll never abandon you."

Renee looked down at the black leather pumps she bought specifically for the funeral. "What if Josh saw Ev and me kissing?"

"No one knows what really happened, so don't torture yourself looking for answers."

Easier said than done, Renee thought and finished the rest of her drink. "I should probably call Ev. I haven't really spent any time with him since—"

"Don't do anything tonight that will upset you," Elise suggested. "We're going to Philly tomorrow, and the next day you lay your son to rest. You don't need to address another emotional situation. Maybe it'll be best if you talk to him when you get back."

Renee put her glass in the sink and returned the bottle to the refrigerator. "I know, but I think I need to at least thank him for his support. I know you're not crazy about him, but . . . whether you or Jerome like it or not, he is my friend."

"Suit yourself," replied Elise. "I'm not going to get into that now. However, after the burial service, I want you to take time for yourself. You've got a lot to think about. There's no rush, but as your best friend, I'm going to help you get your groove back."

"Please don't say we're going to Jamaica," Renee joked, referring to Terry McMillan's novel *How Stella Got Her Groove Back.*

Elise laughed. "I don't think my husband would like me partying in Jamaica without him and the kid, so I'm afraid Florida is gonna have to do. And . . . I'm not accepting no for an answer."

"How could I refuse the chance to see my godson?"

"There is life after tragedy, Renee," Elise said. "God can and He will get you through this."

Against Elise's wishes, Renee called Everett before going to bed. Since the accident, they hadn't been alone together. Everett did call her every night, but that wasn't the same. She needed to see the expressions on his face as they talked.

When Everett answered the phone, it was clear that Renee had awakened him. "I won't keep you long," she said. "My flight leaves at six A.M., so I better get some sleep, too."

"I'm glad you called. . . . I miss you."

"I wanted to say thank you for everything. My sons told me you paid for the limousines."

"No thank-you needed, Renee. I'm sure you would've done the same for me."

After her explosion at the River Forest home, Renee could only imagine the thoughts running through Everett's mind. It had to be hard for him to stay behind the scenes and watch Jerome strut around as if they were still a happy couple. To make matters worse, he had to be affected by the words she shouted at Melanie in the kitchen.

"Will I see you in Philly?" Renee inquired. "The burial service won't be the same without you there."

"I don't think I should go," he replied blandly. "You need to go through this with your family."

"Despite how my husband feels, you are family, Everett," Renee told him.

Not wanting to feel like an outsider, Everett didn't change his mind. "I'm going to London in two days."

Surprised, Renee asked, "Is everything okay?"

"Yes. This is a good time to handle some business with the new hotel over there, and I'll also get to spend time with my daughters."

"Are you sure that's *all* this is? This seems sudden."

"We'll talk when you get back from Philly, okay?" Everett said, avoiding her query.

"Okay," she agreed. Renee didn't want to press the issue. "Once you're settled, give me a call."

After they said good-bye, Renee connected her cell phone to the charger and then walked to the kitchen. There was an obvious distance between her and Everett, and she hoped it was only temporary.

Renee opened the refrigerator and took out the bottle of wine. There were only a few swallows left, so she didn't bother getting a glass. As she headed to the living room, she noticed Elise's Bible on the coffee table. Renee picked it up and then sat down. There was a cloth bookmark dangling from the Bible, and Renee opened the book at that page. Before reading the page, she swallowed some wine.

A passage was underlined in blue ink, and she read it aloud quietly. "Blessed are they that mourn, for they shall be comforted. . . ."

Renee drank the rest of the wine in the bottle and then read the passage again. More than anything, she needed God's comfort. Carefully, she sat the bottle on the floor and returned the Bible to the coffee table. "God, please comfort me," she whispered and stretched out on the couch. "Please, God," she said and laid her head on a small decorative pillow. "*Please* comfort me."

~25~

Jerome

Jerome sluggishly strolled down the hallway to his office. He hadn't been to work in eight weeks, and if Melanie didn't need his help organizing a fund-raiser, he would've taken off another eight weeks. As he passed the offices and cubicles of his coworkers, they offered their condolences and sentiments. Though he wasn't in the mood to speak, Jerome politely responded to each of them without stopping to entertain a lengthy conversation.

When Jerome reached his office, Melanie was inside, putting a cup of coffee on his desk. "I'm glad you're back," she said. "If you need anything, don't hesitate to ask."

Melanie walked out, and Jerome closed the door behind her. He needed the quiet time to help him adjust. After hanging his coat on the rack in the corner, he noticed that his desk was covered with cards, flowers, and small gifts. Jerome wasn't normally an overly sentimental man, but the expressions of love brought tears to his eyes. Before sitting down, he picked up a small glass statue and read the inscription.

> Casting all your care upon him; for he careth for you.
> I Peter 5:7

Jerome put the statue by his computer keyboard and then sat down. He turned on the computer and picked up one of the cards while he waited for it to load. The envelope of the card was addressed to Mr. and Mrs. Thomas. Before Jerome opened the card, he wondered how Renee was coping. He hadn't seen her since they buried Joshua in Philadelphia. After the service, all guests were instructed to leave before the casket was lowered into the ground. This was a new tradition for the family, but Jerome understood the reason for the change. The funeral director explained that families often became irate with the workers handling their loved ones. Lowering the body often required workers to tilt and push hard on the casket. Watching a loved one being covered with dirt was also a traumatic experience for some people.

The cemetery workers tried to talk Renee into leaving, but she demanded they leave her be. "I want to stay here with my son, and I want to do it alone," she affirmed.

Jerome didn't know how long Renee stood at the burial site that day, but it was the last time he saw her. From what he heard from Reggie, she'd been secluded in her apartment since she returned to Chicago. He thought about stopping by her place, but after the explosion during the repast, Jerome didn't know what to expect. Since she'd been drinking, Renee's moods had been callous and erratic. He really wanted to talk to her. If no one else understood her pain and reasons for drinking, Renee knew he did. Alcohol had been the temporary fix to all his problems. From what Jerome could tell, Renee was headed for disaster if she didn't control the habit soon. Jerome wanted to be there for her, the way she'd been there for him, but her issues were much deeper than his were at the time. Jerome had indulged in alcohol because of his insecurities and sense of failure. Renee drank because of her troubled career, Jerome's affair, her teenage stepdaughter, and the loss of her youngest son. Though Jerome wished there was something he could do to relieve her of the pain, he knew this was a journey Renee had to walk alone. All he could do was continue to pray.

Jerome removed the first card from the envelope, and as soon as he opened it, a fifty-dollar bill fell on the desk. He put the money aside as he read the inspiring words, then picked up the second card. When he opened the next one, two twenty-dollar bills fell on the desk. Jerome swelled with emotion. By the time he opened all the cards and read the personal notes, he had close to five hundred dollars. Colleagues, friends, and students from the programs he managed had taken the time to send small tokens of love and care, and he was extremely grateful.

As he placed all the cards into one pile, Jerome thought about sending thank-you notes. That was normally Renee's department, but considering her current state, he had to make other arrangements to get it done. *Maybe Melanie can help me out,* he thought and sent her an e-mail. Though Melanie sat right outside his office door, she was often chatty, and his attention span was limited today.

Jerome leaned back in his chair and looked toward a family poster on his wall. The collage of photographs was a constant reminder of the good times he shared with his family. It had been placed there to cheer him on days he was feeling blue, but Jerome wasn't sure the poster could accomplish its goal any longer. Looking at the captured memories only made him think of Joshua. At some point he would remove it, and the other pictures of Joshua, from his office, just as he had at home. It was too painful to see his smiling face without becoming angry or bursting into tears. Until Jerome was ready, all pictures would have to rest in a shoe box under his bed.

Jerome sat up and stared at the computer screen. *Where do I begin?* he thought. He'd been away from the office too long. Checking his online calendar, Jerome wrote down a few meeting times, as well as the time for Joi's basketball game. *Funny,* he thought. She didn't mention this before leaving the house this morning. That bothered him, but Jerome had to admit he hadn't spent quality time with his daughter since the funeral.

Looking back at his e-mails, Jerome saw a message from one of the NBA executives from New York.

> We like the Future Ballers program you created, and would like to talk to you about expanding your idea. The board and I have come up with an exciting offer that we'd love to share with you. Please let me know when you are available to talk.
>
> Martin Ramsey

Though intrigued, Jerome wasn't sure he was ready for a big change. Mentally, he couldn't handle another huge project. New surroundings sounded tempting, but he just wasn't ready to make that big of a transition. So as not to be rude, Jerome accepted Mr. Ramsey's request to talk. There was no harm in listening to what the top executives had to say.

By the time Jerome responded to all his e-mails and attended two meetings, it was almost 1:00 P.M. His stomach growled a few times, but he wasn't in the mood to eat anything from the cafeteria. If he could hold off a few more hours, he'd treat Joi to dinner after her game.

"Hey, Thomas," Melanie said as she entered Jerome's office. "I picked up thank-you cards while I was out. Just give me the names and addresses, and I'll send them out today."

"Thanks, Mel," Jerome replied without looking up from the computer.

"No problem," Melanie continued. "I also noticed that you haven't eaten, so I brought you a chicken sandwich from Subway."

Jerome stopped working on the computer. "You think of everything, don't you?"

"Well, I am your assistant . . . and friend."

Melanie placed the sandwich on Jerome's desk and then sat in the chair across from him. Jerome couldn't deny that she'd become more than an assistant. But a friend? Yes, they had spent time together and enjoyed one another's company, but Jerome hadn't thought of them as anything more than professionals who worked together. It might look good to have a younger woman accompany him, but his heart was with Renee. Until that changed, he wouldn't be a good man for any woman.

"I've been meaning to apologize for what happened at the repast," Jerome said. Embarrassed by Renee's behavior, he didn't know how to address it, but he knew saying "I'm sorry" was a start.

"No need to," Melanie replied. "I was wrong, and if the tables were turned, I know I would've shown out, too."

"I appreciate that, but I still want you to know how sorry we both are," he stressed, though he wasn't sure Renee was sorry at all.

"Really, don't sweat it," Melanie answered. "We've got happier things to discuss. Do you want to go over anything now? I know there's a lot to catch up on."

"Maybe tomorrow. I'm going to Joi's game at two thirty today."

"I haven't seen her play in a while. I'll go with you."

"I hope I don't offend you," Jerome said, "but I need to go to the game alone."

Melanie said she understood, but Jerome sensed something different.

"Listen, Mel. You're a beautiful woman, and—"

"Oh, dear," Melanie interrupted. "Are you about to recite a Dear John letter?"

For the first time today, Jerome smiled. Melanie had a sense of humor similar to his deceased son's. "No, Mel. I just want to be up front with you. While I appreciate all of your support during such a rough time in my life, I don't think I'm ready to pursue another relationship. I need this time to get my life back on track."

Melanie stood up. "I understand that now isn't a good time, but . . . I'll be around when you're ready to give me a second thought."

As Jerome watched Melanie walk out the door, he knew without a doubt that he'd changed. Not many men would reject Melanie, but no matter how fine she was, he knew better than to string her along. If Renee decided to remain married, Jerome would welcome her back with open arms. And that wouldn't be fair to Melanie.

When Jerome walked into the gym, Joi was sitting on the bench while her teammates warmed up for the game. She was dressed in uniform, but she appeared disinterested in what was about to take place. Joi hadn't even noticed that Jerome had walked into the building.

A little disheartened, he walked to the coach's table and tapped Coach Miller on the shoulder. "Hey, Elaine," he said. "Joi's not warming up today?"

Coach Miller stepped away from the table, and Jerome followed. "Joi hasn't played in a game since February. She's taking her brother's loss hard. She's lost her positive attitude and energy."

That wasn't good. If Jerome didn't step up as her father, Joi could lose everything that she'd worked so hard for. "Do you mind if I have a word with her before the game?"

"Sure. Use my office," Coach Miller replied. "The game starts in fifteen minutes."

Jerome walked close to the bench and called Joi's name. When she looked up, he motioned for her to meet him by the coach's office. As he walked ahead of her, Denver caught his attention and Jerome waved back. Though Jerome was glad to see him there, he couldn't help but wonder why Denver hadn't encouraged Joi to play. Not only had he become a close friend, but he also served as a mentor to Joi in the Future Ballers program. At some point, Jerome would also need to speak to Denver about his plans for himself and Joi. Although he wasn't fond of their friendship, he had to admit that he respected Denver. He had turned out to be a great asset to his program. It was going to be hard, but Jerome was going to loosen up when it came to him dating his only daughter.

"Hey, Pop," Joi said with little emotion.

"Hey, baby girl. Let's talk before the game begins," Jerome said and stepped into the coach's office.

The office was small and cozy, and Jerome remembered his days as a high school athlete. Coach Miller's office was a lot neater than that of any coach he ever had. The walls were filled with framed certificates, newspaper clippings, and photographs of past and present players. Trophies lined the tops of two bookshelves, and autographed basketballs filled a tall display case.

Jerome asked Joi to sit in the wooden chair next to the coach's desk as he browsed the items on the walls. "I hear you haven't played in a while. Want to talk about it?"

Joi didn't answer, and Jerome turned around to find his daughter crying. Unable to face her, or he'd cry, too, Jerome turned his attention back to the wall. "I know this is hard for you, sweetheart. It's hard for all of us," he explained. "But Josh is gone, and there is nothing we can do to change that. What happened isn't anyone's fault. It was an accident."

Joi cried harder, and Jerome lifted her out of her seat. He knew that Joi blamed herself for the accident. But the truth was, everyone had played a small part in Joshua's death. There wouldn't have been a reason for Joshua to drive downtown if Renee hadn't moved out. Renee wouldn't have moved out if Jerome hadn't had a child outside of his marriage.

Pulling her close, Jerome tried to comfort her. "Your brother loved you, Joi, and he's cheering for you in heaven. The last thing he'd want is for you to give up on your dream. You're a true baller. That's what you do, and it's who you are. You've *got* to play. You've worked too hard to get where you are now." Jerome gently pushed Joi away from his chest and stared in her red, slightly swollen eyes. It pained his heart to see her in this state. But he was her father, and it was his job to motivate her. "You've got to play because it's what Josh would want you to do."

Jerome wiped the tears from his daughter's face. "You're a Thomas. Always will be. So, go out and show the world how tough you are."

"Okay," Joi huffed softly. "I can do it for Josh."

The buzzer in the gym sounded. "Right on time," Jerome said.

Joi wiped her face quickly and then headed out of the office. When she reached the door, Joi turned around. "Thanks, Pop."

Jerome's heart warmed. Joi's gratitude was an incentive for him to break out of his depression. He couldn't be a productive father to his children and grandchildren if he allowed his sorrow to overtake his desire to live.

~26~

Renee

The last time Renee searched for a job, Google, Monster, and other online career search engines didn't exist. For the last two hours she'd been sipping on wine and sending her virtual résumé to hotel chains along the East Coast. There were many options to choose from, but Renee realized that her interest in the industry had expired. But what else was she going to do? She had excellent managerial and business skills, but her knowledge was limited to the hotel field.

Renee took a small break and searched the Internet for grants. Last week, during an early lunch, Bianca had asked Renee to help her plan a new business. With Renee gone, Bianca no longer felt secure at Luxury Inn. In addition, she wanted to be closer to her friends and family back in Philadelphia. "I feel like this is what God wants me to do," she had told Renee.

Renee's cell phone vibrated on the desk, and her heart fluttered when she saw Everett's name. "Hi, Ev," she said and took another sip of wine.

"Hey, how are you?" Everett replied.

Renee smiled at the sound of his voice. "I've been better . . . but I'm all right," she said, and it suddenly dawned on her that, no matter how good he made her feel inside, their friendship would forever be strained. Memories of the day Joshua died would surface every time they talked. She had yet to forgive herself for being with Everett on that day. "When did you get back in town?"

"Yesterday," he replied in a monotone, and Renee knew that something was on his mind. "I was just about to go out for a run. Do you mind if I stop by?"

"Now?" Renee questioned. Though it was almost noon, she was still in her nightgown and slippers. She hadn't even bothered to curl her hair in the last two days.

"I could be there in thirty minutes. Is that okay?"

Thirty minutes wasn't quite enough time to pull herself together, but Renee said okay. As soon as she hung up the phone, she gulped down her wine, then rushed into the bathroom to shower.

In record time, Renee jumped out of the shower, threw on a pair of jeans and a New York Knicks sweatshirt, and pinned up her hair into a loose, fancy twist. With the few minutes she had left to spare, Renee threw the pile of dishes from the sink into the dishwasher. The other rooms in her apartment were cluttered, but there was no time to clean up. There was a time when disorganization and clutter bothered her spirit, but now it was easy to overlook the mess. If she had more time, Renee would've done more to make her place presentable, but there wasn't. The most she could do was close the doors to all the rooms so that Everett couldn't see the accumulation of junk that filled them.

Just as Renee closed the bathroom door, the buzzer rang. She quickly scanned the living room and noticed an empty wine bottle by one of the chairs. She ran over to the chair and picked it up and then buzzed Everett inside the building. When she tossed the bottle into the recycle bin in the kitchen, she checked to be sure no other loose bottles were floating around.

Everett knocked on the door, and Renee let him in. "It's good to see you again," he said and gave Renee a hug.

Renee sighed softly when he touched her. She'd missed him more than she realized. In the past few months, she'd known him as more than a friend. "How was London?" she asked and slowly pulled away from him.

"London was good," he said and followed Renee into the living room. "My daughters are growing up too fast."

The light in Renee's eyes disappeared, and Everett understood why. Neither of them had resolved what had happened the day Joshua died. "I bet you didn't want to leave," Renee said and stared at the floor.

"It was hard," he responded and walked over to her computer table, "but . . . I decided to buy a condo there."

Renee looked away and thought about her son. "Yes," she said and walked over to the sofa Under different circumstances, Renee would've been sad he was leaving the country, but losing a child had reconfirmed the short amount of time there was to spend with family. "Good," she added in a mellow tone. "You'll get to spend more time with your girls."

The topic of children was a sensitive one, so he decided to change the course of the conversation. "I see you're looking for a job. I can probably pull a few strings, if you need me to."

Renee started to reorganize the decorative pillows on the sofa. "I'm not sure I want to do that. I think I need to try something new."

"Well . . . whatever I can do for you, just ask," he replied and walked over to the window. "I wanted to stop by and talk about what happened at the repast, but if you—"

Renee cut Everett off and apologized. "I was upset and don't know what came over me."

"No one is to blame," Everett said coolly. "But I understand. What happened eats me up sometimes, too."

Renee stood next to Everett and held his hand. Everett had been a special part of Joshua's life, too. He was with Renee the day her water broke in the middle of a meeting. He also rushed her to the hospital and kept her company until Jerome arrived. Renee had wanted him to be Joshua's godfather, but she knew Jerome would never agree to that title. So instead, Everett had settled for being Joshua's mentor.

"I've known you for a very long time," Everett said as he faced Renee. "You and your family mean a lot to me." Everett let go of Renee's hand. "It really hurt when you told me that Joshua wasn't my son. I mean . . . I'm not trying to be insensitive, and I know it was said in the heat of the moment, but that did something to me."

"Did I say those words?" she said, more to herself than to Everett.

"Renee, I know emotions were at a high. I guess I'm just venting because the words stung. I don't mean to be selfish. I know Joshua wasn't my child, but I loved him and thought I meant more to him than just being your boss. I also thought I meant more to you."

"Everett, I apologize," she stated. That was her only defense. "I really do mean that."

"There's no need to say 'I'm sorry,' but . . . I am curious." Everett grabbed Renee by the waist. "Where exactly does our friendship stand?"

Renee closed her eyes and laid her head on his chest. She couldn't stand to look into his eyes. There was no denying that she had feelings for him, but at this point, Renee was positive that there couldn't be anything more. Saying that she was still married wasn't a lie she could use anymore. Once Jerome signed the divorce papers, she'd be free to date whomever she chose to. She had no choice but to share the truth. "You know that I value our friendship," she said and stepped back. "But I think we'd both be kidding ourselves if we tried to be anything more. Knowing that the accident might've happened because Joshua saw us kissing is something more than I can handle, and until I can, I really don't see how we can be in a real relationship. I hope you understand that."

Everett looked out the window, and Renee stood next to him. "You're going to London to be with your girls. Enjoy watching them mature into beautiful women," she said and gently rubbed his back. "I'm still trying to figure out what's next for me. I'm not sure how long that will take, and it's not fair for you to wait on me."

"I'm not giving up on you. You'll always be special to me," Everett said and then caressed her cheeks with his hands. "I'll be in Chicago another month, and then I'm going back to California. By the beginning of the year, I'll be in London for good." Everett rubbed Renee's arm and kissed her gently on the lips. When he was done, Everett slowly backed away and eased out of the apartment.

Renee stared out the door and watched Everett jog down the street. Inside her heart she knew that her special connection to Everett had come to an end.

Surrounded by pictures of Joshua, Renee sat in bed, reminiscing on the life she'd shared with her son. She'd done this every morning, hoping this would help her accept his loss a little more easily each day. Renee gathered the pictures and placed them back inside of a special box inside her nightstand and then got out of bed.

It was 11:30 A.M., and she still hadn't showered. Though she wasn't in a hurry, she needed to get dressed. Jerome was coming over for lunch. Renee strolled across the room and stepped on a pile of clothes in front of the dresser. She'd been meaning to wash them since Everett left her apartment a few days ago, but she didn't have the energy. Maybe after Jerome left, she'd wash a couple loads.

By the time Jerome made it to her apartment, Renee had set two glasses, plates, forks, and a pitcher of lemonade on the table. She really wanted a glass of wine, but that would have to wait until after lunch and Jerome's departure.

"Hey, sorry I'm late. Panera was crowded," Jerome said as he placed a large bag down.

"Not a problem," Renee said as she eyed Jerome. He looked refreshed. Everything he had on was new, from the dark brown leather jacket to the shiny shoes on his feet. "Make yourself comfortable," she said and put the few dishes in the sink in the dishwasher.

Jerome took the food out of the bag. "It's been almost three months since I've seen you. How have you been?"

"I miss our son," she replied. "Other than that, I guess I'm okay."

Jerome walked to the refrigerator and stopped by the recycle bin in the corner. "You're still drinking?" he asked.

Renee looked at the bin, filled with two weeks' worth of wine bottles. "Don't start, Jerome. I have it under control."

"Are you sure about that? That dishwasher is packed," he replied. "It's not like you to let dirty dishes sit anywhere too long. I'm beginning to worry."

Renee sat down and unwrapped her chicken panini. "Are you here for lunch or to give me a lecture?"

"I'm just concerned, Renee. You can't blame me for asking." Jerome sat next to her and took the lid off of his tomato soup. "Have you found a church out this way to attend?"

Renee silently blessed her food and then took a bite of her sandwich. "I haven't found the strength to go," she said as she chewed her food. Every time Renee thought about going, she was overwhelmed with feelings of guilt. "I've strayed away from God for so long, I'm not sure I can return until I have more control."

"You know better than that," Jerome told her. "You can't fight your battles alone. Church is the place people go to, to get their lives in order. Don't let anything keep you from God."

"I haven't forgotten about God," Renee replied. "I'm still praying at night and reading a little every day. I'm just not ready to be around a bunch of people."

Jerome let out a huge sigh. "The longer you stay away from people, the more liable you are to become depressed." Jerome crumbled a packet of crackers into his soup. "Reggie's coming to town when the Knicks play the Bulls on Tuesday. I thought we could go to the game with the kids and maybe have dinner . . . like we used to do. It'll be a good way to ease you into being around people."

Renee wanted to tell Jerome that the things they used to do were in the past. Soon he'd have to create new traditions. She wanted to go, especially if Joi was going to be there. "I'll think about it," she answered.

"Well," Jerome said, "as much as I don't want to talk about this, I guess we need to discuss the divorce." Jerome poured lemonade in his glass and then drank half of it. "I've been praying about this and realize that I have too much respect for you to drag this out unnecessarily. If this is really what you want to do, I won't stand in your way."

"What I really want is to get back to being happy," Renee responded. She was glad Jerome was no longer putting up a fight, but she still wasn't sure if divorce was the right answer. "Part of our problem is that we never addressed the issues around Joi, and—"

"Let's not go there," Jerome countered. "I know you still have concerns about my daughter, but I don't want to fight anymore. I hurt you and this family, and I have to accept that. I'm dealing with that, but now it's time to put the past behind and move forward. I can't do that with this divorce hanging over me. So, we need to make a decision. Do we live together as a husband and wife should, or do we start new lives without one another?"

"I don't expect you to wait for me to make up my mind. I wish I could be more definite," Renee said, "but I can't. With all that has happened, I feel that I need more time to figure out if what's left between us is more than the love we share for our children and grandchildren."

"Have it your way, Renee," replied Jerome. "I'm not going to rush you, but I can't be put on hold forever, either. This is torture for me." Jerome finished his lemonade and then stared at the empty bowl of soup in front of him. "You know," he continued, "you can't go through the healing process alone. Wine can't help you, either. I'm not preaching, but you and I both know alcohol only makes things worse."

"I'm fine," Renee snapped, though inside she knew she was covering up her pain. "I won't let this get out of control, I promise. Now, can we please enjoy lunch?"

Jerome agreed to back off today, but he let Renee know that he would never stop being concerned about her. They sat together for another hour, and then Jerome went home. When he left, Renee decided to at least clean the kitchen and bathroom. In case she had any more visitors, she didn't want them to see that she'd turned into a slob.

Cleaning the two rooms kept Renee occupied for three hours. She was exhausted but glad she was able to accomplish the task without taking a break. Renee strolled into her kitchen barefoot and automatically took a bottle of wine from the refrigerator. As she poured herself a glass, she thought about what Jerome had said. There was no doubt in her mind that she needed to rededicate her life to Christ, but she was scared. The mere fact that she could fall out of line spiritually in the first place meant that there was no guarantee that she wouldn't again. She knew that God was a forgiving God, but she also knew that she had to be accountable for her actions. Since she wasn't in control yet, Renee wasn't ready to face Him.

Having grown up in a strict Christian home, Renee knew better than to give up on faith. She'd allowed God to take a backseat in her life, and as a result, she'd gradually lost control of all the matters that were important to her.

Renee drank half of the wine in her glass, and as she let the liquid flow through her organs, she tried to recall how many glasses she'd had between last night and this morning. The fact that she couldn't remember frightened her. It was quite possible that she was consuming more than one bottle a day. *Maybe I've lost control of this, too,* she thought. In that moment, Renee started to cry. "Jerome's right," she muttered. "I can't do this by myself. God, please help me!"

Realizing that change would happen only if she showed God some effort on her part, Renee emptied the rest of her wine in the sink. "I promise," Renee told God, "if you give me the strength to get better, I will."

***

Renee couldn't remember the last time she felt so nervous. As she stood outside the closed sanctuary doors, she had to fight back the tears. Though her hands and legs were trembling, she was determined to make it to the altar. With God's help, Renee hadn't consumed a drink in almost a week. In that time, she focused on cleaning up her apartment and helping Bianca establish her new business. Elise had also come back to Chicago for a few days to check on her, and during that visit, she'd helped Renee realize that she needed to go to counseling. Although Renee had had only one session with Mrs. Stroud, she already felt more confident and secure.

When the doors opened, Gloria's eyes widened when she saw Renee. "Good morning," she said with a huge grin. "I'm so glad to see you this morning."

"Sorry I'm late," Renee whispered and took a church bulletin from Gloria's hand.

"Don't be silly," Gloria replied as she escorted Renee to a seat in the front row. "This seat was waiting just for you. Enjoy the service."

Renee sat down and crossed her legs. She specifically chose the 11:00 A.M. service in hopes that she'd avoid running into Jerome and the friends she'd gained during the early services. Today she needed to give all of her attention to the message being delivered through God's vessel, without distracting questions about her marriage and absence in church.

When Reverend Hampton walked into the pulpit, he acknowledged Renee pleasantly with his eyes, and she smiled back. Renee was ready to hear the message, but as she pulled out her paper to write notes on, Reverend Hampton introduced a female guest preacher from his hometown of Columbia, South Carolina. Though she would've preferred to listen to her pastor, Renee positioned herself to hear a word from the Lord.

As soon as the woman preacher opened her mouth, Renee knew God had sent her to speak to her spirit. Almost immediately, the preacher ripped into an emotion-packed sermon.

"One morning you rolled over and realized that you were depressed," she told an excited crowd. "You don't want to do the things you used to. You don't want to be around people. You're always tired. You start doing things that are out of character." The five foot woman lifted her black robe and hopped off the pulpit. "It's time to take off the mask, saints," the preacher said as she strolled back and forth. "Have you noticed that even in your mixed-up state of mind, God *still* granted you favor? You may have lost your job, but God had another one already lined up. You're broke, but somehow your bills keep getting paid and there are still meals on the table."

Renee was on the edge of her seat as the preacher continued. "You changed, but God didn't. You don't deserve His attention, but His favor rests on you. I can't explain why God loves you, but He does. And aren't you glad about that?" she roared. "Your soul was leaking little by little over time, and you didn't realize it. Your resilience was destroyed because you were stretched to your limit. Now it takes longer for you to bounce back from things. Before you changed, you knew without a doubt that God would make everything all right, but now you question whether or not He will. But I've got news for God's children this afternoon. This is your season!" she exclaimed. "You're about to bounce back! Glory to God!"

"Hallelujah!" Renee shouted as she jumped to her feet, and something came over her body. She couldn't keep still. Her hands and feet had a mind of their own, and before she knew it, she was running and clapping around the sanctuary. "I'm ready to bounce back!" Renee yelled and meant it.

Her praise ignited a wave of worship, and other members in the congregation followed her lead. When Renee made it back to her seat, she fell to the floor and cried out to God. "I can bounce back," she sobbed and lowered her head.

Gloria got down next to Renee and prayed in her ear. "God's child has come home. Protect and shield her from the enemy. Put her life and her family back in order."

Renee got up and hugged Gloria as she wept like a baby. "I'm going to bounce back," she said, and this time her spirit really believed it.

~27~

Joi

"I love your dress," Leah said as she played with the rose-colored bow sewn on the thick shoulder strap of Joi's prom dress.

Glad that her sister had traveled with her parents, Joi twirled around in her bare feet and danced across the room. The compliment meant a lot. Unlike Leah and her mother, Joi was not a fashion guru. She had insisted on choosing her prom gown herself, so she was pleased that her selection met their approval. Going to the prom wasn't a part of Joi's original plan. When she moved to Chicago, she hadn't expected to become close enough to someone to consider going to the prom. But Denver caught her off guard. Though they were still only friends, Joi had to admit that there was potential to become more.

"Thank you," Joi chimed as she admired her curvy frame in the full-length mirror mounted on the wall.

Taylor stood next to her daughter and opened a bag full of cosmetic products. "You're almost ready," she added and pulled out blush applicator.

"Do I have to wear makeup?" Joi asked and pushed the applicator away from her.

"A little color won't hurt you," Taylor said as she opened a compact case full of soft eye shadow colors.

"Don't forget the lipstick and blush," asserted Leah.

"What's wrong with the color I have?" Joi said.

"You are beautiful," Taylor replied and rubbed eye shadow on a tiny brush, "but this will enhance the prom pictures."

"All right, Mother," Joi agreed, to make her mother happy.

As Joi closed her eyes, Leah ran up to her with a hand towel and draped it across her chest. "We can't mess up the dress before you leave," she said.

Taylor played around with a few shades of pink and then carefully applied color to Joi's face. Joi stood tall and cooperated. She couldn't wait to see the final product. All she wanted to do was look and feel beautiful tonight.

"Denver is one handsome young man," Taylor said as she worked on Joi's makeup. Leah stood close to her mother's side and studied her mother's moves. "Jerome says he's a nice guy, too. Is his ex-girlfriend still causing trouble?"

"No," Joi replied. "She tried to start an argument one night Denver and I saw her at the movies. Denver was able to calm her down, but she told me that I haven't seen the last of her." Joi cracked a tiny smile. "She said that Denver would come to his senses very soon. I told her that we weren't a couple. If he wanted to be with her, he could."

"Well, you and Denver act like more than friends. Everyone can see that but you," Taylor teased. "But don't worry. You'll be off to college soon, and she'll be history. Will she be at the prom tonight?"

"Dr. Whitmire told her she wasn't allowed to go. Do you know she's been suspended ten times this school year? Dr. Whitmire said she wasn't rewarding anyone who'd been in trouble more than half the school year,"

Joi informed her mother. "I know it isn't right, but I thanked God," Joi shamefully responded.

"Even if she does show up, try to ignore her. You deserve to have a good time. This is a once in a lifetime event. Make it special . . . but not too special. Where are you going afterward?" Taylor queried.

Joi shrugged her shoulders. "I don't know."

"Just make sure it's not to a hotel," Taylor ordered. "A late dinner at Denny's is good enough."

"Denny's?" Joi repeated with a frown. "Can't we go somewhere a little more classy? Besides, that's where everybody will be after the prom. You know I like to be different."

"Excuse me," Taylor sang. "It doesn't matter where you go to eat. Just make sure you remain a virgin."

"Mother," Joi and Leah responded in unison.

"Don't 'mother' me," Taylor asserted. "I don't want you to do anything you'll regret later in life. If Denver really respects you, he'll wait to marry you."

"Don't worry, Mother," Joi assured her. "Babies are not in my five-year plan. Neither is a husband. I have to make it into the WNBA first."

"Okay, I hope you mean that. I'm not going to be in Connecticut with you, so I won't be able to remind you," Taylor said.

Joi mouthed "Thank you," and Taylor playfully popped her hand.

"Is your father okay about UConn?" Taylor asked as she dabbed her cheek with blush.

"No, but he understands," Joi mumbled. "I told him he could visit anytime."

"Well," Taylor said and smoothed on a coat of lipstick, "I'm glad he didn't pressure you to stay here. I know I can be overprotective sometimes, but I do want you to be happy. UConn is a good school, and in the end, that's all that really matters to me."

"Denver's here!" Jerome yelled from the stairwell.

"She's almost done," Taylor shouted back and applied a little gloss to Joi's lips. "All done! What do you think?"

Joi leaned in closer to the mirror and barely recognized herself. Though she couldn't make this a habit, Joi had to admit that she liked the added soft tones on her face. "Thanks, Mother," she said, and suddenly her facial reflection morphed into Joshua's, and tears formed in her eyes.

As if Taylor could read her daughter's mind, she rubbed Joi's arm. "Even though Josh isn't physically here, I'm sure his spirit is . . . and I know he'd be happy for you."

A tear rolled down Joi's cheek, and Taylor quickly grabbed Joi's hand before she rubbed her face. "Don't mess up your makeup," she said and dabbed the damp streak carefully with her finger until it was dry. "Have fun tonight. I'm sure that's what Josh would want you to do."

Leah took Joi's three-inch heels from a box sitting on the bed and handed them to her sister. Before Joi practiced her walk in skinny-heeled shoes for the first time, she posed for various photos as her mother and Leah alternated using a camera to take pictures. A knock on the bedroom door interrupted the informal photo shoot, and Taylor charged to the door. "Men can be so impatient," she said, believing it was Jerome. But when she opened the door, she was surprised to see Renee standing there.

"Can I come in?" Renee asked. "I know you're surprised to see me, but I stopped by to talk to Jerome. I didn't know Joi was going to her prom today. I promise, I'll only be a minute."

Taylor didn't want to let her inside the room. "This really isn't a good time to talk to—"

Joi didn't feel threatened by Renee's presence and tipped to the door in her heels. "It's okay, Mother," she said.

Apprehensively, Taylor looked at Leah and told her to go downstairs, then faced Renee. "I'll give you five minutes," she said. "I don't want to keep Joi's guest waiting too much longer."

Renee stepped into the bedroom as Taylor walked out and then shut the door. Joi walked to the other side of the room as Renee made herself comfortable. "I'm afraid to wear these," she said as her legs wobbled with each step. "I don't know how women can wear shoes this high."

"It's not so bad," Renee said and sat on the edge of the bed. "As you know, anything is possible when you practice. I'm sure you'll be walking like a pro by the time you get to the prom."

"Thank you, but I'm not so sure about that," Joi said and grinned. Renee did, too, and the uneasiness that had always been present between them seemed to disappear.

"You look really pretty," Renee began, and Joi blushed. That was the first genuine comment Renee had given her since they met. "I'm not here to ruin your day, but I'm not sure when I'll see you again, so I wanted to apologize for my behavior. I know that I was mean to you," she said as Joi continued to pace the floor. "I want you to know that my issue wasn't with you. It was with Jerome. I thought it was too soon for you to move into our home. In my eyes, I needed more time to get used to you," Renee said. "I'm sorry, and I do mean that. Adults make mistakes, and I'm admitting that I made a huge one by not accepting you. I want you to know that no matter what happens with Jerome and me, you will still be family. You were a sister to Josh and to my other boys. You're an aunt to my grandchildren, and you're Jerome's daughter. I wish I had the chance to get to know you the way they all do."

Joi walked to her dresser and stopped. Though she was walking better in her heels, she wasn't confident that she wouldn't fall yet. "Thank you, Renee," Joi began. "I prayed that one day we'd be able to talk to one another. I just wish you and Jerome were back together."

Taylor opened the door and poked her head inside the room. "Almost ready?"

"One more minute, Mother," Joi responded, and Taylor slowly closed the door.

Renee opened her purse and pulled out her wallet. She stood up and walked over to Joi. "I don't usually carry cash on me," she said as she took five twenty-dollar bills from her wallet, "but I'm going to a graduation party tomorrow, and I was going to put this in a card as my gift." Renee placed the crisp bills in Joi's hand. "You really are a good kid, and I wish you all the best."

Joi did her best to hold back tears. If only Joshua were alive to actually experience the moment. "Thank you," Joi replied and gave Renee a warm hug. "But you act like this is it. I do expect to see you at some of my games."

"I'll be there," Renee said and ended their embrace. Renee smiled and, when she saw Taylor's fingers on the edge of the door, slowly turned around and headed to the door.

The two women stared at one another once Renee reached the door. "Taylor . . ." Renee began after a brief pause, "I just want to say I'm sorry for anything I may have said or done to hurt you."

Joi watched her mother and stepmother carefully, praying one would not say something to aggravate the other. In that quiet moment, she witnessed a subtle softness in both of their eyes. Without any further exchange of words, Joi sensed that both women had forgiven each other. Renee faced Joi one last time before leaving. "Enjoy your night," she said and then headed downstairs.

"So," Taylor said as she walked into the bedroom, "what did *she* have to say?"

Joi took her time and walked to the door. "That's between me and Renee."

Though Taylor didn't like her daughter's reply, she accepted it. She wasn't going to let anything ruin the night for her child. "You look beautiful, sweetheart. Are you ready?"

"I think so," Joi said, "but go ahead of me. I need to get something from Josh's room."

Taylor nodded and then gave Joi some space. Joi's toes were tingling, but she made her way down the hallway and prayed she could get through the night. In case she couldn't, Taylor had stuffed a fancy pair of flat ballerina shoes in her purse.

Inside Joshua's room, Joi walked to a nightstand and carefully sat down on the bed. She closed her eyes and pretended that her brother was sitting in the chair across from her and talked to him like old times. "I miss you," she began and controlled her tears. "The family is finally coming together. So, I guess we'll be all right. My prom date is a real nice guy," she rambled. "It's weird, but I think he's a keeper. Don't worry, though. I'm still gonna take my time with this one. I promise." Joi opened her eyes and fixated on a guitar in the corner. Joshua was planning to take lessons. He wanted to be an expert by the time he went to college.

In his mind, playing an instrument was his way of attracting female attention.

"I think Pop likes Denver now," Joi said. "Last week Denver came over for dinner, and Pop talked to him for over an hour in the backyard. I don't know what was said, but Denver's been coming over for dinner at least twice a week." Joi sniffed and tried hard to keep from crying. "I really wish you were here, but I guess God needed you more. So, I'll just continue to carry you in my heart." Joi stood up and, before leaving, rubbed a school photograph of Joshua taken months before the accident. *God, please keep my precious angel in Your care,* she said to herself and then went downstairs to socialize with her family and friends.

~28~

Renee

Renee reached for a pen on her lawyer's desk and took a deep breath. Once her signature was on the legal document in front of her, she'd be the owner of Divine Creations, an event-planning business in Philadelphia.

"Renee," Bianca called softly, and Renee turned in her seat to face her. "Are you sure you want to do this?"

Renee took a deep breath and thought, *God has not given me the spirit of fear, but of love, and a sound mind.* "I'm sure," she told Bianca. In addition to her lawyer's review, Renee had read each word in the agreement at least three times last night. Though she trusted her lawyer, Renee was going into business with a friend and wanted to be sure that there were no loopholes or flaws in the agreement. She really wanted to be a part of the business, but it was more important that she didn't destroy her relationship with her protégé.

When Bianca asked her advice about starting a business, Renee never imagined the day would come for them to be partners. But as she helped Bianca with the research, it became clear that Renee should invest more than just advice into her dream. Not only was she in a position financially to start the business, but she had a passion for planning events, and she had already made a name for herself throughout Philadelphia.

Bianca touched Renee's hand. "This is a big move. If you need a few more days, that would be fine with me. I'm not in a rush."

There was a lot going on in her life, but for the first time in almost a year, Renee had never felt more confident about a decision. Somewhere along the line, she lost her confidence. She let circumstances she couldn't control shake her faith and the standard she'd set for herself and her family for many years. When life became too difficult, she stopped trusting God, and as a result, she lost her marriage, her son, and her career. Though Renee reminded herself every day that Joshua's accident was not her fault, what happened would forever hang over her head. Despite it all, God had seen fit to forgive her and give her a second chance at life. And she prayed she wouldn't take his grace and mercy for granted again.

"What a journey this has been," she said and almost shed a tear. "But I'm ready for a new beginning." Renee signed the legal agreement and then faced her new partner. "Thank you."

"No, thank you," Bianca replied, then signed her name right below Renee's. "This is our dream, and God brought us together a long time ago because He knew we were a perfect match."

"We're on to something wonderful, Bianca," Renee said and wiped the lone tear falling from the side of her left eye. "And the best is yet to come."

~29~

Jerome

Any hope Jerome had about reconciliation was squashed when Renee opened the door to her apartment. From the front door, he could see a mound of boxes stacked in the corner, as well as five wardrobe boxes lined next to her computer desk. All the pictures that Renee had mounted along the hallway walls were gone, and on the floor the area rugs lay rolled up and bound by duct tape. "You're moving?" he asked as she locked the door.

"In two weeks I'll be a South Jersey girl," Renee replied. "I was going to invite everyone to dinner in a couple days to break the news."

Jerome followed Renee into the living room, and his heart was heavy. Packing tape, markers, and bubble wrap lay in the middle of the floor, surrounded by open boxes, and he realized that his biggest fear had materialized. Jerome understood why his wife had to leave the state. Losing Joshua was hard on everyone. He, too, wondered if his season in Chicago had ended. Moving to the Windy City was Renee's idea, and although his life had flourished over the years spent there, without Renee around, it would be hard for him to enjoy all the blessings.

"So," Renee said as she leaned against a tall wardrobe box, "what brings you to the neighborhood?"

Jerome stood in the middle of the living room, dumb-founded. Reality had hit him once again with a sharp blow. He had planned to attempt another reconcilia-tion, since the last month had been good for both of them. They hadn't argued or unintentionally offended one another. Their conversations had flowed easily over the phone, and a few nights they'd talked for at least an hour. But staring at all the boxes around the apartment discouraged him, and he moved on to plan B—the plan where he and Renee agreed to amicably part ways.

"I know I said that I'd give you time," he began and took an envelope from his inside jacket pocket, "but I signed the papers. This isn't what I want, but I don't want to block your chances of finding happiness again, and I need to figure out how to move on as well." He removed the papers from the envelope.

"Wow," replied Renee and hesitantly took the papers from his hand. "I don't know what to say. I guess this makes starting over . . . official."

Those weren't exactly the words Jerome wanted to hear. He wanted Renee to tell him that she'd changed her mind, but it was clear that wasn't going to happen. "Well," he said and laid the empty envelope on the cof-fee table, "I don't want to hold you up—"

"I'm not doing anything but packing," Renee inter-jected. "Would you like something to eat? I reheated some seafood ravioli right before you came."

"Sure," Jerome answered. He felt like he needed to spend as much time with her as he could. There would soon be a time when they'd see one another only at spe-cial family events. He removed his jacket and placed it on top of a closed box, then followed her to the kitchen. "Have you found a job in Jersey?" he asked before sit-ting at the table.

"Actually," Renee said, beaming, "Bianca and I are the new owners of an event-planning business in downtown Philly."

Though Jerome was happy for her, he had to admit he was also a little jealous. Renee had found the strength to move forward, while he was still trying to figure out his next steps. "Congratulations! I know the two of you will do well."

Renee put two plates on the table, then divided the ravioli in the pot on the stove between them. "After Darla fired me, I tried to find another hotel job, but no one was hiring. I wanted nothing more than to force Darla into bankruptcy. My plan was to take all my loyal clients and employees with me. She'd never survive this business with me working as competition." Renee put the empty pot in the sink and took two forks from a drawer. "But . . . God knows best. That was evil thinking, and that's why I wasn't getting any interviews. I had bad motives." Renee chuckled and joined Jerome at the table.

"And now you're a business owner," Jerome added. "I'm very proud of you."

"Thank you," she replied with a smile. "Mrs. Stroud has also been helping me get things in order. She's been a godsend."

Jerome looked surprised. When Renee demanded they end marriage counseling, it never occurred to him that he should continue without her. "You've been going to therapy?"

"Yes," Renee responded. "You told me I couldn't get past my issues alone, and you were right. God placed Mrs. Stroud in my life for a reason, and I believe it was to help me sort out this rough stage in my life."

"I'm glad to hear that," Jerome said. Though he wished he could've been a part of Renee's healing process, he was happy that she going alone.

There was a weird moment of silence as they stared
into one another's eyes. It was hard to believe that
almost forty years of marriage was coming to an end.
"Have you heard from the dragon lady?"

"Darla sent a card and flowers, expressing her deep-
est sympathy," Renee told him. "I wanted to burn everything, but when I calmed down, I sent her an e-mail
to say thank you. I told her she blessed me in more
ways than she could ever imagine."

"And what about Everett?" Jerome asked, though he
wasn't sure he was ready for her reply.

Renee stared into the distance and twisted her lips.
It was obvious Everett was a tender subject. "He's going to move to London and run the new hotel there. He
wants to be closer to his daughters," she answered. "I
haven't spoken to him in two months . . . and I guess
that's a good thing." Renee handed Jerome a fork and
then jumped up. "I forgot about drinks. Would you like
some iced tea, cranberry juice, or water?"

Jerome didn't want to dig deeper. It was difficult
enough knowing that Renee had feelings for her former
boss. "Tea would be fine."

"What's next for you?" Renee inquired as she poured
them each a glass of tea.

"I haven't given anything serious thought," Jerome
said, and as he talked, he convinced himself to consider
the second interview with Mr. Ramsey in New York. "A
few guys from the corporate office took me to lunch a
while ago. They like my mentoring program and want
me to help implement one for all the NBA teams."

Renee put a glass in front of Jerome and then sat
back down. "That would be perfect for you," she said
with excitement. "Who would've thought Future
Ballers would go this far?"

"I certainly didn't dream that big," responded Jerome.

"I know you're going to accept their offer, right?"

Jerome cut up a few of the ravioli squares. "I don't know. The job is in New York."

"Really?"

"Yes . . . I'm not sure I'm ready to be uprooted alone. I still look thirty-five," Jerome joked as he rubbed his scarcely grayed beard, "but I'm close to sixty."

Renee grinned. "Do what will make you happiest, Jerome. We've had some pretty tough challenges. It was hard for me to deal with everything at the same time, and I think somewhere along the way I lost myself. I turned into someone I didn't recognize. You tried to help me, and I thank you for that, but I needed to seek help on my own and in my own time. Mrs. Stroud helped me take a long look at my life, and I was able to clear my head. That's why I decided to go into business with Bianca. The business gives me something positive to look forward to, so I don't have to focus so much on all the things I lost." Renee stirred the creamy sauce on her plate as she continued to speak. "I'm so glad to be moving on, Jerome. There are just too many bad memories here."

The soft glaze in Renee's eyes told Jerome that she was thinking about their son. "I understand," he said. Though they had created many pleasant memories in Chicago, these would always be overshadowed by Joshua's death. "I've been going to the altar before work every morning for a while now," Jerome said as he ate his lunch. "Pastor said that was the place where I could find answers. Guess I'll let God show me what to do."

Jerome thought he saw a teardrop fall from Renee's eyes, and he stopped talking. It was clear that her heart still ached for their son, so he changed the subject. "Why don't you tell me more about the business?"

For the next two hours, Renee and Jerome talked about their future plans. Renee had set goals through the next five years, while Jerome was struggling to see beyond the current year. But, as Renee always did, she helped him map out a tentative plan through the end of the year.

As they sat at the table, enjoying lunch, Jerome didn't focus on the fact that Renee would soon be his ex-wife. Instead, he put his emotions aside and enjoyed being with the woman he loved.

At 5:00 A.M. Jerome woke up in tears. For the first time in his life he was alone. He was getting a divorce after being married to the same woman since he was eighteen, his youngest son was dead, and Joi was spending time with her family in Philadelphia before heading off to Connecticut for college. Jerome stared at the ceiling and wiped the sides of his eyes. The humongous house Renee had begged him to purchase was now empty. This was not how his life was supposed to be.

Jerome got out of bed and walked down the hall. When he reached Joshua's room, he slowly pushed the door open. He hadn't gone in there in almost a month. Most of Joshua's clothes had been sorted and donated to the Salvation Army, but there were a few items he and Renee couldn't part with. Jerome walked into the room and headed straight to the closet. The Rocawear denim jacket that he'd given Joshua for his birthday last year was still there. Jerome touched the sleeve and remembered the day Joshua had picked it out in the department store. The jacket was overpriced, even on sale, and when Jerome refused to purchase it, Joshua didn't pout or fuss. Instead, he settled for a cheaper imitation. Any of Jerome's other children would've whined and refused to speak to him for at least two days at his age. But Joshua was different in that way. So moved by his son's actions, Jerome returned the imitation and bought the designer jacket the next day. When Joshua unwrapped his present, the appreciation in his eyes was evident. "You're the greatest, Pop," he had said as he tried it on.

Jerome walked to the bed and sat down, and as he looked around the room, he replayed memories of his son. Soon, he began to cry. He'd never understand why Joshua had to leave the world so young. Only God knew that answer. Jerome just prayed that God would take away the sting of his loss. When he thought about Joshua, he wanted his heart to feel only love.

What's next for me? Jerome asked God as he wiped at his tears. *I've been praying for my family, but the family is more broken today than it's ever been. I'm a mess inside, God, and I have no idea how to rebuild my life from here.*

In the midst of his prayer, Jerome heard a faint voice whisper in his ear, "The answer is at the altar."

Though Jerome didn't feel like going to church, he pushed himself to make it there. If the answer he needed was indeed at the altar, he needed to get there . . . and fast.

The security guard on duty at the church was surprised to see Jerome so early on a Saturday morning. With the exception of the light in his office, the lights throughout the church were not set to come on until 7:00 A.M. "For you, I can make an exception," the friendly guard said.

Jerome followed the guard into the sanctuary and waited for him to turn on the row of lights above the pulpit. "I won't be long," Jerome said. The guard nodded and left him alone to pray.

As Jerome lowered himself at the altar, he cleared his mind of any anxiety and worry. When his spirit settled, he first prayed about the job offer in New York. Weighing the pros and cons, Jerome realized that God had presented him with an opportunity to bless children across the country. *Only what's done for Christ will last,* Jerome recalled. That was what Reverend Hampton had told him years ago, when he was considering starting the mentoring program. Remembering that line, Jerome realized his decision had been made.

Okay, God, Jerome silently prayed. *If this is what you want me to do, I will. But what am I going to do without Renee? How do I keep the family together once we're officially divorced?* In Jerome's mind, he faintly heard the word *stand*. "I've been standing," he mumbled low. "I stood on Your word, and she still wants the divorce."

"Stand," he heard again, only this time it was louder and clearer. Jerome shook his head from side to side slowly, reminding God that he'd been faithful, just as he'd promised. "Stand," he continued to hear, and Jerome stopped complaining. "You win," he said, surrendering. "I'll continue to do as You say. I have no choice but to trust You."

Jerome ended his prayer and stood to his feet. When he turned around, he almost lost his footing. Coming down the aisle and heading straight toward him was his high school sweetheart, and she had an envelope in her hand.

"A smart man once told me that the answers I'm searching for are at the altar," Renee said when she reached him. He could tell that she'd been crying. "I'm not sure I'm ready to get divorced," she confessed.

Jerome was speechless. The moment meant more to him than Renee understood. "Would you like to pray together?" he asked.

"I'd like that," she replied and handed him the envelope.

Overjoyed, Jerome removed the divorce papers from the envelope and placed them on the altar. "Thank you, God," he said and grabbed Renee's hand. Together, they knelt and positioned themselves to pray. Jerome wanted to pray aloud, but every time he went to speak, he started to cry.

"Tears come easy for you at this age," Renee teased and rubbed his shoulders. "But don't worry, babe. I think God wants me to cover us in prayer this time."

~30~
Renee

One Year Later . . .

Overlooking the Manasquan River in Point Pleasant, New Jersey, Renee and Jerome stood in front of Reverend Hampton, admiring the golden sunset. Hand in hand, they listened as their pastor and friend welcomed the few guests seated behind them to the evening ceremony. Though summer had not officially begun, the warm air had reached a temperature of eighty-four degrees. This, added to the private summers Renee experienced at odd times during each week, caused her body to overheat. Most days she'd complain and opt to sit under an air conditioner until the moment passed or the temperature outside dropped. But not today. Today she could tolerate the annoying streams of sweat down her arms and legs. She could deal with the strands of hair stuck to the back of her neck and the tiny beads of perspiration along her forehead. She could stand in three-inch sandals and a crème skirt suit for hours. There was nothing that could keep her from renewing her wedding vows with Jerome.

When Jerome stopped by Renee's apartment, with signed divorce papers, two weeks before she was set to move to New Jersey, she was shocked. Renee had accepted the fact that she and Jerome had grown apart, but she didn't really believe that he'd actually put his signature on the document. She hadn't mentally prepared herself for that, and when he left the apartment, she spent half the night staring at his slanted handwriting on the dotted line.

With papers in hand, Renee recalled a recent visit to Mrs. Stroud's office. In that session, she realized that she never had an open mind when it came to Jerome's daughter. Though it was clear that Jerome should've been up front, Mrs. Stroud helped her to understand that he'd been afraid of losing her. As for the divorce, he had weighed the options, and in the end, he chose to put her feelings first. That had to mean something.

Renee fell asleep that night holding the papers, and in a deep sleep she dreamed that she was in a park with her family, around a table. Not only were her immediate family members present, but Jerome's brother, Brandon, and his family were there, as well as Elise and her family. Taylor and her crew were also present. Everyone sat around the table in harmony, enjoying the food Jerome had barbecued on the grill. Renee sat between Elise and Joi, and she seemed happy. There was a glow about her that she hadn't seen in years. Jerome talked, but in the dream, Renee couldn't make out his words, but when everyone doubled over in laughter to one of his funny stories, she wrapped her hand around Joi's shoulder and laughed, too.

After releasing Joi's shoulder, Renee got up from the table and headed to the serving table under a nearby tree for a second helping of macaroni salad. On the way there, she saw Joshua standing in the grass, wearing an all-white suit, and stopped in her tracks. Instinctively, she wanted to run over to him, but her body was temporarily paralyzed. Joshua's wide grin told Renee that he was pleased by what he saw in the park. The plate Renee was holding fell from her hands, and regaining mobility, she bent down to pick it up. When she stood tall again, she started to speak, but Joshua was gone.

Renee woke up in a panic and full of tears that morning. After wiping her face dry with her cotton sheet, Renee got out of bed. It was early in the morning, but for some reason she felt God pushing her to go and pray at the altar, and she needed to take her divorce papers with her.

Renee couldn't explain how she and Jerome had turned their failing marriage around. Only God could take the credit for the new spark in their relationship. After Joshua died, fifteen months ago, Renee and Jerome spent some time apart. She moved to New Jersey and started her event-planning business with Bianca, and Jerome accepted the corporate position with the NBA and relocated to New York. While it was clear they weren't ready to finalize the divorce, they decided to take small steps to mend their relationship. For months, they visited one another on weekends, talked on the phone well after midnight, and went on dates. They had become friends all over again and discovered new and exciting aspects of life together. It only seemed right that Renee accept Jerome's impromptu proposal to renew their vows on the anniversary of their youngest son's death. As she reminisced about their journey, a tear rolled down Renee's face. Jerome let go of her right hand and rubbed her cheek until it was dry. "Aw, how sweet," Renee heard someone say behind her, and Renee's face turned a light red color.

"If you can still blush and show public displays of affection, you know it's real love. If you can keep the glow she has now, Jerome, then you've done your job as her husband," Reverend Hampton said and then looked out at the guests. "In a world where divorce has become common, as an easy solution to a marriage in trouble, I'm proud to stand before all of you and God to let the enemy know that he has been defeated. Jerome and Renee, the road wasn't rosy—"

"Amen to that," interrupted Renee as she rubbed Jerome's hands.

Reverend Hampton waited for the laughter in the audience to simmer down, then continued. "God never promised an easy journey, but you are a testament to what God can do. It's easy to sever ties during a storm, and although Renee moved out and—"

"I wasn't happy about that," Jerome mumbled, and Renee playfully smacked his arm.

"But she's back with you now," Reverend Hampton added. "Hallelujah!"

"Thank God for that," Jerome cheered humbly, and his eyes filled with tears.

Renee let go of Jerome's hands and wiped at his tears as most of the audience members shed a few tears of their own.

"Before everyone needs a wad of tissues, Jerome and Renee have written short vows for one another. Jerome, why don't you go first," Reverend Hampton said and handed him the microphone.

Jerome closed his eyes briefly, and when he re-opened them, he held the microphone close to his lips. "Thirty-eight years ago, I pledged many things to you, including my faithfulness. With great sorrow and regret, I acknowledge that I broke that vow," Jerome confessed as he stared into Renee's watery eyes. "I realize the enormity of my mistake. Others have come and gone, but you have been the only constant in my life, and I will always love you for standing by me. I believe in this marriage more than ever, and I reaffirm my love and commitment to you." Jerome's voice cracked, and he quickly handed the microphone to the reverend.

Renee listened intently to the words Jerome had memorized. Yes, they had been through a lot, but they'd struggled through all the challenges *together*.

"Renee," Reverend Hampton said and passed the microphone to her.

Turning slightly to her left, Renee faced her daughters-in-law and Joi, who were arranged in a line according to their height. Though her relationship with Joi was not where she would've liked, Renee was finally open to including her as part of the family. No longer did Renee view her stepdaughter as a dark cloud looming over her family. Renee now realized that Joi was a blessing.

Joi stepped forward and handed Renee a folded sheet of paper. "Thank you, sweetheart," Renee said as she took it from her hand.

A mild breeze swept across the landscape, and Renee held on tight to her vows. The fresh calla lily arrangements around them shifted position, and Bianca jumped from her seat in the front row and subtly put each one back in its original place. She was more of a perfectionist than Renee at times. But in their line of work, perfection was needed.

As Renee looked around at the decorations and recalled the extra time Bianca spent putting the ceremony together in a limited amount of time, she wondered why God had been so good to her. After she turned her back on Him, gave up on her faith, and doubted His love, how could God continue to bless her beyond belief? His unconditional love was amazing.

Renee unfolded the paper in her hand and took deep breaths. She didn't want to cry. The day had been flawless. The only thing that was missing was Joshua's physical presence. *I miss you,* Renee thought as the memory of the child she lost came to mind. *Your father and I miss you every day.*

Clearing her throat, Renee held the paper tight and spoke loudly and clearly into the microphone. "Jerome, it seems like only yesterday that I pledged my love and commitment to you. I promised to love you, honor you, comfort and keep you. I pledged to be by your side in sickness and in health, in times of want, and times of plenty, for better or worse, for the rest of our lives," Renee read, afraid to look her husband in the eyes. It would take only a look and she'd burst into tears. "We have had all those things," she continued, "and you have been by my side as we created a family, a home, and a life together. Today, as we begin a new chapter as husband and wife, in the presence of God and our family and friends, I renew my vows to you, pledging my eternal love for you and eagerly awaiting what lies ahead."

Reverend Hampton reclaimed the microphone and eased into the last stage of the ceremony. "Through all the joy and sadness, sickness and loss, Jerome and Renee, you're still standing . . . together. Now, in front of witnesses and the eyes of God, your marriage vows are sealed . . . never to be broken again."

As the guests cheered and shouted well wishes, Jerome didn't wait for permission to kiss his wife. He pulled Renee close and kissed her as if it were his first time, and did not stop until Junior tapped his shoulder. "Enough already," he teased. "All these people are ready to eat and party."

Renee and Jerome slowly separated but glued their hands together. "I love you," Jerome told her.

Renee stared deep into Jerome's eyes and replied, "I love you, too, and I'm so glad we're still standing."

Someone hit the play button on the media system inside the country club building, and "Back Together Again," sung by Roberta Flack and Donny Hathaway, blared outside. Renee didn't know who chose the theme song for the ceremony, but they had chosen well.

As everyone stood to their feet, Renee and Jerome danced down the rose petal pathway, full of joy and ready to celebrate their love with family and friends.

Book Discussion Questions

1. How did Renee's friendship with Everett affect her marriage? Is it possible for married people to have friends of the opposite sex?

2. Describe how Jerome's affair had an impact on his family. How did the affair affect his personal relationships with Renee and his children?

3. What are some advantages and challenges for blended families?

4. Was Renee justified in the way she communicated with her stepdaughter? What should Renee have done differently?

5. If you were Renee's friend, what advice would you give her concerning her relationships with Jerome, Everett, Joi, and Darla?

6. Which character did you identify with the most, and why?

7. What lesson(s) can be learned from the way Renee handled the stress in her life?

8. Did the separation help or hurt Renee and Jerome's marriage? How could they have handled their problems differently?

9. Was Everett at fault for pursuing a relationship with Renee? Do you think that was his goal from the beginning of their friendship?

10. Spiritually, what lesson(s) did you learn from each of the characters?

11. Should separation be an option for married couples experiencing problems? Or should they work out their problems while living in the same house? What are some possible complications with separation?

12. Do you think Renee and Jerome will finally live happily ever after? Or do you think they should have followed through with the divorce?

13. In times of trouble, Christians are taught to pray. In the story, Renee resorted to other methods to ease her pain and find solutions. How do you encourage someone like Renee, who has become bitter and impatient, when she or he is waiting for God to answer prayers?

14. How did Joshua's death affect the family?

UC HIS GLORY BOOK CLUB!

www.uchisglorybookclub.net

UC His Glory Book Club is the spirit-inspired brain-child of Joylynn Jossel, Author and Acquisitions Editor of Urban Christian, and Kendra Norman-Bellamy, Author for Urban Christian. This is an online book club that hosts authors of Urban Christian. We welcome as members all men and women who have a passion for reading Christian-based fiction.

UC His Glory Book Club pledges our commitment to provide support, positive feedback, encouragement, and a forum whereby members can openly discuss and review the literary works of Urban Christian authors.

There is no membership fee associated with UC His Glory Book Club; however, we do ask that you support the authors through purchasing, encouraging, providing book reviews, and of course, your prayers. We also ask that you respect our beliefs and follow the guidelines of the book club. We hope to receive your valuable input, opinions, and reviews that build up, rather than tear down our authors.

WHAT WE BELIEVE:

—We believe that Jesus is the Christ, Son of the Living God.

—We believe the Bible is the true, living Word of God.

—We believe all Urban Christian authors should use their God-given writing abilities to honor God and share the message of the written word God has given to each of them uniquely.

—We believe in supporting Urban Christian authors in their literary endeavors by reading, purchasing and sharing their titles with our online community.

—We believe that in everything we do in our literary arena should be done in a manner that will lead to God being glorified and honored.

—We look forward to the online fellowship with you. Please visit us often at *www.uchisglorybookclub.net.*

Many Blessing to You!

Shelia E. Lipsey,

President, UC His Glory Book Club

ORDER FORM
URBAN BOOKS, LLC
78 E. Industry Ct
Deer Park, NY 11729

Name: (please print):_____

Address: _____

City/State: _____

Zip: _____

QTY	TITLES	PRICE

Shipping and handling-add $3.50 for 1st book, then $1.75 for each additional book.
Please send a check payable to:
Urban Books, LLC
Please allow 4-6 weeks for delivery

ORDER FORM
URBAN BOOKS, LLC
78 E. Industry Ct
Deer Park, NY 11729

Name: (please print): _____

Address: _____

City/State: _____

Zip: _____

QTY	TITLES	PRICE
	3:57 A.M Timing Is Everything	$14.95
	A Man's Worth	$14.95
	A Woman's Worth	$14.95
	Abundant Rain	$14.95
	After The Feeling	$14.95
	Amaryllis	$14.95
	An Inconvenient Friend	$14.95
	Battle of Jericho	$14.95
	Be Careful What You Pray For	$14.95
	Beautiful Ugly	$14.95
	Been There Prayed That:	$14.95
	Before Redemption	$14.95

Shipping and handling-add $3.50 for 1st book, then $1.75 for each additional book.
Please send a check payable to:
     Urban Books, LLC
Please allow 4-6 weeks for delivery

ORDER FORM
URBAN BOOKS, LLC
78 E. Industry Ct
Deer Park, NY 11729

Name:(please print):_____

Address: _____

City/State: _____

Zip: _____

QTY	TITLES	PRICE
	By the Grace of God	$14.95
	Confessions Of A preachers Wife	$14.95
	Dance Into Destiny	$14.95
	Deliver Me From My Enemies	$14.95
	Desperate Decisions	$14.95
	Divorcing the Devil	$14.95
	Faith	$14.95
	First Comes Love	$14.95
	Flaws and All	$14.95
	Forgiven	$14.95
	Former Rain	$14.95
	Forsaken	$14.95

Shipping and handling-add $3.50 for 1st book, then $1.75 for each additional book.

Please send a check payable to:

Urban Books, LLC

Please allow 4-6 weeks for delivery

ORDER FORM
URBAN BOOKS, LLC
78 E. Industry Ct
Deer Park, NY 11729

Name: (please print): _____

Address: _____

City/State: _____

Zip: _____

QTY	TITLES	PRICE
	Into Each Life	$14.95
	Keep Your enemies Closer	$14.95
	Keeping Misery Company	$14.95
	Latter Rain	$14.95
	Living Consequences	$14.95
	Living Right On Wrong Street	$14.95
	Losing It	$14.95
	Love Honor Stray	$14.95
	Marriage Mayhem	$14.95
	Me, Myself and Him	$14.95
	Murder Through The Grapevine	$14.95
	My Father's House	$14.95

Shipping and handling-add $3.50 for 1st book, then $1.75 for each additional book.

Please send a check payable to:

Urban Books, LLC

Please allow 4-6 weeks for delivery

ORDER FORM
URBAN BOOKS, LLC
78 E. Industry Ct
Deer Park, NY 11729

Name: (please print): _____

Address: _____

City/State: _____

Zip: _____

QTY	TITLES	PRICE
	My Mother's Child	$14.95
	My Son's Ex Wife	$14.95
	My Son's Wife	$14.95
	My Soul Cries Out	$14.95
	Not Guilty Of Love	$14.95
	Prodigal	$14.95
	Rain Storm	$14.95
	Redemption Lake	$14.95
	Right Package, Wrong Baggage	$14.95
	Sacrifice The One	$14.95
	Secret Sisterhood	$14.95
	Secrets And Lies	$14.95

Shipping and handling-add $3.50 for 1st book, then $1.75 for each additional book.

Please send a check payable to:

Urban Books, LLC

Please allow 4-6 weeks for delivery

ORDER FORM
URBAN BOOKS, LLC
78 E. Industry Ct
Deer Park, NY 11729

Name: (please print):_____

Address: _____

City/State: _____

Zip: _____

QTY	TITLES	PRICE
	Selling My soul	$14.95
	She Who Finds A Husband	$14.95
	Sheena's Dream	$14.95
	Sinsatiable	$14.95
	Someone To Love Me	$14.95
	Something On The Inside	$14.95
	Song Of Solomon	$14.95
	Soon After	$14.95
	Soon And Very Soon	$14.95
	Soul Confession	$14.95
	Still Guilty	$14.95

Shipping and handling-add $3.50 for 1st book, then $1.75 for each additional book.

Please send a check payable to:

Urban Books, LLC

Please allow 4-6 weeks for delivery

ORDER FORM
URBAN BOOKS, LLC
78 E. Industry Ct
Deer Park, NY 11729

Name:(please print):_____

Address: _____

City/State: _____

Zip: _____

QTY	TITLES	PRICE

Shipping and handling-add $3.50 for 1st book, then $1.75 for each additional book.

Please send a check payable to:

    Urban Books, LLC

Please allow 4-6 weeks for delivery